To
Jayanti

true lo♥e again

saz vora

All the best wishes

saz 2025

PRAISE

A LETTER FROM SAZ

Dear Reader,

I write women's romantic fiction that will make you swoon, salivate, and maybe shed a few tears—but will ultimately leave you feeling uplifted and inspired.

My stories are set in places I know well, around the Midlands and London featuring characters like me, someone who straddles my Britishness and inherited culture. People who've experienced life's ups and downs, but find joy, love, and strength in family, friends, and community.

When you read my books, you're in for more than just a story, you'll discover a new culture, be tempted by mouthwatering menus, and even get a book playlist packed with both uplifting and heart-tugging songs. And if you've ever wanted to learn a few Gujarati words, don't worry. I've got you covered with a handy glossary!

My books are about love, family chaos, and resilience. If you enjoy heartwarming stories with love at their heart than take a chance on me. If you want to find out more about why I write stories about living and growing up in England, while still embracing my South Asian culture, visit my website and read my blog.

www.sazvora.com

OTHER BOOKS BY ME
University Reena & Nikesh Duet
My Heart Sings Your Song - Book One
Where Have We Come - Book Two
Made in Heaven

This book is a work of fiction. Names, characters, businesses, organisations, places, events and incidents either are the product of the author's imagination or are used fictitiously. Any resemblance to actual persons, living or dead, events, or locales is entirely coincidental.

Note from Saz

The spelling used in this book is British which may be strange to American readers, but NOT to those living in Australia, Canada, India, Ireland or the United Kingdom. This means color is colour. I hope this is not confusing and will not detract from your reading experience.

The Gujarati words used in this book can be found in the Glossary at the back.

TRUE LOVE AGAIN

Copyright © 2022 by Saz Vora

All Rights Reserved

www.sazvora.com

Cover Design by Mita Gohel

First published on www.sazvora.com ©July 2022.

Print Book ISBN: 978-1-8381465-3-5

First edition. July, 2025.

To all the single ladies I know who love their lives and have sought paths that aren't the norm, particularly in South Asian society. You are smashing it, don't let the aunties drag you down.

For Gini

TRUE LOVE AGAIN

"Looking back on when we first met. I cannot escape and I cannot forget…"
Atomic Kitten – Andy McCluskey, Stuart Kershaw, Jem Godfrey, Bill Padley

Soundtrack
To enhance your reading experience, you can listen to my soundtrack on Spotify.
There's also a playlist at the back of the book.

DESIGN MY DATE

Meera

Meera wasn't sure why, but there was something about the debonaire gentleman, standing tall and poised that piqued her curiosity. He had the air of an old-world charm, like the gentlemen you see in old movies, dressed impeccably in a tailored suit with perfectly polished shoes. A dainty woman in a flowery dress and light blond hair approached him with a shy smile. She removed a single yellow rose from her black leather quilted handbag and held it out to him. The elderly man nervously stroked the yellow rose on his jacket lapel, his hand trembling slightly. He said something to the woman, and she blushed, her smile growing wider. They turned toward the door, his arm lightly resting on hers as he led her through it. They were both dressed to impress, certainly not your usual Baby Boomer group out for lunch. The yellow roses clearly proved they were on a date. As Meera nursed her coffee, her mind wandered. Could it be a blind date? Were the elderly couple set up by mutual friends, or were they the kind of romantics that corresponded through letters from an advertisement in the newspaper before meeting up? She chuckled softly and shook off the old-fashioned thought entering her mind. They might be old, but everyone she knew from her parents' generation had smartphones and WhatsApp.

She was at her regular monthly lunch with Craig, a fellow department manager who'd joined the Birmingham team at the same time as she did three years ago at Reach for the Sky, the place they worked. They were discussing the recent away day with the Diversity Engagement Group, when she had caught a movement outside the mullion window of the newest place to eat in Birmingham's Gas Street Basin. Curious, Craig turned to follow her gaze, watching the mature couple being led to a table for two in the restaurant.

'Have you ever been on a blind date?' Meera asked. She believed in true love and always loved to hear stories of couples who'd found theirs. Was that why she'd fallen for Kaushik? Was that why she'd forgiven him?

'Look at me, Meera,' Craig chuckled, his manicured finger running up from his head down to his canvas shoes. Do you really think I need someone to hook me up?'

Craig was half Chinese, a quarter English, and a quarter Welsh, but you'd never guess it. His eye shape and complexion were the only tell of his mixed race. He was tall, too tall, thereby defying the Asian stereotype.

'What about you?' Craig asked. Meera didn't particularly enjoy talking about her divorce, but there was something about Craig's genuine interest that drew her out, making her want to share.

'Oh, yes, I have. Obviously, through family introductions. I'm an old divorcee,' she said. Very old, according to the Masi matchmakers, she thought. She'd only just turned 40. 'I've been on blind dates with forty-two men. That's an average of three men per year, and I've been divorced for thirteen years. Of those forty-two dates, ten were introduced by my family or friends of the family.' She paused, reminding herself that they weren't just colleagues, they were friends too. Usually, she kept her private life private.

'The first couple of years were horrible. I had to move back home after my divorce, and every aunty seemed to know someone or the other who was looking for a wife. You know what I mean, hinting that they didn't mind a divorcee.'

She needn't tell Craig of the financial support she'd needed. Only her brother and his wife knew about the monumental debt.

'The first two were in their fifties, with grown-up children. There was this man who barely reached my bust in his Cuban heels. Then, there was one who wouldn't disclose why his marriage broke down, but he was very rich. I mean, who turns up in a red Porsche and drives down to London to the Royal Opera House? I got some seriously bad vibes from him. Then, there was the guy who visited his aunt from Zambia and had a lisp. Also, there was this one guy with the useless arm, and he kept waving it at me.' She shuddered at the thought of that hand touching her. 'I don't mean to be mean, but I couldn't get past the hand, but he was nice enough.'

She then remembered a stream of nondescript men with receding hairlines.

'Wait, I forgot the toupee man!' she exclaimed. 'He had this weird toupee that looked like a flapping crow

3

tethered to his scalp. He refused to walk by the canal with me because of the wind, lest it blew everything up to reveal it all.'

Craig burst out laughing, envisioning the scene.

She immediately put on her best aunty voice and said, 'Arrey, Meera, when are you going to find a suitable boy? You're not getting any younger or thinner.'

Craig snorted, 'That sounds just like Anita aunty, the matchmaker. Yeah, I get it. My Asian aunties are always telling me to find a wife so that I can give my parents grandchildren.' His hazel eyes twinkled, and his smile widened, making his eyes crinkle into tiny slits.

She took a sip of the tepid coffee and told herself not to mention Simon, the ex she'd broken up with on Valentine's Day last year. That was the same day Simon had developed the sudden urge to have sex with his best friend, Janice. That on their date night, no less. To top it off, that same best friend had even prepared a romantic meal for the two of them at her home. The memory was still painfully vivid, the smells from the kitchen, the beautiful table setting and the unmistakable sounds coming from the living room sofa. Later, she'd found out that Janice and Simon had been doing the dirty deed on her favourite sofa and his during every special date he'd surprised her with.

All the reminders of never finding her life partner after Kaushik made the space between her chest ache. Without thinking, she rubbed the spot to ease it. She had really thought Kaushik was *The One*, only to discover he was a psychotic liar, a cheat and a wastrel all rolled into the one man.

'What if we targeted our communities?' Craig

4

suggested, pulling her out of her thoughts. She narrowed her eyes at him.

'Hear me out first,' he said, grinning. 'It's not the usual matchmaking stuff. We're always going on about diverse community engagement, right? How about… a dating app for diverse communities?'

Her mind hummed with the exciting possibility of creating something that would help her community. Besides, she hadn't taken on a new project for a while now and was itching for a challenge to get her out of the heaviness she'd been carrying lately. *So what if she hadn't found a man? So what if she couldn't replicate the marriages of her parents, her brother or her best friend? So what if she was 40? Not everyone has a soulmate, The One, right?*

And she'd already proved to herself just last weekend that she could attract any man when she'd hooked up with that guy from Morgan Stanley, a lust filled, no holds barred type of night. Yes, this sounds like something she could get her teeth into.

'We can create the app, that's a no brainer, but what's going to be our USP? Because we have got competition from websites and aunties. Who's going to be our target audience?' she asked Craig, a bit too loudly.

The restaurant suddenly fell silent, and she and Craig paused mid-conversation. Even the yellow rose couple turned to look at them. Craig's chair scraped against the textured tiled floor, breaking the stillness. Everyone's eyes shifted away from them, and they all turned back to their meals.

'Alright, if you were our target client, what would you want?' Craig whispered in her ear as he settled the bill. 'I'll need to use you for the presentation.'

Before she could respond, he strode to the door, holding it open for her as they stepped out of the restaurant.

Her immediate thought was not me. She didn't need to find a life partner. She was happy as a singleton. And her second thought was, would she be comfortable with creating a dating profile, even if it was just for a presentation and would never go live?

They talked about other possibilities as they strode back to their office at Reach for the Sky. Once inside the office block, they found a meeting room, specially set up for impromptu brainstorming sessions, with piles of Post-it notes and boxes of marker pens. After several failed attempts at a name and a mind map of the unique selling points, they concluded that they had a reasonable idea to present to the board. Meera and Craig were confident that they'd manage to secure a spot on the presentation schedule for the upcoming meeting in two days. Their idea ticked so many boxes for the diversity engagement strategy.

Craig began creating a presentation and found the perfect images from their stock photo drive to bring their vision to life. Meera, who hadn't created a data stream for years, felt a buzz in her fingers as she began coding.

A few hours later *Design My Date* was born. Once they were confident in their initial model, Craig fired off an email to one of their best coders, instructing him to create a prototype using characters from '70s British sitcoms as their clients.

When they finally made their way to the ground floor reception, only Rocky, the security guard, was on duty. The car park was nearly empty, except for two sports cars, a dark grey BMW M3 and a white Audi R8.

'Working late again, Meera, Craig?' Rocky asked as he unlocked the door. They both nodded and asked after his young family and wife. Rocky, whose actual name was Rakesh, always took the night shift as his wife worked during the day at Sainsbury's.

The air bristled with excitement as Craig and Meera walked to their cars. As she pulled the door handle of her Audi R8, Craig, who was just a few spaces away, called out. 'I can feel it in my bones, Meera. We've hit the jackpot with this one. Get ready for a big, fat bonus.' She laughed at his enthusiasm, the sound genuine and happy.

Angus, their CEO, and the rest of the board members would need a lot of convincing. It's not like a dating app hadn't been suggested for new initiatives at nearly every company away day since forever. But this time, it felt different. She felt the simmering hope and excitement at the thought of this one being approved. A perfect way to meet someone through shared interests.

As she drove home, she grew confident that this app would suit people who were searching for companionship and love without the meddlesome aunty network. At least with this, there would be no obligation to date someone who was the nephew of a distant cousin's spouse's sister's next-door neighbour, she chuckled to herself.

WIDOWERHOOD

Krishan

Krishan turned onto the road leading to his parents' house and parked his car in his old parking space next to his father's Volvo, which was now covered with a tarpaulin. His father had recently lost the confidence to drive after a minor scrape at the Tesco car park, where he'd reversed too close to the car behind him. This had become an inconvenience, as now, Krishan had to pick up his children himself, whereas, before his father's accident, he would come straight home to the comforting smell of his favourite food, with his children freshly bathed and ready for bed.

As he opened the door to his childhood home, the familiar aroma of garlic, ginger and freshly baked rotli released all the tension from his shoulders. He placed his car keys on the hook, but a heaviness filled his chest from an earlier memory. He'd seen an elderly couple sharing a quiet lunch date, and the thought that he would never ever be able to do that with Kreena, the love of his life, sent a sharp ache to his chest.

As he spent a brief moment watching them turn towards the restaurant with its old-fashioned wide doors and small windows, he felt a shiver run through him. There, on the other side of the small square glass panes, was Kreena, his wife. He couldn't believe what he was seeing, so he cleaned his glasses, and when he looked again, he saw an Indian woman having an animated conversation with her lunch companion.

He normally ate lunch in the kitchen on the sixth floor of their office block in Birmingham's business district, but today was different. He'd had various investor meetings, starting with lunch at a new three-star Michelin restaurant that had recently opened in the area.

Birmingham City Centre had changed significantly, having become much trendier than the dumpster he remembered from his childhood. The canal basin which used to be full of old trolleys, litter and undesirable activities, was now bustling with professionals in business suits in coffee shops, wine bars, and juice bars.

The day quickly spiralled into one of his least favourites. With both of his parents looking after his children, he himself had to deal with issues related to sites in Northern Italy and the Czech Republic. A job that typically fell on his father's remit, only adding to his stress.

A portrait of his wife, Kreena, a bubbly, smart, and devastatingly beautiful woman, greeted him as he slipped off his jacket and tossed it over the bannister. The walls along the stairs in the entrance hall of his parents' house were adorned with photographs of captured moments with him, his family, her family, and their children. It was a tribute to his wife, who was the only woman he'd loved unconditionally, a shrine lovingly curated by his mother in her memory. She was taken from them all far too soon, especially from him and his children.

When Kreena and he struggled to have children, they'd found out sooner rather than later about IVF. Fortunately, they lived in America, and they had great health insurance. The diagnosis and treatment process took only a few months instead of stretching for years. Although it was expensive, they had access to the best infertility clinics and the latest IVF treatments, leading to a successful pregnancy on their first attempt.

After receiving the good news, they decided that coming back to the UK was the best option for them. Both of their families lived in the UK. There was no way they could have children in the US without support, especially since they both planned to work.

When they returned from California, armed with CVs filled with Silicon Valley experience, they moved in with his parents, and a scenario that not every daughter-in-law looked forward to with excitement. However, Kreena thrived in this environment, glowing from the experience. She got on like a house on fire with his mother, bonding over gossiping, cooking, shopping and bossing around the men in the family. As soon as Natasha was born, Kreena fell deeply in love with their daughter and couldn't bear to leave her side.

He'd been mulling over the idea of setting up a cloud storage solution with server farms in more affordable European countries. After much thought, they both made a bold decision to give up their lucrative jobs and embark on a new adventure, as the likes of AT&T, Microsoft and Google were actively looking out for effective solutions for data storage.

Almost seven years after returning home to Birmingham, he found himself a widower with two precious children: a six-year-old daughter and a four-year-old son. He relied on his parents' support to help him manage his business during the day, and they often stepped in as ad hoc babysitters for investor meetings he simply couldn't avoid.

Krishan had barely walked down the hallway when two small children grabbed onto his waist and legs, squealing with excitement about what they'd done at Ba and Dada's house. He lifted Neel onto his hip and knelt down to let Natasha scramble onto his back. The familiar scents of soap, baby oil and Vicks filled his nostrils.

'Jai Shri Krishna, Beta! How was your day?' His mother smiled as she filled a steel tin with a stack of hot rotlis in the kitchen at the end of the hall.

After he'd had a fill of his mother's delicious cooking, the evening progressed as it often did with his parents. His mother mentioned yet another 'suitable woman' that he should meet, or at least consider looking at her biodata, a term often used by the aunties, or 'masis,' as his mother would say. It was always the same when a family wedding approached. Frustrated, he snapped at her and then immediately regretted his words when he saw the hurt on his mother's face. To make things worse, his father, who was one of the most supportive husbands, also snapped at her for bringing up the Masi matchmaking network.

On the drive back to his home, he regretted making his mother sad. Glancing at the rearview mirror, he checked on his sleeping children in the back seat. The comforting aroma of home-cooked food, packed in ice cream containers for his already full freezer, filled the car.

When they arrived, he lifted Neel, his four-year-old son, in his arms and woke Natasha to take them inside. The lights were off, except for the soft glow from the entrance hallway. Lucy, his daily nanny, always left a light on in the evenings when the kids were with his parents.

'Daddy, can you read me a story?' his adorable daughter, who looked just like his wife, asked. He kissed the top of her head as she went upstairs ahead of him. Neel let out a yawn and snuggled into his neck. God, he loved his children so much.

He tucked his little girl into her bed, sitting in the nursing chair his wife had sourced from an antique store. They'd painted the room yellow and decorated the walls with pictures of ducks in all shapes and sizes before Neel was born, as Natasha loved ducks.

As soon as the little girl's head hit the pillow, her droopy eyelids closed. He waited for a moment before picking up the story of Jemima Puddleduck.

'Have you forgotten what page we're on, Daddy?' she mumbled sleepily.

He turned to the page marked by a blue iridescent duck feather. Not that he'd needed it. He remembered exactly where they'd left the story the night before.

'Ice, I need ice,' he spoke out loud to the empty bedroom after putting his daughter to sleep. He'd been doing that a lot lately, wanting to hear his wife's quiet voice chiding him that diluting good whiskey was a travesty. Sitting in the dark, with the lamp on the bedside table his only source of light, he gazed at the photograph he'd taken of Kreena on the day they'd met. Lately, he felt exceptionally morose and was unable to shake the heaviness in his chest, struggling to make sense of his life. The music system played *"When You're in Love with a Beautiful Woman"* from his favourite country rock album of all time, *Pleasure and Pain* by Dr. Hook. It was the anniversary week of her diagnosis, and the echo of the consultant's words filtered through his mind: 'I'm sorry to say that the cancer has spread to the endocrine system. There's nothing we can do.'

When Kreena hadn't lost her baby belly even a year after Neel's birth, they'd joked about her having a phantom pregnancy because she'd loved being pregnant, loved being a mother too much. It was only after he had stumbled upon an article in the Sunday supplement about the increased risk of ovarian cancer associated with IVF treatments that he'd asked her to make an appointment with a doctor.

As the pain of losing his wife washed over him, tears trailed down his cheek. How could his body react so strongly to the woman he had seen in the window earlier? And how had the thought of finding someone new to replace her even crossed the forefront of his mind? It was just that he missed the companionship, the easy banter, the sessions of thrashing through an idea, and even their occasional squabbles.

He knew why his mother had brought up the topic again. His niece's wedding was fast approaching, and many of the aunties would be quick to point out a divorcee or even an older single woman whom they thought might be 'suitable.'

Maybe he was ready... ready to find someone to spend his life with. The more he thought about it, the more he realised his children needed a mother. At forty-five, he was still young, as his friends and family kept reminding him. It was time to find someone. Wasn't that why he'd spent so long staring at the woman during his walk along the canal basin, his nerves jangling beneath his skin? It was her haircut that had drawn his attention to her; it was the same style Kreena had when they first met, just hitting her shoulders, layered and beautifully shiny. Oh God, he missed her so much!

Sighing, he went to his drinks cabinet and again poured himself a glass of single malt from Scotland, *without ice.*

DATE & MAKE

Meera

Meera had been working long fourteen-hour days, wishing she had gone away for the spa weekend that Lesley, her best friend from school, and Carol, her best friend from university, had arranged for their monthly catch-up. It was supposed to be a day for all of them to re-energise. For Lesley, it meant a day off from the usual weekend routine of ferrying her four children, all under the age of fourteen, to their various activities. For Carol, it was a brief escape from caring for her elderly mother, allowing her to regroup so she could continue supporting women-owned businesses.

However, the prototype she was working on had a few glitches, and the presentation was scheduled for Monday morning. Besides, the developers were working over the weekend, and Meera was not the type of boss who'd swan off while her team was sorting through coding issues. They finally managed to crack the coding glitch late Sunday night and celebrated with pizza and beer.

The next morning, she woke up with a dull, throbbing headache. The gym, located in the basement of their building, was unusually busy, with people in varying degrees of gym wear. She often wondered how some of the women managed to look so fresh even after their strenuous workouts. Sweat trickled down her back as she increased the speed and incline on the treadmill. A good session at the gym always helped her process her thoughts, especially the key points for her upcoming presentation. Afterwards, she freshened up, dressed with purpose, and headed to the office.

'Let's kill this, Meera,' Craig said the moment he stepped into her office on the thirteenth floor to escort her to the boardroom. His enthusiasm always brought a smile to her face. Of all the department heads, Craig was the one who could always put a positive spin on any delays or problems. His go-to mantra was, *'All problems are surmountable.'*

They stepped into the boardroom, where six heads greeted them. Craig handed out tablets that displayed the prototype. Meera logged into her presentation, ready to impress them with their innovative dating app.

The demonstration went exceptionally well, with most of the board members feeling impressed and enthusiastic about the unique solution they'd developed for the dating dilemma faced by the diverse community. As Craig and Meera tidied up their space and got ready to leave, Angus stopped them. His perpetually down-turned mouth hadn't lifted even once throughout the presentation, not even when the rest of the board chuckled at the sayings from aunties of various communities, inspired by sketches from *Goodness Gracious Me*.

'Well done, it was a sound proposal.' Angus's steely blue eyes darted between her and Craig. 'It ticks many boxes for Reach for the Sky's Pie in the Sky strategy.' He gestured towards the two chairs next to him. Craig refilled their glasses with water and settled comfortably into his seat.

'Here we go,' she thought. 'He's going to pick holes, suggest changes, and tell us it needs more work before it can get the go-ahead.'

Instead, Angus surprised them by asking about the costs for the next stage. Meera impulsively blurted out that she had already signed up ten people for the beta team. Craig nudged her foot with his, and she immediately stopped talking.

Angus's tone always made her feel inadequate. He was rarely friendly towards her, often sneering at her failed ideas or unsuccessful beta tests. He had the type of personality that always saw the negative. She often wondered how he'd managed to set up Reach for the Sky, a company whose singular business was all about inspiring people to go beyond their comfort zones and explore new life experiences.

Ten people. What had prompted her to make that claim? The words had just slipped out of her mouth. She didn't know anyone, not a single person apart from herself, who would fit the client profile from her Gujarati community.

Craig informed Angus that he would send him the development timeline later in the day, along with his department's costs. At that, Angus's lips finally quirked upwards. Meera breathed a little easier; her production department's costs were lower than those of developers, so it was likely they'd get full funding for their new app.

As they walked towards the lift, Craig insisted they

stop at the coffee shop and get his favourite red velvet cake to replenish their sugar reserves. While they enjoyed their early morning snack, they wracked their minds, trying to think of anyone they knew from diverse communities. Their company had a diverse workforce, so there was bound to be someone from their own colleagues. However, they would also need to trawl through their friends and family. Meera told herself that it was doable. They could find ten people by next week, but first, she had to convince Craig to talk to Aunty Anita, the Asian matchmaker.

Later that day, as the clock on her desk ticked to 7.30 p.m., she messaged Craig for a quick regroup to discuss their progress on the diversity dating and experience app *Design My Date* (DMD for short).

'So, Aunty Anita won't help. It's a no-go,' Craig sighed, flopping onto the chair opposite her desk.

'Okay, I've got two people. Jex from Design has an older ex who's looking for someone, and Abi from HR has an aunt who's fed up with meeting people from church who don't understand her.' Meera stood by the whiteboard in her office and wrote "Beta Clients," underlining the heading with a squiggly red line. Meanwhile, Craig connected his device to Meera's speakers and played his Queen playlist. Freddie Mercury's voice filled the room, warbling, *"I want to break free."*

By the end of the hour, they had contacted everyone on their list and had five confirmed yeses, two maybes, and eight no ways. Among the five confirmations, there was one bisexual white female, two widows of different genders from the Afro-Caribbean community, one heterosexual woman from Pakistan, and a gay man who'd lost the love of his life ten years ago.

Feeling accomplished, they slapped their backs metaphorically and decided to wind up for the day. Meera tidied her desk while Craig went back to his office to collect his coat before going to her favourite little Italian restaurant. Having missed a few gym visits over the past week, she opted to walk down the stairs. When she reached the reception area, Craig was chatting with Rocky.

'Hey, Meera. Craig has my brother's details. He's frustrated with meeting the same old types of people. You know what I mean?' Rocky winked at her, knowing fully well what he was implying. Rocky wasn't shy about oversharing and told her about his eldest brother, who'd recently gone through a terrible divorce and was searching for a life partner just six days after receiving his decree absolute. Meera thanked him for the recommendation, hoping that his brother was genuinely looking out for a life partner.

During their meal at Paulo's Trattoria, they continued to add friends and acquaintances to their growing list. They'd come up with a unique recognition system, inspired by the elderly couple they'd seen at Gas Street Basin earlier that week. An old-fashioned blind date when people used flowers instead of photographs as introductions. While swipe left and instant rejection was the norm on other dating apps, they had suggested readily found everyday objects like umbrellas, ties and belts as subtle markers. There was even an option to use their own recognition system. But one thing that wasn't allowed was sharing of social media or photographs.

A glass of red wine helped ease Meera's weary mind, allowing her to relax for a moment.

'Angus better stump up the funding for the project. I can't believe I cold-called so many people and convinced them to go on blind dates with complete strangers and actually enjoy the whole experience,' Meera said to Craig, laughing.

The evening continued in good conversation and a feeling of achievement as they enjoyed their Italian meal. Even if she wasn't interested in finding someone, Meera hoped that the app they'd created would allow others to get their happily ever after. When they eventually left the eatery, the area was buzzing with people making the most of the summer evening.

DEVON WEDDING

Meera

A silver SUV pulled up ahead as Meera walked along the narrow, dusty dirt lane leading to the wedding venue. It was perfect, small enough for intimacy, yet large enough for a grand Gujarati wedding, which featured four events scheduled over four days. Exhausting, extravagant and excruciatingly painful. Meera had underestimated the distance from the bus stop, and her poor trainer-clad feet were throbbing in protest. She hesitantly walked toward the vehicle, her tender soles feeling every sharp stab of the sandstone and flint along the track.

Just then, the SUV's window rolled down. 'Are you in trouble? Can I give you a lift?' She stopped at the driver's window, her eyes widening slightly as the stranger's deep, penetrating voice rumbled through her stomach. His concerned gaze scrutinised her face.

'I'm heading to Carlington Manor. You wouldn't happen to be going there for Jaimini and Keval's wedding, would you?'

He certainly didn't have the Devon twang of a local. With his dark tanned complexion, dark eyes and thick dark brown hair, he fit right in with the expected wedding party. His head tilted slightly as a smile shone in his eyes.

'Where did your car break down? We can get your bags. Hop in.' She heard the car doors unlock with a click. She explained to him that she hadn't driven but had simply miscalculated, thinking the walk from the bus stop would be much shorter.

She lifted her red weekend bag and said, 'This is all I have. The rest of my wedding outfits are with my parents, who arrived by car.'

The boot of the car opened automatically as he stepped out, taking her bag from her. He was tall, at least a couple of inches above six feet, which was taller than the average Indian man. His sky-blue shirt stretched tightly across his broad shoulders, and his sleeves were rolled up, revealing muscular forearms. He strolled back to where she stood.

'Hi, I'm Meera, the bride's guest,' she said, holding out her hand. He didn't look like a serial killer or a rapist. And they say if you build a rapport with someone who gives you a lift, they're less likely to want to kill you or rape you. Why had that thought even come into her mind? She questioned.

'Krishan,' he replied, shaking her hand. 'I am the bride's guest too. Jaimini is my cousin brother's daughter.'

Meera racked her memory, trying to recall if she'd ever seen him at any of the family gatherings that she had been obligated to attend. She was certain she would have remembered him, the five o'clock shadow on a powerful, chiselled jaw, and those exceedingly long eyelashes that no man had any right to possess were impossible to forget. But most of all, she would have remembered his height. At five feet six inches tall, she was regarded as tall, much too tall for a lot of Gujarati men. Except for Kaushik, who stood at six feet one inch, was as vain as a peacock, and spent all his time at the gym and in other women's beds.

She exhaled, pushing the thought of her ex-husband back into a box. The new project had a lot to answer for. Reading the application brought back painful memories. Memories of displacement, destitution and debt that had grown into… well, into the top end of tens of thousands of pounds. She instinctively touched the diamond pendant on her necklace for comfort.

'Have we met before?' she asked him.

She was at most of Jaimini's milestones, except when she was with Kaushik. He'd never liked coming to her family gatherings, often making excuses to avoid them or simply disappearing.

She recalled the waiting and waiting… until it was too late. How she'd eventually give up, undressed and wallow in the sadness of missing yet another opportunity to catch up with her family.

But that was then. After her divorce and a few years in Copenhagen, she had started attending close family celebrations again. So why hadn't she met him or his wife before? The odds of not meeting him before were very slim, especially since she belonged to a tight-knit Gujarati community.

'I'm afraid we haven't. We lived in California before, if that helps.' He opened the passenger door for her and jogged to the driver's side. Before getting in, his eyes wandered to the back seat. She turned to follow his gaze and saw a little girl with her hair styled in several bunches held by yellow ribbons, and a boy sucking his thumb, his hand clamped around his curly hair. Both the kids were sleeping in their car seats. He pointed to them, whispering, 'That's Natasha and Neel. They're napping. Two of the other reasons we didn't socialise much.' He chuckled. 'Chickenpox, teething, colds, unexplained fevers. The list of ailments is endless.'

Meera nodded as she reached for her seat belt, her thoughts drifting to the children's mother. They were cute, with their little button noses and pink cheeked, cherub-like faces. She wondered what sort of woman his wife was. Undeniably beautiful, no doubt.

The little boy resembled his father, but the girl had a round face and cupid bow lips above a delicate chin. She was a lucky woman to have a husband who had brought the kids to Devon all alone, while she arrived ahead to enjoy the Mehndi party. The very party Meera was now late for, thanks to a rescheduled meeting with a new client.

She glanced at the special rear-view mirror, designed to check on the children in the backseat, and a pang of sorrow filled her chest. The only regret she had was not finding someone earlier so she could have had children. She'd turned forty earlier in the year, which meant it was highly unlikely for her to have kids now. Statistically rare, not impossible, but definitely uncommon.

She didn't have a boyfriend anymore and wasn't planning on getting one anytime soon. She'd also thought long and hard about donor insemination. Being a parent was tough enough, and the idea of single parenthood didn't appeal to her. She loved working far too much to give that up. Juggling the responsibility of both a small human and a department full of twenty-year-olds wasn't her idea of a happy life.

'I hope you don't mind speaking in whispers,' Krishan interrupted her thoughts.

'No, not at all. To be quite honest, I like the silence,' she said, flashing her broadest, brightest smile at him, hoping it would tell him that she wasn't usually this anti-social. She just needed to build up her strength for all the inevitable aunty remarks.

Fifteen minutes later, they arrived at a bottle-green sign with gold lettering announcing Carlington Manor.

'Finally,' Krishan whispered, 'I thought this winding road would never end.'

'Oh… I'm sorry, I didn't notice,' she replied, her eyes meeting his. His eyes twinkled with mirth as he asked her where she was staying. She told him that she was staying in the main house, and he made a point of mentioning that he was staying in the cottages with his family.

The sweeping driveway revealed a grand Georgian manor with classical pillars supporting a colonnade that sheltered the stone steps. The house was elegantly covered in ivy, adorned with large, small-paned windows on either side of the centred double doors.

It was impressive, an unconventional choice of venue that could accommodate all the guests for large Indian weddings. Jaimini and Keval had found this place and had brought both sets of parents to negotiate the deal. They secured sole use of the property for their guests over four days, with external caterers providing authentic Gujarati vegetarian food for the wedding.

A small voice muttered from the back seat. 'Are we

there yet, Daddy?'

Krishan glanced at the rearview mirror and told his daughter that he was getting Meera's bag and that they still needed to drive to the cottage. The child waved at Meera, and she smiled, waving back, telling her she'd see her later. Krishan opened the boot and took Meera's bag out.

Just then, a young woman in a crop top and baggy track pants rolled up above her knees ran down the stairs. Her face was perfectly made-up, false eyelashes, shimmering eyeshadow and an elaborate hairstyle.

'Meera Fai! Thank God you're here!' she exclaimed breathlessly.

Krishan's head dipped. 'Meera Fai?' His face was full of questions. She was surprised that he knew nothing about her and her failed marriage. Perhaps he was cut from the same cloth as her, happy to stay out of people's lives.

'Thank you for the lift. See you and your wife tonight,' Meera said, waving to Natasha again. Krishan's lips curved into a smile, but a dark shadow of sadness fell across his face.

'Hi, Krishan Kaka. See you later.' Jaimini held out her cheek for a kiss and then popped her head into the open car door. 'Natasha, do you want henna too? Get Risha to bring you up to the house.'

She turned back to Meera. 'Leave that, Meera Fai,' Jaimini said, pointing to the suitcase and a man in a dark green jacket standing beside her. 'They'll take it to your room. I've kept the henna lady back just for you as you are the only one left to apply mehndi.'

'Hello, honey. Stop calling me Fai. It makes me feel

old,' Meera said with a laugh.

Jaimini's eyebrows disappeared behind her fringe. Meera kissed her on the cheek and said, 'Show me your mehndi first.'

Grinning, Jaimini held out her hands, palms up, then turned them over before pointing with her splayed hands to her flip-flopped feet.

'You shouldn't have made the ladies wait. All you needed to do was ask them for a cone. I would have applied the mehndi myself,' Meera said.

'Oh no, not this time. It's my wedding, and you are going to get dolled up like everyone else!' Jaimini exclaimed.

Meera chuckled. When her brother got married, she was only sixteen, and her job was to keep the kids entertained. Jaimini, who was just a little girl back then, had fallen in love with her and followed her around with the other children. Meera had always loved that role when she was younger, keeping the kids busy at family gatherings, both religious and social.

She still enjoyed hanging out with younger people. They were fun to be with and were far less judgemental.

She wished her mother's friends would stop trying to find a suitable man for her to marry and stop commenting on her age. She took a deep breath and rubbed her tired eyes as she followed Jaimini into the grand house.

Could the app she was developing find her an ideal match? She slapped the thought away. She needed a stiff drink and a good night's sleep.

SANJI NIGHT

Krishan

As soon as Meera smiled at him, Krishan immediately realised that he'd seen her before at Gas Street on the day of his investor meeting. Recognition hit him instantly. She reminded him of Kreena, not only her looks but even her voice was the same. Soft and lilting. His innards vibrated from her nearness, at the haunting familiarity of her. Yet there were differences too. The way she couldn't sit still, her leg jiggling. The way her jaw jutted out as she mulled over an idea. The nervous way she touched the stone pendant on her necklace. And then there was the full curve of her hips, the voluptuous breasts, the narrowness of her waist. How could this be happening? He recalled the flash of memory that had burst into his mind when she'd sat in his car.

His thoughts drifted to another wedding a long time ago.

Joshna, his cousin sister, had pointed Meera out to him at her own wedding. 'That's my husband's younger sister,' she'd told him. 'She's brilliant and a Maths whizz. I think you have a lot in common, Krish. She'd be perfect for you.'

He'd watched Meera from a distance, jingling her wrists like a Pied Piper as she escorted the children to the garden. A broad smile filled her lips as she'd turned to face him. A current so sharp ran through his body. He'd taken off his glasses and wiped the lens, worried that they'd turned into magic goggles that made every young Indian woman resemble Kreena.

He'd been seeing Kreena for eighteen months, eighteen glorious, unpredictable months. Every day spent with her was different, her enthusiasm for life's experiences addictive. As Joshna's wedding day approached, he'd finally mentioned marriage to Kreena, and to his delight, she'd accepted. However, they'd decided to tell their parents only after graduation, so he'd kept the news that he was dating a secret, even from his own sister, Kalpana.

Of all the events he had started attending, fate had somehow placed his wife's doppelgänger in his car, both of them heading to the same wedding. He'd heard about the ex-husband who had left her and how she'd moved back to live with her parents after her divorce. He'd also known of the many jobs she'd taken on while she was newly divorced and starting again. He'd checked her left hand and was surprised to see she wasn't married. She would impress any man with her resilience and the ability to bounce back from nothing.

Suddenly, a thought struck him. Why wasn't she on his mother's list? He wouldn't mind an introduction to Meera. The thought surprised him, and he quickly pushed it aside. Who was he kidding? No one could ever take up the space Kreena still occupied in his heart.

Later that evening, he didn't recognise her at first until she grinned. An excited anticipation stirred in his stomach as he took his time gazing at her. Her layered hair was swept into a loose bun at her nape, and the parting in the middle was adorned with a crystal encased tika. Matching leaf-shaped earrings brushed against her neck, and a matching necklace rested just above the curve of her perfectly rounded breasts. His eyes explored the exquisite display of skin, especially the small diamond pendant she unknowingly fiddled with, sitting in the dip between her collarbones. She wore a sleeveless choli in a deep purple, while her magenta and purple chaniyo was tied low on her shapely hips, accentuating her gorgeous body. A sheer chiffon chundadi draped elegantly over her left shoulder, completing her ensemble.

An idiotic grin spread across his face as his heart beat a staccato tempo in his chest. Meera was finally approaching their table. Ever since they'd gathered in the large dining area, she had been busy meeting everyone from Keval's side of the family, and he had tried really hard to stop his eyes from following her.

'Hello, Krishan. And Jai Shri Krishna, Ramchandra Fua and Kavita Faiba,' Meera greeted warmly, acknowledging his parents and everyone at the table with a smile. Then she crouched down to Neel's height and held out her hand to shake his. 'Hello, I'm Meera. Pleased to meet you.'

Before Neel could respond, Krishan's mother gently corrected him. 'Meera Aunty. Call her Aunty,' she said, grabbing Meera's hand and turning it over to inspect both the back and her palm. It was covered in an intricate, dark red pattern from the mehndi ceremony she'd been whisked away to earlier.

'Goodness, it's dark maroon. Looks like you'll find a husband this year,' his mother teased with a knowing smile.

'Is she related to us, Ba? I'm sure I've met everyone in our family,' Natasha inquired curiously.

'Beta!' His father's stern voice immediately quietened her, while her grandmother's mouth opened and closed at her granddaughter's question.

'Sweetheart, it's a sign of respect, like masi, fai, mami, kaki. Everyone here knows Meera as Meera Fai,' Krishan explained.

'But she's not your sister, Daddy. Can I call you Meera instead?' Natasha asked, her face scrunched in confusion.

Meera was doing her best to hide her hands behind her back. He had seen the hurt in her eyes at the mention of the superstition. Apparently the darker the colour of the mehndi, the more a woman's husband loved her.

'Sure, I'm too young to be an aunt anyway,' Meera laughed.

Natasha wrinkled her nose at her. 'But you look old.'

'Natasha!' Krishan admonished his daughter, his voice firm but tinged with embarrassment.

Meera's face lit up, and she smiled at his blunt daughter, holding out her mehndi-painted hand. 'We're going to be great friends. I like your attitude to not have too many aunties.'

She then stood up and told Krishan that she was

heading to her table and would see them later when the dandiya raas started.

Later in the evening, when Krishan was standing at the bar waiting for an orange juice with a double vodka, Meera appeared at his side, waving at the bartender to place her order.

'Two Absolut and lemonades, one without a slice of lemon, and a Bombay Sapphire and tonic with the works, please.' She leaned in, her eyes narrowing thoughtfully. 'Can I see the lemonade?'

The bartender held up two bottles, and after a quick glance, she pointed to one she wanted. She picked up the drink placed in front of him and sniffed it.

'Vodka? Is your wife coming tomorrow morning or have I missed meeting her?' she asked.

'My wife is dead,' he snapped.

Her smile faltered.

He hadn't intended to sound angry, but he had just been cornered by a gaggle of aunties at the buffet table, outside the restrooms, and in the garden. They had been telling him about a suitable match from the bevy of single women who'd come that night and would be there the next day.

'I'm sorry, Krishan,' she gently placed her hand on his arm. 'I didn't know.'

'Really? Everyone in the country knows about poor Krishan. Widowed too young, has two bright children, a big lonely house in Sutton Coldfield and a thriving computer technology business. They all say the same thing. So young to lose such a lovely, beautiful wife.' He exhaled sharply, shaking his head. 'How have you

32

managed to escape the aunties and the gossips? You're divorced, aren't you? Hunting for a life partner?'

Her eyes glistened with unshed tears and she instinctively touched the stone pendant on her necklace. He hated that he had made her feel nervous around him.

'I'm sorry, Meera. That was uncalled for. But seriously, how do you cope? How do you get past... the matchmaking?' He almost whispered the last word. She released a slow breath, the tension between them shifting to that of mild understanding.

'I don't cope. I've already had a neat vodka before coming down, and I've learnt to drown out their voices by trying to remember song lyrics. That's probably how I missed putting two and two together. Obviously, I've heard the whispers; I'm not impermeable to the Masi grapevine. But the moment someone mentions "a suitable man," my mind just... strays. I am so sorry. How are you and the children doing?' she asked, her fingers touching his forearm. The warmth of her touch seeped through his jabho shirt, stirring something inside him.

'I'm okay,' he found himself saying. 'I have loads of help from both sets of family. Natasha was three, so she remembers Kreena and sometimes wakes up asking for her mother. Neel was just a baby... so his life isn't as complicated. Birthdays and anniversaries are the hardest. I try to make things as normal as possible.'

Why was he telling her his life story? His eyes rested on her hand, and she quickly pulled it away.

'Sorry again,' she murmured. 'Any mention of a suitable man makes me zone out. I never, ever want to marry again.' She then picked up her drink, glugged it back, and signalled for a refill. She repeated the words as if reaffirming it to herself, 'Never. Ever. Marry.'

'Don't drink alone,' she advised with a teasing glint in her eyes. 'Go and find a table full of men. The aunties won't bother you then. Do you like dandiya raas, Krishan?' she asked, cocking her head. She then lifted her tray of drinks.

He told her he did. She beamed and promised to find him when the dandiya raas started. She told him that dancing helped her relax and that drunk dancing was the best at these events.

As soon as the DJ announced that the dancing would begin, Krishan took his daughter's hand and went to collect the dandiya, looking around for Meera. A stab of disappointment hit his stomach when he couldn't find her on the dance floor.

The DJ asked everyone to pair up and create a circle. As Krishan stood waiting with Natasha, trying to find anyone else with a young child, Meera called out Natasha's name. He turned towards her voice and saw Meera leading a line of teenagers and young children to the centre of the dance floor.

'Join us, and bring your daddy. This circle is for young people only,' Meera said, grinning. His mind flashed back to Joshna's wedding, remembering how she'd gathered all the teenagers and children up to play ball in the garden. He loved how much she drew the youngsters to her.

Much later, as the evening progressed, the die-hard guests were still engaged in a battle of Antakshari, a competitive singing game among the aunties and uncles. Krishan finally excused himself and got up from his table. His parents had already gone back to the cottage with Natasha, and Neel was snuggled against his neck. He suddenly realised that he hadn't seen Meera in a while.

During dandiya raas, she had swapped places with the young girl next to him, twirling and changing partners every fifth beat. He hadn't let himself enjoy dancing to the raas in ages, but with Meera, it felt natural. And she'd even pulled him to the dance floor afterwards when the DJ had put on a Bollywood dance song, *"Banke Tera Jogi."* They had laughed and danced until the tempo slowed down, and the slow dances began.

He wished the rest of the people at his table goodnight and walked through the lobby towards the cottages. And then he saw her. Meera was cradling his daughter in her arms in the quiet reception of the hotel, a notepad by her side. He'd left Natasha with his parents and hadn't thought once about his daughter since then, and a wave of guilt washed over him. He hadn't enjoyed a social gathering like this in a long while. He'd been lost in the easy conversations about cars, films and sports, a rare evening where no one mentioned his wife's tragic death, and no one reminded him of the fact that he was a single father.

He approached Meera and apologised to her, switching Neel to one arm, and motioning for her to pass Natasha to the other.

She waved him off. 'I'm fine, Krishan. Go settle him down first and then come back for Natasha. I'd volunteer to come with you, but have you seen these?' She lifted her foot slightly, showing off her gold high-heeled sandal.

When he returned to take Natasha, Meera was fast

asleep, cuddling his daughter even tighter. His heart pounded in his chest on seeing her like this. He sat next to her and gently shook her shoulder, her skin soft and velvety under his touch.

Suddenly, her eyes flew open in fright. 'What? Where am I?'

'You're okay. Let me take Natasha off you and walk you to your room,' he reassured her softly.

Carefully, he lifted his sleeping daughter and laid her on another sofa, instructing the man at the desk to watch out for her. Then, turning back to Meera, he reached for her hand and helped her get up. She leant into him as he escorted her up the stairs.

Just then, Joshna stepped out of the bathroom in the hallway.

'Can you look after Natasha, Josh? I'm just helping Meera,' he said. His cousin's face lit up with a smile as she nodded before heading towards the lobby.

He opened her door with the key and asked Meera if she needed any help. She was more awake now and had stopped leaning on him. He immediately missed the feel of her against his side.

'Thank you, I'm fine. Goodnight.' She smiled at him and held the door as he wished her a good night.

As he returned to the lobby, Joshna smiled at him and asked if he had a good evening.

'Yes, one of the better ones,' he admitted, scooping Natasha into his arms. He kissed Joshna goodnight and stepped out into the cool night air towards the cottages.

Hope and excitement filled the air. Perhaps he was

ready to meet someone new.

Only he remembered what Meera had said. That she'd never ever want to marry again. But looking back, when he thought about her experience, he understood why she felt that way.

THE BEACH

Meera

Meera couldn't remember how many drinks she'd had last night, but she knew it had been many. She hated weekend wedding events since there was no escape from the aunties, who constantly reminded her that she wasn't getting any younger. How she was a constant worry to her mother. How no man would accept her body shape. How she needed to exercise and get thinner, because according to them, only a man would make things better.

So far, she'd managed to go to these gatherings on the day of the ceremony itself. She would exchange greetings with the bride and groom, congratulate the parents on the spectacular occasion, eat, and then leave. But she couldn't do that with Jaimini. Never Jaimini. She loved her too much, having seen her grow into a confident, eloquent and successful young woman.

At the crossroads, Meera halted, panting to get her breath while clutching the stitch that had bothered her throughout the run. She debated which route to take. According to the map from the hotel, she could either do a full five-kilometre circle or take a straight two-kilometre path up or down. At breakfast, she'd tried to persuade her bhabhi, Joshna, to come with her, but Joshna had shown her a notebook with the list of tasks she had in the morning. The throbbing headache she'd woken up with still lingered on her forehead. She recalled a vague memory of being helped to her room, held by strong, protective arms, sad chocolate eyes, and a distinct scent that she couldn't quite place.

A familiar SUV pulled up beside her, the driver's window rolling down.

'Morning, Meera. Say hello to Meera, kids.' Smiling, she poked her head through the open backseat window and asked the children where they were going so early.

'Daddy promised to take us crab hunting,' Natasha said excitedly.

'And to the beach for paddling and sandcastles!' Neel added, holding up his red bucket and spade as proof.

'Did he now?' Meera grinned. 'It's a gorgeous day for crab hunting. Morning, Krishan! No hangover?'

He leant closer towards the passenger window he'd opened, whispering, 'I feel like Es Etch Eye Tee. Thought the sea air might make it better.'

'You said a bad word!' Natasha gasped, her eyes wide with shock. 'You know I'm good at spelling, Daddy.'

'What bad word? Tell me,' Neel giggled.

Krishan chuckled. 'Sorry, sweetheart. I won't do it again,' he said, glancing back at his daughter.

Meera told Krishan she was contemplating running the full 5K. He asked her if she had any tasks for the day. She told him that she would be helping set up for

39

the pithi ceremony under the gazebo in the orchard with him later. Friday was mainly a rest day before the full day of ceremony and celebration. Some families had already left for sightseeing, taking packed lunches from the hotel.

'See you later, Natasha and Neel. I want to hear all about your morning at the beach.' Meera waved and smiled at them, thinking that the full 5K would be worth the pain. She selected a running track on the music app, tapped her earbud and took off to the right.

A few minutes later, just as she was about to turn onto a well-used path, a car horn startled her. She turned to see the SUV pulling up onto the verge. Before she could react, Krishan jogged up to her and stopped just inches away. A pleasant scent of lemon and herbs hit her.

'Would you like to come to the beach?' he asked, his dark chocolate eyes holding her gaze. 'We'd love your company.'

Meera didn't have to think twice. She could always go back to her room. It was the safest way to avoid the aunties and their relentless commentary. But it would be a shame to be cooped up inside. The warm breeze was already brushing away the wispy clouds, revealing a cornflower blue sky.

It took her only a second to decide, as the early summer sun warmed her skin. She'd love to spend the morning on the English Riviera with Krishan and the kids.

'I would love it. You don't mind me dressed like this, do you?' she asked, hesitant. Krishan was wearing a red polo shirt, with navy blue shorts that hung off his hips, his toned muscular legs on full display. The children were just as smartly dressed, Natasha in a strappy red summer dress and Neel in green shorts and a red t-shirt. Earlier, Meera had thrown on an oversized yellow t-shirt with a tropical beach scene over her turquoise running shorts. Every contour and curve of her body was visible for all to see.

'It's perfect for the beach,' Krishan said, his warm hand touching her elbow as he led her toward the car.

'Yay!' The children cheered and clapped in excitement as she sat in the front passenger seat.

She turned to them. 'A couple of rules before I come with you.'

Natasha and Neel looked at her with curious eyes. 'I won't touch crabs or slimy seaweed. Instead, I'll collect seashells and expect ice cream, the kind with all the sauces and a flake. If you agree to my rules, then I'm all in for a morning at the beach.' She winked at Krishan and raised her left eyebrow questioningly.

'Agreed,' Natasha replied.

'Neel?' Meera inquired.

'Why won't you touch the crabs? They are the best thing,' he asked in confusion.

'Just agree, Neel. We'll sort the crabs out when we find them,' Natasha said.

Meera laughed and grabbed her seatbelt. 'We're off to the beach, beach, beach!' She sang in a sing-song voice.

Krishan reached over and squeezed her hand, and a spark jittered all the way down her spine. Flustered, she quickly turned to stare at the hedge outside to figure out what just happened, and why it had happened at all.

'Do you need to call or text anyone?' Krishan's voice interrupted her thoughts. She pulled out her phone from her shorts pocket and sent a text to Joshna.

Meera: Off to the beach. Promise to be back by lunch.

A reply came instantly.

Joshna: That's too far to run. You'll be exhausted.

Meera: Not running, driving.

Joshna: Who are you going with?

Meera: Krishan and the kids.

A second later, Joshna replied with a smiley emoji. A smiley emoji was never a good sign. Her sister-in-law had a habit of planning her wedding at the slightest hint of a man in her life. But why hadn't Joshna Bhabhi ever mentioned Krishan to her? What had happened to his wife? Why hadn't anyone mentioned him? Had he already rejected her before she even knew there was something worth going for?

'Did Joshna Bhabhi know about your trip to the beach?' Meera asked.

'Yes, I told her this morning when I asked how you were.' Krishan replied.

Meera blinked. 'You asked about me?'

'Do you remember anything about last night?' he asked, studying her intently.

'Yes, of course I do. Most of it, anyway. Natasha and I hung out together, didn't we?' she asked as if to confirm.

'We played noughts and crosses, Daddy,' Natasha chimed in.

Meera laughed. 'I remember you found us. The rest is all a blur.'

She explained to him how she had been working fourteen-hour days on a new app she was developing. The wedding, although full of aunties, would also help her rest and recoup, as long as she stayed away from them and their interfering matchmaking.

He nodded, but his face fell at the mention of the aunties. She sucked at the straw from her water pack until only air gurgled out. Krishan then told her about the cool bag in the footwell. Grateful for the distraction, she reached for a water bottle to avoid staring at his face.

'Natasha, Neel, water?' Meera asked.

They held up their cups.

'Aah, I see you're prepared. What about you, Krishan?'

He nodded, and she took a water bottle, twisted the lid and passed it to him.

Just as he took the bottle, her mobile rang. A distraught bride-to-be's staccato bursts declared she needed her. Jaimini.

'Honey, take a deep breath,' she said gently, glancing at Krishan, who slowed down.

She heard a pause, then a deep exhale.

'Much better. Now, go back to bed. It's too early to get up.'

Jaimini didn't listen to her. She cried out that she wanted Meera to sit by her side for the pithi ceremony.

Meera frowned. At the planning meeting, she had convinced Jaimini to pick someone younger and closer to her age for the role. Besides, if anything went wrong– No, she wouldn't allow those thoughts.

'You can't do that. We agreed. Sarina will get upset, and she'll look much better in the photos,' Meera pacified her softly.

Jaimini sighed. 'But you'll be there, right?'

Meera smiled and agreed that she would do her best to be by her side.

'Promise,' Jaimini was still not convinced.

'Yes, promise. I love you. Now go back to sleep.'

With that, the call ended.

'Do you want to go back?' Krishan asked with concern.

She shook her head. 'No, I'll send a couple of texts. She'll be fine. Keval will calm her down.'

'Okay, kids. Car Karaoke time!' Krishan flicked through his playlist, and Taylor Swift played on the car speaker.

'Yay, she's one of my favourite singers,' Meera grinned and began to sing, "Once upon a time, a few mistakes ago…".

❋ ❋ ❋

Within half an hour, they had parked and climbed down to the rock pools with buckets and nets in hand, ready to collect crabs. Meera loved finding out how young children responded to rules.

The truth was she wasn't actually frightened of crabs

nor did she think seaweed was slimy. She'd said that only to let the family crab hunt together, not wanting to be an interloper in their special time with their dad. Not wanting to intrude, she wandered off along the shore and returned with a bag full of seashells and shiny pebbles.

Neel approached Meera shyly to show her his bucket. She asked him to lift the crab, and when he did, she faked a scream, pointing to the uniqueness of the crab.

'Don't be scared Meera. My Ba told me that crabs lift their claws and snap them because they're frightened. It's a survival mechanism,' Natasha said, patting her gently on her shoulder as she knelt on the sand.

Meera grinned at her and Neel. 'Your Ba gives good advice. Most creatures react the way they do because they're frightened. Did you know that this is one of the best beaches for crab hunting?'

She looked up at Krishan who was watching her intently, his camera poised in his hand, ready to capture the moment. His expression changed as understanding dawned on him. He picked up a seaweed and waved it at her.

'You don't mind seaweed either, do you?'

'Nope, have you seen the bladderwort that's ready to be collected over there?' She pointed to the wiggly line of mottled green and olive that meandered along the beach.

By eleven o'clock they'd built a sandcastle, added seaweed curtains, decorated it with seashells, and had taken countless photographs with Krishan's professional-looking camera kit. After that, they had their well-earned ice cream cones. All the sauces for her and the kids, and strawberries for Krishan.

Meera liked the seaside. It was one place she'd love to escape to, although Norfolk and waterways were her go-to spots. She liked the children too. Neel was less talkative than Natasha, whose inquisitive mind was constantly asking questions. And Krishan didn't speak to them like parents normally did. Instead, he answered every query, no matter how unexpected it was, even when they found a decaying rat with skeletal babies.

Once the children were safely buckled into their car seats again, Krishan gave them Tupperware containers, each filled with sliced fruits to eat as they drove back to the manor house. Natasha's endless questions kept both of them occupied, some of which neither of them could answer.

When they reached the hotel, she kissed the kids goodbye and thanked them for letting her in on their special time together. Her stomach lurched when she saw the aunties gathered outside on the benches, looking at them with curiosity. Quickly she turned and ran into the main house.

She'd enjoyed the morning with Krishan and his children, especially as she'd avoided the same aunties' prying eyes. It was a shame they'd seen her get out of Krishan's car. She sighed, knowing very well they'd definitely have something to say about that later.

KALPANA QUESTIONS

Krishan

Krishan was hesitant about attending weddings because one aunty or another would invariably bring a woman to meet him. He'd declined so many invitations, citing sick children or a busy work schedule as excuses. However, he couldn't back out of Jaimini's wedding. He was her kaka, the younger male sibling of the bride's father, a first cousin, and in Gujarati families, that's practically the same as a brother.

Although his family was very close, with lots of impromptu meet-ups, he'd kept his distance. The sight of all the happy couples often made him resort to drinking, a habit which he was desperately trying to break. Perhaps he could handle a gathering again. So far, it hadn't been as bad as he'd expected. Or was it because, instead of sitting with his parents, he'd taken Meera's advice and sat with the men?

Their mission to find him a wife had begun just a year after Kreena had left them. Only one year.

In that short time, Tara Masi had introduced him to a woman, the daughter of a close school friend. She spent the entire birthday party telling him how much she loved children but never wanted any of her own. She told him how her small beauty product business was too important to give up while caring for a baby.

Then there was a timid widow in her mid-twenties from Malawi, who still dressed in pastel colours because her parents objected to her wearing bright colours when she visited them. How could he even consider someone who couldn't stand up for herself and so readily complied with her parents' wishes?

There were others, but the fifty-year-old spinster, who'd lost her mother at the same time he lost Kreena, still burnt in his memory. She had cared for her elderly parents until their passing. She'd said she wanted companionship, conspiratorially whispering she wouldn't mind if he had girlfriends to satisfy his sexual urges. She had such a low benchmark for a marriage, only wanting someone to care for her. He remembered meeting them at a puja at the temple, the poor woman had ended up marrying a sixty-five-year-old who wanted a new wife just months after his first wife of forty-three years had died of a heart attack. He recalled how the old man couldn't keep his hands off her and the woman's eyes being fraught with fear.

Tara Masi still badgered him, telling him at every opportunity that he'd mourned long enough, and should find a wife and mother for his young children. But Tara Masi knew nothing about Kreena. If he'd accepted any of those women, Kreena would have turned in her grave. Not that she had a grave. Besides, she believed in reincarnation and had told him her time with him was up. His dying wife had told him that he would meet someone very special, someone he would spend the rest of his life with.

He unlocked the car doors, and the children ran into the cottage, and he stayed outside, wondering again why his family had never introduced him to Meera. The thought that she'd already rejected him made him more upset than he cared to admit.

'Krish, do you want chai?'

He turned towards a petite woman in jeans and a loose white linen shirt knotted at the waist. She was holding up a teapot at the kitchen door. Kalpana, his sister, was the spitting image of their mother. 'Like two peas in a pod,' their mother would often tell people. They had identical personalities, identical mannerisms and identical taste in clothes. He leant against the garden gate. Shrieks and laughter from inside the house brought a warmth to his chest.

'How was the beach? Didn't know you asked Meera to accompany you?' Kalpana said. He took his mug of brewed tea off his sister.

Krishan had enjoyed Meera's company, her good sense of humour, her fun personality and her calm manner. After what she had told him last night, he had relaxed. He'd taken her advice and wasn't on high alert from the Masi Mafia anymore. No one knew how he really felt. No one would understand the sadness that bombarded him like a hailstorm, painful, bruising, knocking him off his sheltered path.

'We bumped into her,' he replied after a long beat of silence.

She let go of a deep sigh. 'I saw you dancing with her last night, and Josh told me you helped her upstairs. Anything I need to know?'

Krishan exhaled sharply, shaking his head. 'Really,

Kalu? I danced with a divorced woman and escorted her up the stairs because she had spent the entire evening playing with Natasha. We just went to the beach, and you already have our wedding planned?' His voice stern. 'And to top it all, none of you ever mentioned her to me. You all knew how similar she looks to Kreena,' he accused. He turned around and strode into the kitchen. His sister's face fell from the accusation in his voice.

Meera looked too much like his wife. *Is that why he'd felt a weight lift from his chest the moment he met her?*

'Woah, Krish, Krish, come back,' she screeched and followed him. The kids looked up at him as he walked into the living room.

'But I have to explain,' Kalu said by his side.

'End of conversation, Kalu,' he said firmly, raising an eyebrow as she stood beside him.

With a deep breath, he diverted the topic. 'What model are we making?' he asked his nephew Jaisan, who was sitting with Neel and Natasha, collecting pieces of Lego. His niece Risha was going through the instructions, while Hiran, his youngest nephew, was on his phone, watching a YouTube video.

For the rest of the morning, they, including his parents, made walls, turrets, towers and parapet walks out of Lego. His children eagerly told their older cousins about the fun they had at the beach with Meera. As they strolled up to the hotel for lunch, his mother also enquired about Meera, curious to know if they had met through work. Knowing they both worked in technology, she thought he might have bumped into her at the conferences. He informed her that they hadn't crossed paths before and that he had only just met her. He watched his mother's mind sifting through the gossip, making sure she was suitable. She smiled at him but not with her eyes.

Meera was already at the serving station, her arm linked with Jaimini as they filled a plate with salad and baked potatoes. She checked the cold buffet, which included both vegetarian and meat options. She had changed into a simple summer dress in red with white daisies, cinched at the waist with a matching tie belt, the hem hitting her knees. Damp strands of hair fell loose to air dry, and a natural wave shone through its gentle layers. It was nothing like Kreena's hair, which was straight as an arrow.

Another difference.

When had he begun noting the differences between Meera and his wife? When Meera returned to the serving table for pudding and coffee, Kalpana waved her over to their table. Meera approached them with a hint of reluctance in her eyes, the aunties following her every move. Nothing escaped the Masi Mafia, especially since they had WhatsApp on their phones. There was no stopping the messages and interference.

Krishan's mother thanked her for helping with the children last night and again this morning. He watched Meera's shoulders relax as she eased into friendly chatter.

'Meera Fai, can you tell him?' Jaimini yelled, pointing her manicured finger at Keval.

Meera sighed, an apologetic expression crossing her face as she turned towards Jaimini.

As she turned to leave, Krishan said, 'See you in the orchard, Meera.'

Then, turning to his family, he informed them that they would be decorating the gazebo later in the afternoon.

Under normal circumstances, Krishan would have dreaded being nudged toward a so-called suitable woman at these weddings. But he knew Meera was just as frustrated by the matchmaking aunties as he was. Besides, he remembered their conversation from the Sanji night, the night she'd told him she would never, ever, marry again.

BURNT FLOWERS

Meera

Jaimini was panicking like a bride in a rom-com. Meera had sneaked off after lunch to her room for some respite from the knowing looks of the aunties and woke up to the sound of furious knocking. A distraught bride stood in the hallway, waving a piece of paper with a checklist. Meera guided Jaimini to the armchair, made her some tea, and quickly texted all of Jaimini's friends. Half an hour later, the once frazzled bride was laughing with her friends as they left her room to find another gathering spot. Once Meera was certain Jaimini was surrounded by sensible friends and was in good hands, she made her way to the orchard. She unravelled the gem-coloured bunting from the boxes, lovingly crafted by Leena Bhabhi, Jaimini's mother, from old sarees, kameez churidars and chaniya cholis.

Krishan arrived soon after, apologising for the delay as it had taken longer than usual to get Neel down for a nap. They settled down to work together, unrolling and tying the bunting onto the branches of the apple trees. Before long, excited shouts from Krishan's nephews and a few of Jaimini's friends filled the space. With everyone's help, the orchard transformed into an exotic location reminiscent of India.

Krishan and Meera stepped back to admire the decoration.

'How did Leena Bhabhi find the time?' Krishan said in admiration.

'I know! A busy GP surgery, all those trustee positions, and yet she still managed to sew this special bunting for her daughter's wedding. She's a legend. One final touch, and we deserve a cool glass of lemonade,' Meera said, tying the last piece in place.

The younger volunteers waved them goodbye as they headed out of the gate towards the main house. Krishan and Meera strode toward the wooden gazebo, where the discarded boxes lay, and lifted out the painted panel of Krishna and the dancing gopi, which would hang on one of the hexagonal sides facing the seating area.

As Krishan gathered the now-empty boxes that had contained the yards of bunting, Meera took photos of the gazebo.

Suddenly, a panicked cry from Joshna drew her attention and Meera ran towards her sister-in-law. 'What's wrong, Bhabhi?' she asked, noticing Joshna wiping the sweat from her forehead with the back of her hand.

'I need a favour from you and Krishan,' she said.

Meera turned to see Krishan already striding towards them. 'What's up, Josh?' he asked.

They listened as Joshna told them about the florist's car accident, which meant the wedding flowers were nothing but burnt cinders lying somewhere in a ditch along the motorway. Frantically, she recounted the countless phone calls she had made to find replacements for the floral decorations she needed.

'It's a logistical nightmare. Do you have any idea how many weddings are happening this weekend? I need drivers to pick up flowers after the pithi ceremony,' she cried.

'I'll help in any way I can. Natasha and Neel have plenty of people to keep them busy,' Krishan reassured her by taking her hand and cupping it in his.

'Great. But no one breathes a word of this to Jaimini. She's already freaking out, wanting to change things at the last minute.'

For the pithi ceremony, everyone was told to dress in shades of yellow. Meera wore a pale yellow saree from her mum's wedding trousseau, a Banarasi silk with silver brocade embroidery and small flowers in pastel pink. She paired it with a full-sleeved matching chiffon blouse that their trusted tailor from Leicester had custom-made for her. It had two narrow straps, one at the waist and the other at the back of her neck, leaving her back entirely exposed. Most women her size chose to wear full cropped tops, but Meera had stopped listening to the fat shaming voices a long time ago. Her only concession to stop the gasps of displeasure was to wear her hair loose, it wasn't long enough to cascade down her back like her old hairstyle, but she'd been persuaded by her hairdresser to try a new look.

She beamed as Krishan arrived with his family. All men were dressed in mustard yellow jabha. While he and Ramesh, his brother-in-law, paired theirs with navy dress trousers, his father opted for cream pyjamas. His nephews wore short shirt-length jabha with white dhotis. Recently, she'd noticed that many of the youngsters wore dhoti instead of the traditional churidar, influenced by the latest fashion trends from Bollywood. Even her nephew Sachin had opted for a mango yellow kediyu with a black dhoti.

The women in Krishan's family were just as elegantly dressed, all in matching mustard yellow sarees with antique embroidery, while Natasha and Risha, his niece, wore canary yellow chaniya cholis. Natasha's hair was tied in two bunches, each secured with yellow ribbons with tiny ducks. Meera had learnt from their time together that ducks were Natasha's favourite birds, and she possessed an encyclopaedic knowledge of them.

Throughout the ceremony, Meera stayed close to Jaimini, almost forgetting her divorced status, until she overheard Tara Masi.

'Why is *she* in the gazebo? Leena needs to tell her to move,' Tara Masi said.

'Shush, Tara, they'll hear you,' Hetal Masi whispered, trying to quieten her younger sister. Tara was modern in her dress, being the only elderly woman in an Anarkali suit instead of a saree but was too traditional in her outdated views.

'It's an auspicious occasion, Hetal. Divorced and widowed women should stay away,' she insisted, only this time louder.

Meera's mother narrowed her eyes at Meera, a silent message for her to move away from the bride.

When it was time to give money for luck, she lifted her phone and walked to the end of the orchard. When would they stop blaming her? Kaushik was the culprit.

She'd forgiven him for lying so many times and had kept their mounting debts a secret, not wanting either of their families to worry. His constant cheating was the final straw. No man would make her go through that again. Taking a deep breath, she dialled her oldest friend.

'Which Masi was it?' Lesley's fuming tone vibrated through Meera's earpiece.

She had known Lesley since their first year of primary school. They lived two streets apart, growing up on the outskirts of Coventry, went to the same secondary school and were inseparable throughout their school days. University had sent one to York and the other to Durham, yet that hadn't dented their closeness. The only time they'd drifted apart briefly was when Meera had tried to keep her marriage woes to herself, as Lesley was already struggling with her first child and postnatal depression. It was a weak moment in both of their lives.

'It was Tara Masi,' she sighed.

Tara Karia was married to a wealthy business owner and had been born with a silver spoon in her mouth. Her two children were perfect, beautiful and successful, each married to equally successful and attractive spouses. Both the children gave her the mandatory grandchildren, in the right order, boys first, then girls. There was no conflict in her family. She perceived she had the right to express her opinions without regret, showing not one ounce of sympathy or empathy for others.

As she dawdled back to the hotel, everyone was enjoying their Indian high tea, complete with an assortment of snacks, all accompanied by lively chatter. Meera decided to retreat to her room with a plateful of food, telling Jaimini that she needed to work for a couple of hours. It was a white lie; everything at work was fine. She just felt raw and hurt from the whispered taunts from the aunties.

Jaimini & Keval's Pithi Ceremony
Afternoon High Tea

Idli

A soft & fluffy steamed cake made with fermented rice and lentil batter served with sambar - a lentil, and vegetable spicy soup - and coconut chutney

Mini Masala Dosa

A crispy pancake made with fermented rice and lentil batter pancakes stuffed with a potato and onion curry served with sambar, lentil and vegetable spicy soup and coconut chutney

Wati Dall Bhajia ane topra ni chutnee

Deep-fried ground Black-eyed pea and split mung beans fritters, and fresh ground coconut chutney

Bateta Vada ane tameta ni chutnee

Deep-fried flatbread stuffed with spiced smashed potato balls coated in gram flour batter and fresh tomatoes and red onion chutney

Paneer Pakora ane dhana, marcha ni chutnee

Deep-fried Gram flour batter coated fresh Indian cheese squares and coriander and green chilli chutney

Pani Puri

Deep-fried wheat breaded hollow spherical shell filled with a combination of potatoes, chickpeas, and a special water made with a blend of spices.

Pau Bhaji

Pan fried bread rolls with smashed spiced vegetable, chopped shallots and a knob of butter

Bombay Sandwiches

Toasted sandwich made with tomatoes, cheese, onions, boiled potatoes and coriander chutney and special spice blend

Assortment of vegetarian sandwiches

Lasun Mogo

Deep-fried cassava chips served with garlic chili chutney

Bateta ni Chips
French Fries

Assorted Chutney

Ambli Khajjur ni chutnee
Sweet and sour tamarind and date chutney

Tameta ni chutnee
Tangy and spicy fresh tomato and red onion chutney

Dhana Marcha ni chutnee
Fresh Coriander and Green chilli chutney

Topra ni chutnee
Freshly ground Coconut chutney

Sweets

Mango Shrikand
A Gujarati strained natural yoghurt dessert made with mango and sugar

Topra Paak
Sweetened ground coconut and milk sweet

Boondi na Ladwa
Beads of gram flour fried batter soaked in saffron and cardamom infused sugar syrup formed into balls with raisins and chopped pistachio

Fruit and Plain Scones served with Devon clotted cream & strawberry preserve

Assorted Cakes

Drinks

Masala Chai
Brewed black tea with milk and sugar with ginger and a combination of fragrant spices

Badam nu Doodh
Sweet brewed milk with powdered almonds, saffron and cardamom

Assortment of fresh fruit juices and fruit teas

Later in the afternoon, she met Krishan by the exit gate. He had changed into a pair of dark jeans and a white t-shirt, and he wore dark-rimmed glasses. He held up a wicker basket with a checkered cloth hiding snacks for their upcoming journey.

She had also changed into a pair of jeans and a yellow top with a slashed neckline that sat perfectly on her shoulders.

'Glasses?' she questioned.

'Hay fever and lack of sleep,' he replied, adjusting them slightly. 'Neel's been having trouble settling. Don't you like them?' he asked playfully.

She grinned and told him he looked like Clark Kent, and he laughed, the rumbling sound penetrating deep into the pit of her stomach.

The journey on the M5 to Bristol was uneventful. Krishan and Meera spoke little, opting to listen to his playlist. When Atomic Kitten's *"Whole Again"* started playing, Meera looked at him, arching an eyebrow.

'Don't raise your perfect eyebrow at me. I like ballads,' he said in defence.

She liked being with Krishan. He hadn't passed judgement. unlike many men she had met in their community. After three years of marriage, Meera had been the one to instigate the divorce, leading to many accusations. After all, Kaushik had been a good suitor. The youngest son of a heart surgeon, privately educated, worked for a Swiss Bank, then an Investment Bank, a Hedge fund, and eventually managed his own funds. Many viewed her as the unsupportive wife of a husband who hadn't found his place yet.

Only a few people knew of Kaushik's debts. Even after thirteen years, many of his women still found her on social media, attempting to hold her accountable for their debt.

Once they arrived on Gloucester Road in Bishopston, a suburb of Bristol, Krishan parked behind the row of shops. Inside, the florist pulled the haars out of their boxes, exquisite garlands of red, cream and orange roses, one for Jaimini, and the other for Keval. The woman handed them a cardboard crate containing matching flower displays and assured them that Joshna had already paid for everything.

Curious, Krishan asked her how she knew about the haar. Smiling, she pulled out her phone and showed him a photograph of herself with her best friend, an Indian bride, proudly posted on her social media.

Krishan then video called Joshna and showed her the haars and other flower arrangements to ease her mind, and gently asked her if they needed to go anywhere else before heading back home. As they prepared to leave, the florist requested them to help promote her new florist's business on social media using a hashtag #indianweddinghaar.

As they were leaving Bishopston, Krishan suggested to Meera that it would be wise to eat in Bristol, and at that very moment her stomach rumbled, making the decision for her.

He laughed and commented on how that reminded him of Natasha's often rumbling tummy. 'Are you a frequent snacker too?' he teased.

'No,' she replied indignantly, pointing to the clock on the dashboard.

He turned towards her, grinning. 'The Quayside has great places to eat,' he suggested.

She felt a small flutter in her belly. *He has a lovely smile, she told herself. That's all. Nothing more.*

As they drove, a nugget of an idea came to her mind. But first, she had to get him in a good mood. She needed to find out his opinion on dating again.

BRISTOL DINNER

Krishan

People were waiting at the bar at the Greek taverna for a table. Krishan ordered a soft drink for himself and a white wine for Meera after she had gone through the wine list. He had noticed that Meera was quite discerning about her drinks the night before. She had been very particular about the brand of vodka and the type of lemonade they stocked.

He, on the other hand, had asked for any old vodka with orange last night, not wanting his parents to see him drowning himself in alcohol again. His usual tipple was a decent, neat whiskey, but last night's choice, 45% alcohol without a distinct smell had thankfully not raised any suspicions. Suspicions he couldn't afford, not when he was already reluctant about being at this wedding, surrounded by the Masi Mafia.

Once they were seated at the table, Meera asked him if he would share a bottle of red with their souvlaki. He agreed to just one glass as he was driving. Conversation with Meera felt easy. She listened attentively, making encouraging sounds as he talked about his work and balancing life with two young children.

'How long have you been alone?' she asked.

He thought about his response. Should he be honest with her? After all, Meera was Joshna's sister-in-law. Surely, she would have known about Kreena. He glanced at his empty plate, took a deep, steadying breath and told her about his beautiful wife. He spoke of how he still talked to her in the home they had furnished and decorated together in anticipation of their baby boy. He also told her about how Neel had come into their lives, without any help from hormonal treatments or checking fertility cycles. Their miracle baby, as Kreena had called their son.

He then told her about Kreena's diagnosis and how they'd lost any hope for a cure. He shared how difficult it had been for them all. Retelling the story was never a problem for him. He'd had to repeat it so often that, at times, it felt like he was sharing someone else's life story. He described how he would fall asleep from exhaustion, everywhere in the house as he tried to keep working. Then, when Kreena had finally gone into a hospice, he couldn't function anymore and had become like a walking corpse, requiring the same type of care as his young children. He also told her about the help he'd received from his and Kreena's family and how they spent weeks with him until he had finally recovered.

'I'm so sorry, Krishan,' Meera said, squeezing his hand. He felt the beginnings of a tingle, but quickly dismissed it as something that he'd imagined. He loved Kreena. She was his one true love, his only love.

But he missed true companionship. The odd one-night stands were tempting, and the Tech conferences were full of people who wanted to hook up. He was a full-blooded man and hadn't lost his sexual appetite, but the guilt always stopped him from going through with it. More than once, he had walked away, leaving the women confused and unsatisfied. So, he learnt to bury it deep within him, and when things got tough, he satisfied his urges like most men did, but he still felt guilty about emotional connections. Dating was difficult for him.

'I miss her. Miss her so much that my heart's sore,' he confessed, and her brown eyes darkened with sadness. She didn't offer meaningless comfort. Instead, she just nodded at his confession and quietly took one last sip from her glass.

They arrived at their manor house at 11.30 p.m., a huge traffic jam delaying their return. The place was quiet now. Everyone was back in their rooms, readying themselves for a day full of ceremonies ahead.

'Want a bedtime tipple?' Krishan asked after they'd taken the flowers to the cool room. Meera looked at her watch, two thin creases appearing across the ridge of her nose as she instinctively reached for her necklace.

'It's just a drink, Meera,' Krishan coaxed.

'Sure,' she nodded, meeting his eyes.

He led her toward the hotel bar, his hand resting lightly on her elbow. She was tall for an Indian girl, he'd noticed that when they had danced. Kreena wore killer heels and still only reached his lips, but with Meera in heels, they stood eye to eye. He was pleased to note another difference.

'Brandy?' he asked as they approached the bar. She gave a nod.

'Two Calvados, please,' Krishan signalled the barman.

She laughed, a tinkling crystal sound. He felt an unexpected thud in the pit of his stomach.

'I was beginning to think you didn't know your alcohol after ordering any old vodka and orange,' she teased.

He smirked. 'No, I know my spirits too well.' He looked down at the wooden bar top as the barman set down two coasters.

'But?' she prompted, curious.

He exhaled, leaning slightly against the bar. He told her that his mother worried if he drank too much of the hard stuff in her presence. 'Besides, the masis had collared me, and I lost my senses.'

She nodded in agreement and turned towards the comfy armchairs by the fireplace. Cheering echoed from the games room, breaking the quiet. And they fell into their usual moments of silence and comfortable conversations.

Later, he walked Meera back to her room, giving her a kiss on the cheek.

'Goodnight, see you in the morning.'

She caressed her cheek lightly, a small smile playing on her lips.

'You're quite a catch, Krishan. Maybe you should think about finding someone.'

He thought the same thing. He wanted to spend more time with her. A question burst through his mind, and he had to ask her.

'What about you? Would you be interested?' he said,

gauging her reaction. She laughed, that wonderful sound making his belly queasy.

'You're so sweet,' she said as she unlocked her door. 'But I'm not looking for anyone. Never. Ever. You remember?' She smiled, but her eyes held a quiet sadness.

As he returned down the stairs, he saw Tara Masi closing her room door.

Had she been there all along, spying on them?

He exhaled sharply, hoping this wouldn't cause any more problems for Meera.

6

6
68

JAIMINI'S BIG DAY

Meera

Meera adjusted the neckline of her off-the-shoulder dress, pulling it up slightly from the armpit. She had spent the best part of the morning running around, searching for people. Jaimini, overwhelmed with wedding day jitters, suddenly wanted to speak with someone or the other. Instead of standing in her beautiful white lace wedding gown, Jaimini tugged and paced.

At least the weather gods or as her mother and Jaimini's grandmother would say, Lord Ganesh, had set aside all obstacles to make the wedding weekend glorious and perfect. The flowers decorated over the heart-shaped arch smelt divine. Their fragrance permeated through her nostrils as she leant to whisper something into Jyoti, Keval's mother's, diamond-encrusted ear. Even the replacement florists had come up trumps, providing exquisite last-minute displays.

Throughout the morning's ceremony, not once did the aunties comment on her presence. Some were even nice to her, complimenting her on the choice of clothing she'd brought with her for the Ganesh Puja. A few minutes ago, just as she came out to fetch Jyoti,

Tara Masi had clutched Meera's hand to her bountiful chest, gushing over her pale lilac gown, a snip at the John Lewis sale, perfectly suited for the pastel theme of the civil ceremony.

As they hurriedly walked back to the manor house, Meera explained Jaimini's nerves to Jyoti. Krishan was seated next to his parents, his pale grey suit fitting him perfectly, as expensive handmade suits often did, and displayed his broad shoulders, the lapels showing off his powerful pecs. Underneath, he wore a pale pink shirt with a striped, pink tie in gradation of magenta to light pink. His children sat in the row behind. Neel was dressed in a pale grey suit that matched his father's, and Natasha in a cream dress with embroidered ducks on the bodice.

Krishan raised his eyebrow in a query. Meera threw her brightest and happiest smile at him. He didn't need to know the ins and outs of Jaimini's pre-wedding nerves. It was between the women who mattered to Jaimini, and Meera was part of that inner circle.

Leena Bhabhi and Joshna Bhabhi had tried to calm Jaimini to ease the fright that was clear in her eyes. Jyoti, despite her four-inch heels, ran to her future daughter-in-law and engulfed her in her arms, rubbing her exposed back gently, whispering words of comfort. They'd been doing that in turns, holding her tight, reassuring her and telling her it was normal to feel panicky before the wedding.

Jaimini took deep, calming breaths and thanked her mother-in-law for rushing to comfort her. Lifting her head up high, she turned to the other women.

'I'm ready. Meera Fai, tell Keval to get ready to meet

the most beautiful bride he's ever seen,' Jaimini said with a small shy smile plastered on her face.

With that, Meera walked back to the manicured garden, where the registrar was waiting with Keval.

'What did my mum say, Meera Fai?' he asked, curious.

She'd told him so many times to call her Meera. She shook her head with a smile at his insistence on calling her Fai.

'Et tu, Keval,' Meera clutched her ribs, feigning a blow as she turned towards her seat. She sat next to Joshna and her brother in the front row, directly in front of Krishan. The familiar, comfortable smell of his cologne hit her nostrils, wrapping around her senses.

She'd enjoyed the previous day's mad dash on the M5 to Bristol. Krishan had a self-deprecating personality, making light of his wealth, his intelligence and the multi-million-pound company he single-handedly owned. After closing the door on him last night, she'd googled his company. But that wasn't what kept him on her mind. She was physically attracted to him, and yet she couldn't do anything about it. From their conversation, she knew one thing, Krishan was old-fashioned. Someone who had married his first love and wouldn't even think of a quickie or a fumble under the covers. And certainly, never with her, because of their family connections.

The violinists played *"Suraj Hua Maddham"* from *Kabhi Khushi Kabhi Gham*. All eyes turned towards the manor house as Jaimini walked down the path, with her mother to her left and her mother-in-law to her right. Joshna squeezed Meera's hand while Hasmukh Bhai waited ahead for his beautiful daughter to join him.

The legal ceremony went without a hitch as the bride and groom declared their vows, many shed tears as they watched the newlyweds walk back up the aisle. As they made their way to the marquee, Krishan stepped beside Meera, casually plucking bits of confetti from her shoulder. 'You look stunning today, Meera. I love the hair,' he said softly. Then, with a sigh, he added, 'The ringlets... How long did they take?'

She wasn't sure if he was being honest or ironic. The hairstylist had assured her that the cascading ringlets would soften over time, but three hours later, they were just as springy. Lifting her chin in the air, she told him to stop teasing and ignored him as they carried on walking towards the marquee, which was set up for a hearty wedding breakfast. Just as they reached the entrance, Krishan pulled her to the side, right behind a metre high pedestal adorned with the gorgeous flower arrangements they'd picked up the day before.

'It's a compliment, Meera. I really like them.' His voice was low as he deliberately curled his forefinger around one of her ringlets by her jaw. Her breath hitched, and his gaze zeroed on her lips.

Suddenly, a voice interrupted them.

'Arrey, Krishan! I've been looking for you.' Tara Masi approached us from the other side.

'Can I grab you for a moment?' she said, placing her small hand lightly on his formidable forearm.

Meera watched his broad back slump as Tara Masi escorted him towards a petite woman dressed in a floral pastel dress in silk chiffon, someone Meera had briefly met on her first night here. She was a family friend from Keval's side and had spent the mehndi night vividly describing every horrid and acrimonious detail of her divorce as they sat with wet henna hands.

A sudden pang of regret washed over Meera. If she ever considered marriage again... if at all... then Krishan ticked all her boxes. But she wasn't looking. She would never be interested.

The thought upset her, but she swatted the feeling away. As she continued watching them walk away from her, he suddenly stopped and said something. Tara Masi turned towards her and widened her eyes. And then, a small smile spread across the interfering aunt's face. She squeezed Krishan's forearm and walked alone towards the newly divorced woman. Meanwhile, Krishan walked back to her.

'Why did she glare at me? What did you say to her?' Meera's breath hitched.

'Tara Masi saw us last night,' Krishan informed.

Her heart thudded. He'd only kissed her on the cheek, but she had placed her hand on his honed chest, letting it linger longer than normal. Was that the reason Tara Masi had complimented her today? There was none of the usual body shaming nor the questions about her inability to find a man to fill the void in her life, in the words of the aunties, not her. Her man-less life was perfectly acceptable to Meera. She was happy. She was content. She didn't need a man to complete her life.

'I told her I liked you,' Krishan revealed.

A small feeling of warmth soaked into her heart, but she ignored it.

'Honestly, Krishan, didn't you listen to me? I'm not looking for a match.' She moved towards the table their family had gathered around.

'Just hear me out. I have a plan.' He fell into stride beside her, their steps perfectly in sync.

She stopped and faced him. 'Go on then, explain?'

His eyes scanned left and right. Curious, she turned her head, too. Their family's attention was fixed on the two of them. Tara Masi stood triumphantly beside her mother's chair, looking smug.

'Daddy!' Neel screamed as he ran towards them. Krishan immediately picked him up.

'Hello, Meera. I wore a suit. Do you like it?' Neel said, showing off his new outfit.

She concentrated on talking with Neel as she walked with Krishan towards the table, pointedly ignoring the feelings she'd built up at his words. *I like you*. Krishan was one of the good ones. If the aunties had matched her with him earlier, she might have even considered it, because a few years ago she was open to meeting someone, open to a relationship. But not anymore. She would let no one break her heart again.

She wondered what he meant by *a plan*, letting the excitement nudge its way into her chest. As they reached the table, Krishan leant in and whispered, his warm breath caressing her neck, 'Meet me in the orchard afterwards.'

With that, he walked to the other side of the table, leaving her curious and confused.

Masi Mafia

Krishan

He explained his idea to her as quickly as his breath would allow, his nerves all over the place.

'MASI MAFIA?' Meera's eyes narrowed.

'Aren't you fed up with them? Always pulling you to meet some unsuitable man? Giving you those cutting looks at the Puja?'

'Cutting looks?' she repeated, incredulous.

He laughed. *She made him laugh.*

Earlier, he'd waited for her in the orchard, only she hadn't come. But he knew he'd see her again; after all, they were at the same wedding. Did she think she could avoid him?

So, he'd waited quietly at the bottom of the stairs in the manor house. His children were with his parents, and for once, he wanted to speak to Meera alone, without any interruptions.

When she'd walked to the top landing, his breath had caught in his throat. His eyes were like telescopes, locking onto her face, searching for any sign that she'd seen him waiting. The wooden staircase, with its

75

curved balustrade, seemed to carry her gracefully down to him. Her springy curls from earlier were tamed in a style that rested on her nape, and he waited for her to come to him, unable to stop admiring her. The Gujarati style saree she wore was in a heavy turquoise silk with a parrot-green and gold brocade border. The side parting of her hair from the morning had changed to the centre, a line of crystal adorning it. A diya-shaped chandlo glittered on her forehead.

She was flanked by Jaimini's friends, young men and women in their twenties. He had watched how they were drawn to her, like bees to a bright flower. He saw her making an indistinguishable remark, and they all burst into laughter.

Revealing himself, he stepped into the centre of the atrium. Immediately, the youngsters scuttled past him, calling out to Meera that they'd see her in the food marquee, where pre-wedding teas and coffees were set up. Krishan asked Meera to follow him. She didn't ask why; she simply dipped her head as she strode next to him.

They were now facing each other in the library of the manor house, just beyond the games room.

'Do you intend to keep repeating what I say?' he asked, amused.

She snapped out of her stupor, her gaze locking onto his.

'So, let me get this straight. You want me to be your fake girlfriend and accompany you to the next set of gatherings we have over the summer, just so the–' she air-quoted. '–"Masi Mafia" will leave you alone?'

Krishan nodded, affirming that she had got the gist of

his plan. Her perfectly arched eyebrows scrunched together, forming the shape of a flying bird.

'Who gave me cutting looks? Why cutting?' she asked, puzzled.

He told her about the aunties' behaviour at the Ganesh puja and the pithi ceremony, how their disapproving glances and whispered gossip had irritated him. He told her how it upset him that they'd sprinkled gangajal on anything Meera brought to the ceremonies.

'Oh, that,' she said with a shrug. 'That's normal. I'm used to it. Being born under an evil star has its consequences.'

'My stars are aligned badly, Krish. It was meant to be.' Kreena had said believing the astrology to be true.

His wife's words echoed in his mind, a flashback from the day they discovered she couldn't conceive without help. A familiar ache settled in his chest. No. He couldn't think about Kreena's last words to him. He was not ready to revisit that memory. *Not yet.*

Without thinking, he grabbed Meera's hand, and it felt like it belonged there. The thought struck him so suddenly that he immediately pushed it away. He had to remember why he was doing this. It was because he loved his wife too much to let go. And as long as he could hear her voice in his mind, she was still with him. This only confirmed that his plan was right. They both had a motive, his was to adjust to being alone, and Meera's was to stop the endless arranged marriage introductions.

'You can't believe that. The next thing you'll say is that your horoscope predicted everything that happened to you,' he scoffed.

Her lips pursed tighter. Her free hand absently stroked the gem on her necklace and her eyes dropped to their joined hands. For a fleeting moment, he felt her tug, as if meaning to pull away, but she didn't.

'Do you agree?' He wouldn't give up her hand, gripping it firmly. He realised then that he liked holding her hand.

She led him to the sofa in the centre of the room and sat down gracefully. She took a slow, deep breath and released it softly. He turned to face her.

'I'll agree if you also do me a favour,' she said.

He dipped his chin slightly, listening.

'You know that app I'm working on? But before that, you have to agree not to tell anyone.'

He'd known about the app she was working on and questioned why she hadn't asked him for help yet. A part of him hoped it was because she liked him too.

'I hope it's not cyber trawling or cloud data harvesting, because I won't do that. My company's reputation rests on my honesty and integrity,' he clarified, in a pompous tone, unable to stop the smile twitching on his lips. He wanted to bring that smile back on her face.

'No, nothing like that,' she laughed. 'You watch too many dystopian thrillers.'

And there it was, that laugh again. He felt a sliver of warmth spread in his chest.

'Do you agree?' she asked again.

He met her gaze and told her he did.

'We're working on connecting like-minded people together to go on an experience. It's like a dating app but designed for new experience seekers from all minority communities.'

'And... you want me for what?' he asked, intrigued.

'First, I want to add your details to the database. Then, you have to go on dates. And since you'll be on the beta list, I want your detailed feedback on the experience. It's still new. We haven't fleshed it out with community liaison or marketing yet.'

He exhaled sharply. 'One reason I asked you to be my fake girlfriend was to not go on dates. I love my wife, and I'll never ever want to replace her. She is the only woman I will truly love. You're making me do what I don't want to do.'

'But these aren't Masi Mafia dates,' she countered. 'They're people who want a life partner. The people on my app are like you and me. People who want companionship, who want to learn new things and who want to get the aunty brigade off their backs.'

Having someone who'd accompany him to dinners and award ceremonies didn't seem like a bad idea. He'd stopped going to the cinema or the theatre alone. He'd stopped meeting up with friends too. The only people he met regularly were his family or parents at his children's school. He'd stopped doing things he loved and had to find new hobbies as a single parent of two young children.

'It's only a few dates with like-minded people Krishan, and a couple of drinks with me afterwards.' She added.

He thought about meeting with Meera after the

wedding for drinks without prying eyes. That's what cinched the deal for him. The space between his chest warmed.

'Okay, it's a deal. Let's seal it.' He held out his hand, as she shook his hand her smile reaching her eyes. He'd never noticed the tiny golden flecks that radiated from her dark pupils. Kreena's eyes had been black, another difference he added to his growing list.

As they walked out of the hotel, she took his hand.

'You'd better ask permission from my brother if we're going to fake it to believe it,' she said, teasingly.

He hadn't considered that. Lying to the aunties was one thing, but to his family? Could he deceive them too?

'By the way, who came up with the term Masi Mafia? Was it you?' she asked.

She tilted her head to look at him, her sparkling earrings grazing her long, slender neck. His skin heated as a lustful thought of his lips on her neck smacked in his mind.

'No, Piyush told me,' he informed her.

'Piyush! The guy who said, "Wanna come see my Ferrari Portofino?" while pointing to his crotch? Ugh, when did you speak with him?' she asked, shuddering.

'You told me to go sit at the men only table, remember?' he reminded her.

'I meant married men only table, not the "I'm too sexy and single man table".'

She rolled her eyes.

'Krishan, Krishan, Krishan. I am so glad you're my fake boyfriend. You have a lot to learn.'

'My friends call me Krish,' he said.

Just then, her brother strode purposefully through the arch of the marquee.

'You tell me that on the third day, Krish?' She laughed again, and before he knew it, he was laughing too. For the first time in years, he didn't feel guilty about a little joy. But he felt something else… something he couldn't quite place. When had she even met Piyush? A strange feeling nudged at his heart.

Suddenly, her brother was in front of them, an unreadable expression on his face, as he asked, 'What's going on with you two?'

DATA & DATE

Meera

The alarm on her phone rang while she was in the middle of updating the DMD app, the third version of the fifth iteration. They'd added sixty people so far, which was good going, considering it was only company employees, friends and of course, Krishan, once he had agreed to join. She'd asked some of the other single people at Jaimini's wedding. Who knew there would be a lot of interest in meeting up for shared experiences? One candidate had actually referred to it as the best thing since sliced bread, and cost effective too.

She closed her laptop, grabbed a holdall from under her side table and went to change out of her clothes into an evening dress and killer heels. Tonight, she was off on her first fake date with her fake boyfriend, Krishan. The plan was to spread the word and meet the people who needed to know at Warwick Art Centre at Nitin Sawhney's concert. She knew that everyone related to the Masi Mafia would be out there in full attendance. It was the best way to send the news along the gossip vine.

As she stepped into the lift, she reflected on how well

the rest of Jaimini's wedding went. It was the best time she'd had in a long while at a Gujarati wedding. Tara Masi and her gang were all smiles and congratulations, beckoning her to the front of the festivities, instead of the disparaging remarks they'd made to make her leave the area.

Krish had wandered over to her often, resting a protective hand on her lower back. Even her mother's eyes had sparkled when Harish had told them about Krish asking for permission to date Meera. Which was a pity, as their fake relationship had an expiration date and would end by October. By then, all the gatherings and celebrations would be done. Diwali was usually a small family event with her family and friends. She'd have to create a falling out so her mum wouldn't be too upset, something that wouldn't paint Krish in a poor light. She'd also agreed with Craig that it was enough of a trial period to get Angus to fund the project.

Krish stepped out of his car to come towards her as she stepped through the revolving doors. He was handsomely dressed in a Navy Nehru suit with black satin collar and buttons, adding a touch of elegance. His trousers were jodhpur style, sculpting his well-defined thighs and tapering beautifully over his muscular calves. For a fleeting second, an image of a naked Krish briefly shimmered in her consciousness, and she gulped, heat pooling in the pit of her stomach. She silently reprimanded herself for conjuring the image. He loved his wife, even now. He'd told her often enough that she was his true and only love.

He stopped in front of her, and his intense, appreciative gaze slowly, deliberately roamed over her body.

'Wow, another exquisite dress.' His eyes immediately locked onto her lips. 'Can I kiss you–' he whispered, his breath fanning her face, '–on the lips?'

'There's no one here to witness this kiss,' she breathed out softly, trying to steady her trembling heart.

'They're everywhere, Meera. We have to cover all bases.'

She brushed her lips against his, a soft caress, and pulled away, rubbing her sweaty palms on the ruche bodice of her emerald chiffon dress as she walked towards his car. His warm hand moved to rest on her lower back as he guided her to sit inside. She liked the feel of his hand. Just a bit too much.

Stop thinking about him like that. He's unavailable.

'How was your day?' He turned towards her before starting the car.

'Good, thank you. And yours?' she asked.

He laughed, a deep, rumbling sound that reverberated in her belly. 'Good, thank you?' He shook his head. 'We know each other better than that.' Then, as if realising what he said, he added, 'Sorry. I shouldn't have said that.'

'No, it's good. It feels nice that someone actually wants to know how my day went. It doesn't happen often.'

'Don't your parents ask?'

'They don't call me every day. It's never really been their thing. Do yours?'

'Mine call every night to say goodnight to the kids. So yes.' He shrugged his shoulders. 'They've been really supportive. I don't know how I'd juggle everything without them.' She felt happy that his family was there for him.

The small bistro in Leamington Spa buzzed with pre-concert goers. Once they'd ordered their food, Meera pulled out her phone and set it to record. Krishan's head cocked to the side, and her tummy wobbled at the small gesture. She let out a slow breath, steadying herself.

'Questions… kill two birds with one stone,' she said, and he gave a subtle nod.

'What activities do you enjoy doing in your free time?'

'Rock climbing as in real rocks,' he explained. 'Back then, when we lived in California, we'd spend weekends in the mountains. It was exhilarating. But here, I go to the climbing centre. Actually, Kreena and I met at a climbing centre. We were on opposite teams and reached for the flag together.'

His lips quivered, and a thin, wistful smile appeared on his face as he stared at the salmon tartar on his plate. After a brief moment, he lifted the fork to his mouth and took a small bite. Krishan then looked at her and began to fill her in on what else he liked to do.

'Skating, mainly ice skating. We used to go a lot. It's fun. Do you ice skate?' he asked.

She told him she did and asked about spectator sports.

'My friends and I used to go to hockey games and basketball in America. Kreena and I used to go all the time.' He talked of Saturdays spent at football matches with his dad. 'One day, I'd like to take the kids, but it's changed a lot. Not sure that it's a spectator sport for families anymore.'

'You like Nitin Sawhney. Who else?' she asked, leaning forward.

'Anoushka Shankar, Norah Jones,' he smiled, 'and their dad, too. You know I liked Atomic Kitten when I was younger. Oasis, as well. I've been to all their concerts,' he beamed.

'Any other types of musical entertainment?' she asked, taking a bite of her goat's cheese salad.

'Ballet. No musicals, the odd small musical concert. No festivals,' he answered.

'You seem to be the type who likes music festivals. Am I right, Meera?' He tilted his head slightly. She liked the fact that he wasn't the type who only spoke about himself. If he seriously joined the list, she was certain there would be a queue of women for him.

'No more replies until you answer my questions,' he said firmly.

He put his cutlery down and watched her. She told him about her love for music festivals and musicals.

'What about theatre, Meera? Do you like going to the theatre?' he asked.

She promised to answer his questions once he'd finished answering hers.

'Do you like going to see plays?' she asked.

'Prefer repertoire, but I don't mind the usual. I'll try anything once even food. And I'd love to learn something new. I'm not closed off to suggestions,' he chuckled.

She nodded happily and told him that was the end of her questioning. She also informed him that she liked plays too, mainly at Stratford or The Rep in Birmingham.

They spent the remaining time discussing amateur productions that she went to see with her friend, Carol.

At the entrance to Warwick Art Centre, they bumped into people from the community, Rashmita Aunty's son, Girish and his wife, Lata. As they exchanged air kisses with them, curiosity was evident on their faces at seeing Meera with Krishan. She stood quietly by his side as they asked after his well-being. Without hesitation, Krishan pulled her closer to his side.

'How old are your children now?' Lata asked Krishan, and he told her his children's age.

'Old enough to be left with babysitters,' Lata smiled. 'Hope to see you two more frequently. We're having a small mehfil if you're interested, there's a new group from India performing, we're raising money for the cataract train.'

Krishan gave Girish his business card and said, 'Call me with the details.'

The concert was amazing. Meera had heard Nitin Sawhney on the radio before, but had never been to a live performance. It was something else altogether. They met more people during the break, and Meera was sure the gossip vine would soon reach the Masi Mafia and, hopefully, they would move on to their next prey.

Krishan pulled up in the car park outside her flat and

opened the car door for her.

'You don't have to walk me to the door, Krish. Goodnight,' she said, unbuckling her seatbelt.

'It's my duty as your fake boyfriend. I always walk my dates to the door.'

She raised a brow. 'Dates? How many dates have you had?'

'Before Kreena, I dated two girls. And before your hackles go up, I'm not being derogatory. They really were girls. Maya was in junior school and Rachel in secondary school. Then I met Kreena. I'm a loyal boyfriend.'

'Unless you go on dates for my app. Then, you'll be disloyal to me,' she said, her voice unsteady.

'It's data gathering. There won't be any inappropriate behaviour, I promise.' He crossed his heart and kissed her softly on her lips as they waited by her flat door.

'Goodnight, Meera, and thank you for a wonderful evening.'

She watched him walk down the corridor. He stepped into the lift, turned and waved at her. She slipped into her hallway and leant against the front door, her heart swelling at the comfort of finding someone who made her happy.

She brushed her finger over the tingle on her lips.

It's not real. None of this is real.

LEISURE CENTRE DATE

Meera

She found Krishan and his parents at the children's activity area in the Leisure Centre in Sutton Coldfield.

Meera greeted his parents politely before taking Krishan by the elbow to a quiet area. It wasn't until she reached the car park minutes before, that she realised the stupidity of her actions. She could have simply called him, but the excitement of new members joining through word of mouth had made her impatient. Besides, once she'd driven across Birmingham, there was no point in abandoning what seemed like a good idea earlier in the morning. Developing this new app had brought back the thrill she hadn't felt in a long time.

'What are you doing here?' Krishan said, surprised.

'I need to show you the new people who've joined recently. You've already met a few of the matches. Are you open to seeing some more?'

'Not for a couple of weeks. I'm busy with a new contract I need to iron out. I'm also out of the country for a few days,' he replied.

'Look at the bios I'm sending you now. I think a few of

them would be a good match.'

She copied the new people's profiles from her spreadsheet and emailed them to him. She looked up at him and found him watching her. She had slipped on her flats with her turned-up boyfriend jeans and a strappy top. Even her hair was tied up in messy, uneven bunches. Whenever she was sorting out design and user experience, she often unconsciously reverted to her wardrobe from her college days.

'Please, Krishan, if the sample is bigger, we'll have a better chance at funding.'

'Why did I agree to this!' he said in exasperation as he opened up his personal email. His fingers immediately went straight to his head. He was nervous. She'd noticed that was an obvious tell that he hid really well with other people, only touching his forehead lightly. But he didn't bother to hide it from her, his full hand raking through his luxurious black hair. A warmth filled the space beneath her ribs at the gesture.

'Because you wanted the Masi Mafia off your back. Remember, there's peace at the end of this charade,' Meera reminded him.

'Okay, let's go for a coffee.' Krishan informed his parents that they were going to the coffee shop on the ground floor of the complex.

They picked up their drinks, a latte with double espresso for him and a mocha for her, and settled at one of the small round tables. Meera took a sip and the taste of the chocolate and coffee slid soothingly down her throat. She needed the chocolate to help with the lack of sleep. She hadn't expected the participants to spread the word and recommend the app to so many people in the minority community. Confident, she was beginning to feel better about suggesting it to the board and was desperately hoping that Angus would now stop micromanaging them.

When she looked up from her phone, Mitra Patel was waving at them from across the café. Meera stopped scrolling through the bios as Mitra weaved through the tables to join them.

'I couldn't resist. Look at you two, hunched over your phones. What are you doing?'

'We're trying to coordinate our calendars,' Meera replied smoothly, without hesitation.

'Aww, how sweet. You two are so lucky to have found love again.'

'Yes, we are very lucky, Mitra Masi,' Krish murmured, his soft lips brushing the side of her head.

'Mitra!' the woman at the till shouted. The older woman gave them a wiggly finger wave before walking away.

'That was good, right?' She felt his warm breath on her neck and the hairs on the back of her neck prickled.

'Yep, a real boyfriend move.'

'I knew she'd be here. She always has her grandchildren on Sunday mornings,' Meera said, tilting her head to the side, amused.

Krishan's mouth fell open. He tugged her hand, and she looked up from her phone.

'Genius idea to come see me here. We're bound to meet with my family. This is going to light up the Masi WhatsApp group.'

Yes, it definitely would. But right now, she was more

interested in seeing the sparkle in his eyes as he gazed at her. She let herself observe the calmness being with him brought to her mind and basked in his gaze.

He thought she was a genius, no-one had said that lately.

MEHFIL DATE

Krishan

Krish: Fancy going to Girish & Lata Shah's Mehfil night on Friday?

Meera: Sure, that works for me. I need a break from the computer, and it will be an excellent fake date. Send me the details.

Krish: I'll come pick you up at yours. Eight, okay?

During the dinner break, as they mingled among the guests, Lata turned to them and asked, 'When did you two know you wanted to keep seeing each other?'

Krishan placed his hand on Meera's lower back, and for once, she didn't arch away to create a distance. He began to weave the lie; he'd read somewhere that a good lie always contained a speck of truth.

He told her of the day they'd spent decorating the gazebo and the unexpected romantic drive to Bristol to get replacement flowers. He added how he'd noticed the constant jiggling of her leg when she was nervous and how she used her index finger to push her hair off her forehead.

As he mentioned these things, Meera stilled. Lata held her hand to her chest, mesmerised by the retelling of

93

their story. For his finale, he turned to face Meera, their chests almost touching, and talked about the drink in the bar. How they both liked calvados and had stayed up until 2.00 a.m., chatting about anything and everything.

'It just felt comfortable. It felt like we'd known each other all our lives. You know, that has only happened to me once,' he said in a low voice.

Lata became flustered as Krishan tucked a strand of Meera's hair behind her ear.

For a brief moment, he saw Meera's eyes darken. Almost immediately, her gaze dropped to the ground, creating a distance that only he noticed.

When he had asked Meera if she wanted to come to the mehfil that they'd heard of at the concert, she'd agreed straight away, and he'd been excited to spend another evening with her. Being with Meera felt comfortable, almost like he'd known her all his life. Earlier, when he'd picked Meera up, his heart had slammed hard against his chest. She was dressed in a cream sheer saree, with a border of rani pink embroidery and crystal stones. Her sequined cream blouse clung to her curves; the halter neckline low enough to make his breath hitch. Her jewellery was relatively simple, a pair of small diamond earrings and the necklace she always wore.

The first thought that came to his mind was that Kreena would never have paired that type of saree with a halter neck. He liked that Meera was different, but her face... Throughout the evening, he would catch a glimpse of her and his heart would lift. But then, the pain would slash through the joy. She looked too much like Kreena.

During the first part of the mehfil, he had daydreamed for a while about his wife's body filling out like Meera's, only to be reminded of her final days. Kreena's gaunt face, her frail body, and the way the illness had taken a toll on her health. His eyes had watered, and he'd felt Meera squeezing his hand in reassurance.

When Lata moved away to speak to the other guests, Meera turned to him.

'Was that really how you felt?' she asked, her eyes sparkling.

He huffed. 'Course not, but that's what they wanted to hear. You've heard the song requests tonight. Young love and longing.'

He knew she had been enchanted by his recollection of that day, and he couldn't bear to see the hope shining in her eyes. Krishan knew that meeting with Meera had stirred something within him, something he wasn't ready to name or acknowledge. And he could feel that she was also being drawn into the web of lies they were weaving.

How could he tell Meera his heart was closed? That he'd already found his only love, and it hurt too much to expose his heart again. His children and family were the only people who could have a piece of it. She was his *fake* girlfriend. Nothing more. Once they reached their expiry date, she would move on and go off to build the successful life she deserved.

And he?

He'd go back to living in the past, in the memory of his one true love.

GOLF DATE

Krishan

Krishan watched as Meera came down the steps from the clubhouse towards where he was waiting. She had a white cap on her head, her ponytail slipping through the back. Her long-sleeved pale yellow zip top was left open, revealing a mint green polo shirt and matching skorts. He couldn't help but admire her body, curvaceous and fully honed. He'd noticed those thighs before, back when he'd seen her running in her summer shorts. There was not a wobble in sight.

A flutter stirred in his lower belly as her lips quirked to a full smile. She walked up to him and kissed him quickly on his cheeks. He suddenly had the urge to turn his head so their lips would meet, but he resisted it and asked instead, 'I thought you didn't play golf. Did you get the gear especially for today?'

'No. All borrowed from Carol. Lucky we're the same size.' She pulled at the waistband of her skort. His eyes rested too long on her waist, and he remembered the sight of her in her chaniya cholis at Jaimini's wedding.

He cleared his throat. 'I've got you some clubs, so let's get this started. By the way, have you ever played golf before?'

'Yes, crazy golf on holiday, but I will warn you I'm usually tipsy. But today, I'm sober as hell.'

He chuckled. 'We can rectify that.' He called over a young man dressed in the club colours of royal blue and white and ordered a jug of white wine spritzer.

Meera stood in front of the ball he'd placed on a tee, gripping the driver, her arms straight and her feet hip distance apart. She pushed her bottom out slightly and swung her arm. Then, she put her hand on the rim of her cap to watch.

Her lips pouted, and her eyes scrunched. 'Where's it gone Krish? Can you see it?'

He pointed to the ball still sitting untouched on the tee.

Disappointment washed over her face but quickly disappeared when a server came with their drink. She poured both of their glasses and gulped down hers before filling it up again.

Krishan took his shot and hit the 150m point. She clapped and cheered, excitement evident on her expressive face.

As the afternoon progressed, he was enjoying watching Meera try her hardest to hit the ball with the right force and direction. As the jug of spritzer emptied, Meera's golf swing became better, but she still hadn't managed to get anywhere near the first flag.

'Krish, you have to help me. I can't give this back to Carol without hitting a target.' She pulled at her top in frustration. 'I have to score. This is getting embarrassing.'

His tummy did a little flip. He had been avoiding the

urge to stand behind her to guide her into the right stance. She was so close. She only needed a little adjustment, and she'd get her target.

He placed his right arm beneath hers and grabbed her hand, placing it higher on the club, his left palm skimming up her back, straightening her posture slightly. Leaning in, he whispered to her to bend her knees and put all her weight into her hips. His left hand wrapped around hers firmly. She inhaled sharply, and for a beat, he worried that his thundering heart would betray him.

A burst of laughter escaped her. 'I was doing it all wrong.'

A buzzing warmth hit his cheek as it touched hers, and he huffed, 'Swing, Meera.'

She did. The ball whizzed through the air and hit the 100m mark. He stepped back. Meera jumped up and down and squealed. She turned around to face him, stepping closer, and the pit of his stomach clenched.

'Are they looking?' She glanced over to the tables where the Gujarati golfers were eating.

'Yes.' His breath hitched, his heart escalating.

'Put your hand around my waist and pull me closer,' she said excitedly.

He loved the feel of her in his arms. It felt too natural, too perfect. Except today, he felt other things too. Things he should definitely ignore.

She was his *fake* girlfriend. But recently, he had to stop himself from touching her. It was becoming too embarrassing. Moreover, he was enjoying spending time with his fake girlfriend. She smiled up at him, her delicious eyes drawing him in.

'Are you okay?' she whispered as fine lines appeared at the corner of her eyes.

Those were new. Krishan hadn't noticed them before. He scanned her face for any other changes. Her lips were plumper now, and his eyes homed in on the tip of her tongue poking through her lips.

Slowly, he leaned closer. Their noses touched, and she tilted her head slightly, their lips melting into a soft kiss. He felt her quick inhale and pulled his lips away to see her cheeks darken with a red tint.

'Brilliant,' she whispered. 'Now they'll all be in a flutter and won't stop talking about us.'

She moved away from him, and he had no choice but to let go of her waist. He wanted to haul her back to him and kiss her properly. God, what was he thinking?

This was just an arrangement. She'd only agreed to *fake* date him in exchange for his participation in developing her dating app. It was also a way for them to get the Masi Mafia off their back. Nothing more.

But then, why did it feel like something... something more?

CHOCOLATE MAKING

Krishan

Krishan informed the children that they were off to a chocolate-making workshop, one of the experiences that Meera had signed them up for through the Design My Date app for the afternoon.

He had forgone their usual Sunday breakfast of tikhi puri and masala chai for the adults, badam doodh for the children, and the rest of the Gujarati essentials of far-far, various athunu and fried green chillis.

Instead, he'd spent the entire morning at the gym after a productive dinner with his new investors the night before, which was fuelled with far too many wine pairings at every course.

When he arrived at Meera's flat, she was ready and waiting, her hair tied back into a loose ponytail, with auburn strands framing her face. He couldn't help himself, his eyes automatically roamed down to her feet before trailing leisurely back up to her face.

Her feet were clad in a pair of classic white Adidas trainers with rainbow laces, which she had paired with cropped faded jeans and a soft pink t-shirt tied at her broad hips. A crossover bag with a cream cap attached to its straps completed her look.

He'd begun to notice that her work-mode style consisted of slouchy, comfortable clothing and minimal makeup. Just a hint of lipstick, a touch of kohl lining her eyes, and no mascara on her long lashes, which fanned her cheeks whenever she looked down. A small smile appeared at the edge of her mouth as she closed the front door of her flat.

'How's your head this morning?'

He told her he had sweated out the alcohol and was raring to go for the chocolate-making workshop.

Two eager faces watched as he parked the car in the driveway of his parents' house. Meera grinned at him. 'I love how full of enthusiasm the children are. Don't you?'

He hopped out of the car to open the passenger door for her, and as she climbed out, two eager children ran out of the house, grabbing her hands. Meera turned her head to look at Krishan from the threshold of the house, her eyes sparkling with happiness.

'They are excited to see her,' his father chortled as a squealing Neel dragged Meera toward the pond to see the insects.

His daughter, always concerned about other people's feelings, asked cautiously, 'Do you like frogs?'

Meera laughed. 'Just as much as crabs.'

'She's brilliant with the children. Those two haven't stopped talking about what combination of chocolate they are going to make,' his father remarked, watching his grandchildren run along the hallway towards the back of the house.

Krishan couldn't help telling his father of their first time together.

'They had a great time together when we went to the beach with her, Dad. She's great with the children.'

His father nodded, knowing Meera's family for years. 'She's always been lovely with the young ones, even when she was a teenager. She looks so much like Kreena that we were worried you'd be upset on seeing her. If only we'd known.' His father took a deep breath and continued. 'Everyone can see the resemblance. I'm sorry we took so long to suggest her to you, son.'

'Dad!' Krishan groaned. 'It's still early days. I expect Mummy to plan a wedding, but you too?'

'I just want you to be happy, son. You look a lot brighter, more… taller. At ease. It's like a heavy boulder has been lifted from your shoulders.'

Krishan couldn't deny it. He did feel calmer and lighter after meeting Meera. Even the obligatory dates on the app seemed easier, knowing that he would meet Meera afterwards for a debriefing.

Those meetings were his favourites. They didn't have to fake or pretend anything. They just had to be themselves. He really did enjoy the feeling he got when he was with Meera.

Was that wrong? Especially when he was seriously considering finding someone to marry. Meeting women through the app had made him realise how much he missed the companionship. Perhaps he could find a real match.

But soon, he shook that thought away. All this dating nonsense was making him lose his final goal. He just wanted to be left alone to treasure and cherish the memory of his late wife, Kreena.

PARK DEBRIEF

Meera

Meera parked the car on the road opposite the park and made her way to the children's playground. This wasn't one of their fake dates; Krishan had told her the kids wanted to meet her.

She'd repeatedly told herself that this wasn't a *real* relationship. That she was just doing this to get the Masi Mafia off her back, and so far, it had worked. Not once had they sent her mother any biodata about an eligible man she had to meet. This summer had been one of the quietest in a long time. She'd even enjoyed the mandatory family gatherings.

But mostly, she loved spending time with Krishan and the kids.

When he told her he was open to meeting more matches, she felt a little sad that he, too, would find someone, and she'd be back to spending time with the single, younger crowd again. Not that she didn't enjoy that. But she felt old, far too old to hear of their binge drinking and sexual encounters. Perhaps she needed to lay down some boundaries with the twenty somethings.

She saw Krishan in the distance, dressed in a charcoal grey t-shirt with an image she couldn't quite make out and beige shorts. Her tummy did a little flip, she loved it when he wore his glasses. He looked so much like Clark Kent, the alter ego of Superman.

Her mind went back to their trip to Bristol, a day she'd dreamt of more times than she could count. She tugged at the smock bodice of her sundress, making sure her breasts weren't too exposed. Strapless dresses for women of her size were difficult to get hold of, but she'd had this one specially made by Carol's mum, who found the softest cotton indigo block print with tiny white hearts.

The children were on the swing, and Krishan was taking turns pushing them. She waved at him and he stopped pushing and pointed toward a bench just outside the play area. He'd gone on one of the DMD dates the night before, and it had been too late for their usual debrief. She reminded herself that this meeting was just for her app, and seeing the children was an added bonus. Nothing more.

She opened the centre pocket of her bag to take out her phone and sat on the bench after she'd waved and said hello to the kids. A moment later, he opened the gate of the cordoned off area and walked leisurely towards her. Soft lips kissed her cheek, staying for a second too long as he leant toward her. Then, as he sat beside her, their thighs touched, and his warmth seeped through the fabric of her dress.

Her heart thumped hard against her chest. *No! This can't be happening.*

She turned to her bag, creating a distance between them and rushed out her words.

'Thanks for doing this for me, Krish,' she muttered.

To stop her heart from thundering, she concentrated on opening her notes. The questions were cemented in her brain now as she'd been doing this for weeks, but her mind was still processing the way her body was behaving. The air around them, the sounds, the smell of his aftershave… everything sent her skin into hyper alert mode.

Natasha shouted that they wanted to go on the roundabout, and another parent let them get on it.

She asked Krishan questions about his experience, the venue, the staff and finally his date. Trying her best to avoid those sultry eyes that often held her gaze, she told herself he needed to focus on getting this done as quickly as possible. Her eyes locked on the children, and when an older boy in dirty football kit began to turn the roundabout, Krishan laughed at the kids squealing in glee.

'Are we nearly done, Meera?' he asked.

'Sajan! Stop frightening the children.' A sing-song voice pierced her ears.

'Oh, hello, Meera.' She looked up to see a slim woman with a pair of tortoiseshell-framed sunglasses that covered most of her face. She was wearing a navy linen dress, cinched at the waist with a Chanel belt. For a moment, Meera couldn't remember her name. She was definitely the daughter of one of the Masi Mafia.

'Hi, Anita. Is that your son?' Meera inquired.

'Yes, he's shot up since he turned ten.'

Anita twisted a strand of copper-highlighted brown hair as she stared at Krishan expectantly.

'Anita, this is Krishan. Natasha and Neel's father and my–'

'Friend,' Krish added smoothly, holding out his hand to Anita. 'We haven't met in a while. Your mum and mine, Kavita Meghani, volunteer together at the Geeta Mandir on Wednesdays.'

'Oh, yes, Krishan. Sorry, I haven't seen you in ages. You've decided to date again?'

'Well, it's not really a date. Meera and I like each other's company.'

Without thinking, Meera took his hand and lifted it up, her fingers tightening around his. Anita's gaze dropped to their entwined hands.

'Except we *are* dating. I'm surprised you haven't heard,' Meera smirked.

She didn't like the way Anita lifted off her sunglasses and put the tip of the metal arm between her pink lips, revealing her hazel eyes. Hazel? Meera was confused. Anita had dark eyes like the rest of them, and just because she had a coffee-with-cream complexion and a slim body didn't mean she wasn't Indian.

'I'm not into all that gossip. They are like *The Mean Girls*. It's embarrassing to have a mother like that.' She gave them a small smile and called out to her son again. 'Sajan! Come on, you'll need a shower before we go for lunch.'

'Bye,' Neel cried after the boy as he ran up to his mother.

'Thank you,' Natasha added politely.

'They're cute,' Anita said with a smile, this time flashing her perfect white teeth. 'Enjoy your park date.'

As soon as the mother and son left the playground area, Krishan released her hand. And she instantly lost the warmth and calmness she had felt while holding it.

'We weren't on a date, Meera! This was just two people meeting up at a park.'

'I know,' she muttered, shaking her head. 'You are so... never mind.'

Krishan raised his eyebrow, waiting.

'She's seen us together, and you're a single parent. It's only natural that you and I spend time with your kids. Wouldn't you want your children to get to know anyone you're seeing? To find out if Natasha and Neel like her.'

'I hadn't thought about that. Is that why you asked me to pick you up before we went to the chocolate making workshop?'

'Of course. I wanted it to look authentic.'

He looked at her in awe. 'How do you even know all this?'

'I don't.' A nervous laugh gushed out of her mouth. 'Lesley reads romance, and we had a bit of a brainstorming session about our fake relationship.'

'Your best friends know?' he asked.

'Yes. They know everything that happens in my life. Can I ask you something?' She paused, suddenly unsure. Was she being too needy for a fake girlfriend? 'Have you told your friends?'

He grimaced. 'I mostly text them, and it's usually sports-related or the odd conversation about the kids.

But I'm meeting them soon.' He looked away from her. 'Yes, I'll tell them then.'

She stood up and went into the children's playground to the roundabout to push it faster for the kids. Krishan sat for a while on the bench, lost in his thoughts. She wondered if he would tell his friends about their fake dating or just call it their new friendship.

She pushed away the sadness of never being his girlfriend. This man was finally ready for a serious relationship, while she knew she would never put herself in that situation again. She needed to make the app a success. Once that happened, her career would send her to New York. And once she was there, she could be whoever she wanted to be. *Don't lose sight of the goal, you're not his type.*

She'd seen the look on his face as he waited expectantly for an introduction with Anita.

BABYSITTING KRISHAN'S KIDS

Meera

Neel toppled over a red paint pot, and the thick liquid splattered across Meera's silk top before dripping onto her jeans. A shrill wailing sound pierced the air. His eyes scrunched, his face turned red and his little fists clenched as he stomped his feet in fear.

'Please take it off. Take it off. Take. It. Off,' he cried, and then ran into the wide hallway.

Meera rushed after him, with Natasha sprinting up the stairs, just as he disappeared behind an open door.

When she entered, Neel was pulling open the drawers of a wide dresser that ran along one of the softly painted walls of the main bedroom. That's when her breathing stilled. Her eyes locked on a large photograph of a woman smiling at the camera. It was her own face mirrored on the wall, a carbon copy of her except for the eyes. While hers were brown, her doppelganger's were black.

'Is this okay? Neel, stop crying. Meera can change into these,' Natasha said.

She turned towards Natasha as the little girl picked up fresh clothes from the floor, lifting a pair of pyjama bottoms and a t-shirt that belonged to Krishan.

'Wash it off, Meera, please,' Neel repeated, tugging at her hand. He then pulled her out of the bedroom and pushed her into the main bathroom. Natasha came behind him and placed the clothes on a chair.

'Come on Neel, give her privacy,' his elder sister said firmly, pulling the door shut behind her.

Meera stood frozen, her heart hammering in her chest. She'd heard from Joshna Bhabhi that Krishan's wife looked similar to her, but she never ever imagined they would be so alike. Her chest ached from the shocking revelation. No wonder he was so open with her, asking her opinion, grabbing her hand at any opportunity, fiddling with her hair. Meera had built up hope from those intimate touches and let herself dream of a stupid future with him.

She gripped the edge of the basin and gazed at herself in the mirror. How had she let herself develop feelings for him? He wasn't interested in her. He was reliving a false dream, chasing a memory. The photo of his wife proved it. She looked too much like her for it to be anything but an old habit.

Krishan had gone on a date with another one of their Beta testers, and she was here to babysit the kids since his nanny, Lucy, was unavailable.

Meera had expected to cajole him, or even threaten him into it, but he'd agreed straight away. His date, Radhika, was one of the many women who matched his profile on the app. She was a friend of Craig's who had lost her husband, a sweet, kind and fierce woman who had similar interests to Krishan.

A sudden, loud thumping sound startled her. She

hurriedly pulled off her stained top and jeans, ran the cold water over the stain on her silk blouse and changed into Krishan's PJ bottoms and t-shirt.

When she opened the bathroom door, Neel was still crying, his fist clenched, snot smearing under his nose. She grabbed a tissue and knelt in front of him.

'The stain will come off. Look, it's almost gone.' She pointed to the sink, trying to reassure him.

'Did you know they invented jeans to wear for work? People wore them for weeks and weeks without washing them. Nothing stains them. Besides, these are an old pair, and the paint stain.' She wiggled her eyebrows. 'I can pretend it's something gruesome, like blood.'

Neel wailed again.

'He doesn't like blood. He's scared of blood.' His older sister patted the little boy's shoulder.

'Come here, honey.' Meera pulled him to her chest. 'It's just red paint, nothing else.' She soothed his back with gentle strokes and felt the little boy relax under her embrace.

Later that evening, when Meera was putting Natasha to sleep, the little girl whispered.

'Are you Mummy? Have you come back to us?'

Meera's throat tightened, tears threatening to spill over.

'Oh, no, sweetheart,' she murmured, brushing Natasha's hair from her forehead. 'It doesn't work that way. I just look like your mummy. Many people look alike. It's a coincidence, that's all. A wonderful coincidence.'

'Will you be my friend, Meera? I know Daddy's gone on a date tonight. He'll find someone. He's too handsome not to. And then, you won't come anymore,' Natasha said, her voice low.

Meera's heart melted at the worry in the little girl's voice.

'Of course, I'll come to see you. I'm glad I get to spend time with you guys. Besides, your daddy will want more babysitting, not less,' she assured her.

Natasha shook her head. 'No, you're too pretty. If he finds someone, she'll tell Daddy to ask Lucy to babysit, and we won't go to the park or family outings together with him anymore. He'll ask her, not you.' Meera couldn't lie to Natasha; the little girl was too clever.

Krishan might find someone. Even though he'd told her he couldn't, wouldn't find anyone to replace Kreena, she knew he would eventually meet someone who would mean more to him. And then, their relationship, too, would end. By Diwali, she wouldn't be his plus one anymore.

'I don't want you to worry too much. It's a long way ahead. I won't stop being your friend.'

She was going to add *'I promise,'* but stopped herself. She didn't want to give the little girl false hope. She knew that, ultimately, they would drift apart. She'd let her guard down and had begun to hope, but she needed to stop herself. She would have to let go, eventually.

Never. Ever. Marry. She chanted the mantra silently again.

Natasha suddenly sat up and pulled out a small notebook and pencil from her bedside table.

'Can you write your address and number in here, please?' The little girl handed the book and pencil to her. Meera added her name and address below the rest of her family.

After Natasha fell asleep, she again soaked her blouse in fresh water and went downstairs. She couldn't help but think about Kreena, the woman who looked like her twin.

She turned on the TV, filled a double measure of brandy with ice in a glass, and settled in to watch *The Notebook*.

It was a mistake.

The melancholy felt like a boulder on her shoulders. She was always going to be alone. She'd built up an insidious hope that Krishan liked her and that they'd both be each other's plus one for longer than their agreement. That he'd get used to her being his go-to number, the person he instinctively turned to.

She had to distance herself from him and remind him of their arrangement. She'd misunderstood him completely. He was spending time with her not because he wanted to be with her, but because of her resemblance to his dead wife. How foolish of her to think otherwise.

She heard the sound of the front door shutting in the hallway. As Krishan stepped into the snug, she stood up. His gaze swept over her, his eyes travelling down her body.

'Why are you in my clothes?' His face was stern and emotionless. 'Take them off. Now!'

She froze in shock at his tone. He stiffened like a statue, glaring at her, his fist clenched, his knuckles white.

Saz Vora

Meera ran past him and up to the bathroom, blood thundering in her ears. She snatched up her jeans, thankful she hadn't soaked them. She then hurried back down the stairs.

Krishan was waiting at the bottom, and when she tried to explain, his jaw clenched even tighter. His face was expressionless, and the air around him vibrated with barely restrained anger.

She didn't wait. She grabbed her handbag and her jacket and slammed the door shut behind her.

Once inside the safety of her car, she forced herself to steady her laboured breaths, trying to understand his reaction. He had never once mentioned that she looked like his dead wife. Not even once.

Anger rose at the thought of her family. They knew. They had manipulated her again. When will she learn? People can't be trusted. Ever.

Furious rage coursed through her body. How dare they withhold that piece of information?

A sharp knock on the window made her turn. She started her car and rolled down her window.

'What? What do you want, Krish? Do you want this?' she snapped, pinching the t-shirt she was wearing. She yanked it over her head and threw it at him, not caring that she was in her cream lacy bra that was stained red.

Krishan caught the t-shirt. 'I'm sorry, Meera. I overreacted. Come back in again.'

Overreacted? He had yelled at her. Dark, angry eyes had looked at her like a piece of dirt. Like she was nothing.

'Please, I haven't debriefed you yet.' His lips twitched

114

upwards, and he cocked his head.

She huffed angrily. 'I don't want a debrief.'

The image of Kreena, her carbon copy, simmered in her mind. She was close to tears, and she would never ever show him or anyone that side of her again. She pulled out of the parking space, concentrating on the way ahead. She took one last look in the rear-view mirror as she pulled out of his road.

Krishan was still watching her.

That night, she slept fitfully, haunted by the memory of his angry, guilt-ridden eyes. As the dawn chorus twittered outside, she dragged herself out of bed and drove into Birmingham early. She needed a distraction. Anything to take her mind off Krishan.

'These arrived for you. A new admirer?' The receptionist asked, carrying an enormous bunch of flowers for her, blue hyacinths, lily of the valley, white roses. The fragrance filled her office, overtaking the scent of freshly brewed coffee from the kitchen.

Meera read the card that came along with the flowers.

I was an idiot. Please forgive me. I want to tell you about Cynthia and what happened.

- Krish.

She thought of ignoring him as she'd already spent too much of her time and energy thinking about Krish's reaction. But then, curiosity got the better of her.

Cynthia? Who was Cynthia?

Her first thought was what had she done to him. She

shouldn't want to know; he wasn't her boyfriend. She reminded herself again that it was just a fake relationship.

But the bouquet and the note? Didn't feel fake, it felt like real.

FAMILY PICNIC

Krishan

He had a fitful night, haunted by his actions. He had overreacted when he saw Meera in his PJs. Shame and guilt had slammed into his mind. It was the same combination of t-shirt and pyjama bottoms that Cynthia had worn, except on Meera they looked better, like she had belonged in his clothes. The thought alone filled him with regret. Meera was his fake girlfriend. Cynthia had been Kreena's best friend, and he'd taken advantage of her vulnerability to satisfy his own needs. To fill the emptiness that soaked his heart after Kreena's passing. Seeing Cynthia reminded him too much of the loss of his wife, but he'd promised Kreena that he'd make sure that his children knew about their mother's best friend and their shared childhood. Only he'd ruined that. He had slept with his wife's best friend.

'Krish, promise me you'll find someone. Promise me you won't deny love.' He recalled Kreena's plea to find someone who would love him back, but he hadn't made any effort to honour her wish yet. How could he when he was broken, a husk of the man he was once? His constant drinking, wallowing in tears and relying heavily on his family and friends was beyond the

norm. And eventually, he'd begun to call and rely on Cynthia more than anyone else.

She had been just as vulnerable. She had known Kreena since junior school. They'd holidayed together, laughed together and cried together. It was Cynthia who had flown to California to support them when they heard about their infertility journey. Who'd hidden her own pain and kept the news of her breakup from them. Cynthia who'd been their rock, and he had smashed that trust by taking her to his marital bed. How could he have done this to Kreena's childhood friend? What had been a close relationship felt strained, and whenever she visited, he made sure she had time alone with his children.

Krishan had sent the flowers to Meera because of the guilt, hoping desperately that it was enough to get Meera back in his life.

They hadn't met or spoken since his outburst, but at least she'd accepted his apology, albeit grudgingly. She'd sent him a photo of the flowers along with a sad face, a neutral face, a black heart and a poo emoji.

'Can we come too, Daddy?' Natasha asked as he parked the car outside Meera's flat.

They were having another fake date, a family and friends' picnic at War Memorial Park in Coventry. The annual gathering had started when he was just a child. The Saturday of the autumn bank holiday weekend always meant a get-together to play rounders or other games with his family and his parents' friends and their families. There would be at least fifty people, each bringing their own food and more to share.

This year, his mother had made methi na thepla and sukhu bateta nu shaak. Everyone else brought something, and then there was the natural yoghurt and the usual pickles. Some of the masis even brought homemade barfi – delicious Indian sweets made from nuts and milk. . When he was younger, he joined in the activities, but as a teenager, he preferred bringing his bike and often went off exploring with some of the other boys who weren't interested in babysitting younger siblings.

When he met Meera, he'd often wondered why she never came to any of these gatherings. A nervous energy rippled through his belly. Was there a reason for her absence? Had the Masi Mafia's viscous tongues hurt her so much that she stayed away?

Pushing that thought away, he opened the car door to let his children out. Then, he reached into the backseat for the silk blouse he'd sent to a specialist dry cleaner, his small attempt to make things right.

He knocked on Meera's door and waited, a nervousness in his belly. When she opened the door, Krishan's throat tightened, and he found it difficult to swallow. The yellow off-the-shoulder dress she wore made her skin glow, accentuating her long, slender neck. As their eyes met, she absently stroked the stone on the necklace she always wore, resting in the dip between her collarbone.

The children rushed in to explore her flat, but he waited outside for her to invite him in. He'd dropped her off plenty of times, even after they'd met for debriefs, but he had never stepped inside her home.

She turned to watch the children run down the narrow hallway. She had tied her hair in a high plait, the yellow clips keeping the layers off her face. A sadness penetrated Krishan's chest; he loved the way the layers framed her face. But he couldn't blame her for tying them.

He knew he should have told her. But how do you raise the subject?

By the way... you could be my dead wife's twin.

'Sorry, they wanted to see where you lived,' he said apologetically. He wanted to touch her, to close the space between them, but there was a distance in her gaze that kept him from doing so.

'Come in. Do you want a drink before we leave?' she asked.

She followed them inside, leaving the blouse on the coat hook. A feeling of discomfort nudged at his chest. He'd invaded her private space by bringing the children up. She'd babysat for him out of necessity as his parents were away and Lucy was busy when he'd gone to meet Radhika, a match on the *Design My Date* app. Meeting in their own homes was never a part of their fake dating rules.

He followed her into the kitchen, aware that his children had disappeared further into her apartment. She reached up to pull out some glasses from a tall cupboard.

'You don't have a guest bedroom? Just an office?' Natasha said as she strode into her small kitchen.

Meera picked up the small tray of drinks and walked into the living room. She told the children to sit on the cloth sofa and offered them their juice. Once she took a sip of her drink, she explained to the kids that it had a sofa bed.

'Can we come to stay?' Neel asked eagerly. 'I like sofa

beds. What's a sofa bed, Daddy?' His brow furrowed curiously.

Meera laughed. Krishan loved how the tingly sound of her laughter hit the base of his stomach. He gulped his juice, trying to ignore how much he missed her. The children put their empty glasses back on the tray, and she told them to follow her. He watched, leaning on the door frame of her office, as she took off the seat cushion and pulled out the mattress. She straightened the duvet and propped the seat cushion against the backrest.

'Ta-da, guest bedroom.' Neel quickly took off his shoes and climbed in.

'I like sofa beds. It's magic,' he said, wrapping himself in the geometric patterned quilt.

She was wonderful with the kids. Other people wouldn't have shown the children what a sofa bed was. But Meera did. He'd already seen her patience at Jaimini's wedding weekend, and she was specifically good with younger children. A memory from when Joshna had first pointed Meera out to him warmed his chest. He had seen from afar, a young girl rounding up the children at the noisy wedding and guiding them out in a neat line. It brought a smile to his face.

As he stood there, Meera slipped past him, walked down the narrow corridor to the front door, and handed him a crisp envelope from the hall table.

'Tickets to watch West Brom's Women's F.C. for next Sunday,' she said.

'Are you coming too?' he asked, leaning in to kiss her cheek.

She turned her head away, and his lips met the slick

strands of her tied-back hair instead. 'No, I'm busy,' she replied, her voice cool.

'Time to go, Natasha, Neel,' Meera called out, her back still turned to him. She was different, a lot more distant and subdued with him. If only he'd kept his emotions in check that night when he saw her in his clothes.

The park was full of families enjoying the final long weekend of the summer. When they'd first agreed to the fake dates, this day was the one they discussed the most. He knew that if she'd made an excuse not to join him at this picnic, the whole group would have spent hours dissecting the nature of their relationship. Meera wasn't too keen on the picnic, telling him it would make no difference. In the end, it was Natasha who'd won her over by asking if she'd come with them.

As soon as they'd parked, Neel insisted on being carried. With a smile, he knelt down and hoisted his son onto his shoulders, while Natasha took his and Meera's hand. The guilt of finding someone to replace Kreena squeezed his heart. How could he keep that promise when she still owned his heart?

They found their group in a big patch of lawn marked out with picnic blankets and rows of tables and chairs for the elderly. His sister, Kalu, shouted and waved at them excitedly. The children dashed ahead, eager to meet the family. Krishan tried to take Meera's hand, but she subtly moved away from him.

'I'm sorry,' he said, and she stopped. 'I shouldn't have shouted at you that night. I'm really sorry.'

'We need to talk, Krish, but later.' She ran towards her

family.

For the rest of the picnic, he felt devastated as she ignored him and stayed close to her family. He missed talking with her, laughing at her anecdotes about the dates that were happening, and her amazement at the matches that worked. The dread that he'd lost her choked his breath. Krishan racked his brain for an idea to make things right between them. His head felt too hot as he pushed his hair away from his face. He had to find a way to get her to forgive him.

The realisation that he wanted Meera in his life hit him hard. He couldn't let her go now that he'd found her. He liked her too much to lose her. He let the thought settle deep into his mind.

'Mama, we're playing rounders. Do you want to join?' Jaisan, his nephew, approached him as he sat in the shade of an old oak tree.

A game of rounders was bound to get her shouting and laughing again. He got up and went up to where she was sitting with his sister and her parents.

'Meera, come and join me for rounders,' he said.

She took off her sunglasses. Her eyes dull with sadness, an ache seeped through his chest. He'd made the sparkly teasing woman sad. It was his fault she wasn't enjoying this gathering.

'I'm okay, Krish. I've got my book,' she said, lifting the paperback she was reading.

'Come on, Meera Fai. I was coming to ask you next. Joshna Masi, you too,' Jaisan said by his side.

Her eyes moved to his nephew, and her lips curved into a wide smile. His heart pounded. He really needed her to forgive him. He wanted her to smile at him again.

The game was exciting and competitive, with Meera shouting and running around with the younger children when their team was fielding, making sure they took the credit for her catches. And with batting, she shouted words of encouragement at everyone. At the victory embrace, she high-fived and hugged everyone, including him. He held onto her a little longer than what she was comfortable with. Just then, Tara Masi shouted.

'Ow, so cute!'

Meera quickly moved away and ran to the drinks table. Krishan followed her and asked her to join him for a walk. She glanced at the group of parents, whose faces were turned to them, watching them with keen interest.

'We have to keep pretending, and I also have to explain,' he murmured, touching her elbow lightly.

She filled a glass of water for him and drank her own water in one thirsty gulp.

'Alright, I have questions for you too,' she said, setting the glass down.

He'd expected her to ask questions, and in that moment, realisation struck. She had changed her hairstyle. The new style was for his benefit. She had deliberately hidden the layers.

A conversation from Jaimini's wedding came to his mind. 'I can't stand having my hair up,' she'd said, pulling at the back of her neck. 'It gives me a bad headache.'

Was her resemblance to Kreena the only reason he liked her company?

'I'm sorry,' he admitted, his voice quiet. 'I should have told you that you look like Kreena when we first met. It's quite uncanny, really. Even her cousins don't look as similar to her as you do.'

Her face hardened. 'Is that why you asked me to be your fake girlfriend? Are you just reliving a fantasy?'

Krishan pulled out his wallet and handed her a photograph. Her sad eyes examined the image of his wife with their children. He explained that the photo on his bedroom wall was of when they'd first dated. He told her his wife's hair was long and straight, unlike her wavy and layered look.

'But I look like her. Do you understand why I'm upset?'

'It's only a passing resemblance. You and she are very different.'

He'd said that to placate her, but deep down, he couldn't deny that she did remind him of his wife. Was he unknowingly searching for a replica of his wife? It wasn't fair to the beautiful, gregarious woman to compare her with Kreena. Meera was unique, vibrant and full of life. He knew that in his heart. He owed it to her to be honest about his feelings.

Perhaps meeting Meera had felt safe, like he wasn't truly betraying his wife with another woman, because she looked a lot like Kreena. But Meera wasn't just a placeholder, right?

Meera gave his wallet back to him. 'We're going to have to set some ground rules. I need to know more about Kreena. Her likes and dislikes, favourite colours, favourite foods. I'll make sure I don't remind you of her ever again. And promise me we won't go to your favourite places with her. Otherwise, we can stage a huge fake row with everyone as our witness right here, right now. Because I don't want to feel this way again. I've vowed to avoid relationships again, and I don't intend to get hurt by a fake one.'

'I'll do anything you want, Meera. No more secrets. Can I explain about Cynthia now?'

They walked away from their families, the hurt still lingering in Meera's eyes. But at least she was walking next to him.

He took a deep breath and told her about Cynthia. How seeing Meera in his pyjamas and a t-shirt brought back memories of how he'd betrayed his wife. How he'd slept with Kreena's best friend when she came to support him, just because he was lonely and sad. How he'd come downstairs afterwards and seen Cynthia in the same pyjamas. How the guilt of that night gnawed in his mind, a cruel reminder of what he'd done. How he'd felt dirty and dishonourable to his wife and her best friend. The recollection of that night made his skin crawl with disgust. He'd let someone close to Kreena touch him like that, tempting him into a night of passion and making him feel those emotions again. The worst thing was that it had happened only weeks after Kreena's death. He'd cheated on her too soon.

He didn't know why he felt the need to confess to Meera, to tell her of his disloyalty to his wife. But the only thing that mattered to him was that she listened to what he'd done. He wanted Meera to know, not just about his mistake, but that he'd once let someone get close to him.

'You must forgive yourself, Krish. We're only human. We all crave comfort. I'm sure Kreena would want you to have a happy life.' She squeezed his hand and a warmth raced across his skin. He knew Kreena wouldn't want him to mourn forever, but he wasn't ready to give up on his memories or his wife. *Except he was making new memories with Meera.*

'You give good advice. It's a shame you don't follow it,' he murmured, turning his head to lock eyes with hers.

Meera let out a small breath. 'I never said I don't seek comfort in men's company. I just don't do relationships.'

Meera's remark hit him hard, and he stopped in his tracks. She looked back at him, her arm stretched behind her. His hand had instinctively taken hers as they walked back. It felt so naturally comforting, so right.

'Don't tell me you're shocked. I hate this the most about our culture.' She pulled her hand out of his and faced him. 'So, it's okay for men to have sexual gratification? But we're supposed to be chaste and untouched until the next man is willing to make us his.'

He thought about her remark. He wasn't shocked, but the thought of Meera with another man bothered him. It bothered him too much for him to understand.

'What did your ex do to you?' Krishan asked in a quiet voice.

She pursed her lips and walked towards the picnic group. When he caught up with her, she said, 'I won't talk about Kaushik. That part of my life is not up for discussion.'

His curiosity peaked at the remark. What had Kaushik done? Why hadn't she come to the family picnics with him, and why hadn't she returned since her divorce?

Krishan made a mental note to ask Joshna later. He wanted Meera to be happy, and he wanted to be the one to make her happy.

Was that wrong? Was he wrong in thinking that he could?

She was his *fake* girlfriend. He couldn't have feelings for her... could he?

CELEBRATION

Meera

Angus had announced an impromptu party at Birmingham's exclusive nightclub for a soft launch of the dating app, and Meera was annoyed. Craig and she knew that the idea was viable, but she was still analysing the data. They'd set up twenty unique dates, found thrice as many candidates, and the concept had a favourable response. Especially with the follow-ups that she and Craig had scheduled with the participants. It was still too new, too early. They hadn't even conducted a stress test or ironed out the kinks yet.

It wasn't just that the data was still new. She was now tasked with chasing the PR team to get social media influencers and people from the experience providers at short notice. Meera's workload had doubled. Craig's was even worse as he had to deal with the venue, entertainment and catering. And Angus, being Angus, had invited all his friends, mostly middle-aged men with several divorces behind them.

'How do you want your hair, Meera?' Sharon, her hairdresser, asked.

'Can you pull it up off my face? No curls or waves on

my jawline,' Meera said firmly. She was never ever going to be anywhere near Krish with her hair looking like his wife's.

'But you have such a beautiful round face, and the curls accentuate it.'

'Stop the flattery, Sharon. I need to look professional. It's a work event.'

Sharon sighed and began sectioning her hair, clipping it back into neat segments.

As soon as they'd fixed a date for the soft launch, Meera had sent a text to Carol, hoping she'd come as her plus one. Her best friend rarely went out on a weekday, but tonight, she wanted a shield against Krish's attention. This wasn't one of their fake dates, and he was beginning to behave too much like a real boyfriend.

Was it wrong of her to protect herself?

The Night Owl was a club that specialised in retro music with a live band, the music her best friend loved; northern soul, Ska, Reggae and Britpop. Carol loved to dance, and when Craig had secured the venue, all it took was one final push, resulting in Carol sending her a thumbs up and a smiley emoji. Her best friend was on board to dance the night away.

As Meera sat in Sharon's chair, sending out last minute emails, a text arrived from Krish.

> **Krish: Do you need a lift? I can swing by your place tonight.**

She quickly replied, telling him that she was busy with the set up. Sharon lifted a mirror to show the back of her head, a sleek chignon, without a curl in sight.

Krishan turned up dressed in a pair of black jeans and a tight black t-shirt that clung to him like second skin. She'd seen him in casual clothes before, but this was different. The snug fit showed off his pecs and so much more, and she couldn't help but notice.

He'd joined her at the bar for a drink and they talked about the children briefly. Once Radhika arrived, she, Krish and Craig took themselves off to a booth.

She'd met Radhika, a university friend of Craig's, at one of their work parties. She had lost her husband to bowel cancer and was going through the same thing that Meera had faced, being constantly paired with unsuitable men. Craig had asked her to join the Beta list, and she'd met with a few men who fitted her ideal profile. She'd even been paired with Krishan. They had attended a sushi workshop the same night Meera realised just how much she looked like Kreena.

Meera was hoping the party would go well. Besides, she needed to let her hair down, metaphorically speaking. She tugged at the strands of hair at the base of her neck to loosen her updo. Ever since she was a child, she hated wearing her hair up, but tonight, she did it to avoid Krishan's sultry gaze. Taking a long sip of her vodka and lemonade, she tried to shrug off her nervousness.

'Hello, this hairstyle doesn't suit you,' Carol said, greeting her with a kiss. 'You look like an air hostess,' she added, sitting next to her at the bar.

'I know, but Krish is here, and I refuse to look like his wife,' she shouted in Carol's ear as *"Uptown Top Ranking"* blasted through the speakers.

'Why do you want to look different? He needs to get over himself.' Carol's eyes widened. She was known for her honest, no-nonsense advice. Her friend pulled down the lime-green clingy top that showed off the small mounds of her breasts. She'd matched it with a pair of psychedelic flares that rested on her wide hips. She'd created the whole '70s vibe, her big, bold afro showing off her glorious black hair.

Carol took several gulps from Meera's drink, slammed the empty glass back on the counter and pulled her to the dance floor.

A mixed-race woman, part Asian and part black, joined them on the dance floor and asked if they were on the dating list.

Meera was surprised to hear Carol reply, 'No, but you might persuade me to join.'

She hadn't asked Carol to join, thinking that she'd rather meet people the usual discreet way, just as she had been doing since declaring she preferred the company of women to men. Making a mental note to ask her later, she left the dance floor as she felt that she was cramping her friend's style.

Meera glanced around the club and went back to the bar, where the rest of her team were busy drinking shots. She watched her young team with wonder. They worked hard and played just as hard. She'd been like that once with not a care in the world, until her life unexpectedly unravelled. Shaking away the thought, she dismissed the idea of ordering tequila shots and opted for sparkling water instead. Free booze was bound to result in one or two of her team members needing help later that night.

By the end of the evening, Craig had found someone

from the experience marketing team, a brunette with endless legs who was at least three inches taller than him. Carol had already informed her she was going off somewhere quiet with Akemi, the Japanese Nigerian paramedic, leaving Meera on her own. She never mixed her personal and work life, so she danced with a few colleagues and drank with the others, unlike Craig, who had left a trail of broken hearts among the women they worked with.

As the evening wore on, Meera excused herself from the dance floor and perched herself at the bar. She hadn't seen Krishan or Radhika for a while and wondered if they'd gone home. She felt a pang in her chest. She told herself that this wasn't a fake date. He was one of her clients, not a fake boyfriend, and he could go home with any woman he wanted. But it still hurt that he didn't even come to say goodnight to her.

When she eventually stepped into the dark but spacious area of the ladies' toilet, she found a couple of women from her team helping a young Goth with multiple piercings on her face, including nose rings and a septum ring too. Meera did what she always did when something like this happened. She asked one of them to go home with the incapacitated coder and called and paid for a cab to take them home.

As she was helping the young Goth out of the club, Krishan called her name, instantly making her stomach flutter. He approached her, asking if she needed any help. She coolly told him that it was under control.

As he turned, the sight of his tight trousers and perfectly sculpted rear sent a stir through her stomach. She watched him for too long, admiring his muscular glutes as they clenched with each step. Then with a final wave, he headed back into the nightclub.

The groan from the young woman leaning on her shoulder snapped her back to reality. Just then, her colleague arrived with their coats, pausing mid-way to gape at his retreating back. Meera sneered at her. Krish's tight t-shirt and narrow trousers were a real lady magnet, and her reaction to the young woman's attention was wrong. Krishan was her fake boyfriend and nothing more.

Three days later, the funding had been approved, and Craig and Meera were suitably tipsy at the celebratory party by the time Krish showed up. Craig greeted him with a nod and moved to a nearby table after ordering another bottle of champagne.

Earlier in the week, Krishan had gone on a ghost tour of Birmingham with Gayani, a 33-year-old widow from the Sri Lankan community. According to their agreement, he'd come to give Meera his feedback. He talked a lot more about Gayani than Radhika, and Meera felt the need to ask.

'Would you consider seeing Gayani long-term?'

Krish's lips pressed into a thin line, and his intense eyes bored into hers.

'I'm only doing this for you, Meera. I want this to be a success for you,' he replied, his voice low and husky.

Her breath caught at the way his voice rumbled in her stomach. He was wearing glasses again, different from the dark-rimmed ones he'd worn when they'd gone to get the flowers. These were Ray-Ban Clubmaster, and he looked like Dean Cain in them.

Ever since watching *Lois & Clark*, the '90s TV series, she had a thing for dark-haired men in glasses. And now, as if her imagination had a mind of its own, an image of Krish in a Superman costume flashed before her.

'Meera?' Krish frowned, his gaze seeping into her soul.

'I like some of the women I've met. I've enjoyed their company as well as the new experiences. But no one will replace Kreena here.' He pointed to his chest, his eyes darkening with sadness. Meera's warm body instantly chilled as she concentrated on his hand.

'Hey, Meera,' The guitarist from the retro band shouted as he entered through the door. Craig beckoned him to join his table.

'Is he your next debrief?' Krish asked, raising a brow in surprise.

She laughed. 'Does he look like someone who wants to go on experiences?'

Krish's eyes narrowed as he examined the guitarist. He was in a pair of ripped jeans, a worn black leather jacket and red cowboy boots. Then he pulled off his jacket, making sure Meera saw him giving her a once-over from her chest to her face. He pushed his hair off his forehead with a ring laden hand. The faded snug t-shirt rode up to reveal the tuft of hair on his stomach and his low-slung waistband.

She smiled, hoping to share a conspiratorial look with Krishan, but instead, she saw his lips curl with disdain.

'Your date? Wasn't he the guitarist from the band at the club?' Krishan asked, an unreadable expression on his face.

'Yes, we exchanged numbers,' Meera told him. 'He's taking me to an impromptu gig in a basement later.'

Krish's gaze locked on hers briefly before he released a slow breath. He looked away and pulled a blue scarf from his squidgy-worn leather briefcase.

'Thanks for this,' he said, giving it to her.

She wrapped the scarf around her neck, which was a mistake, as his lemony, herby scent penetrated her lungs, making her breath stutter.

Unlike hookup apps, they'd knowingly made it a point of not adding photographs on their dating site, making it more about connections than appearances. It was all part of the experience, a "get out" clause, a unique colour signal. It didn't matter what it was. If they liked each other, they'd keep it on, if not, they'd hide it. They still had a great experience, even without the blind date element.

Meera stood up as Craig called Krish over for a drink, but he declined. Meera gave Krish a quick peck on the cheek and went to join Craig and the guitarist for an eventful night with a member of a Britpop band. The guitarist wasn't her type, too much of a rock star, too much into himself. There was a reason she avoided men like him. Like Kaushik.

Only that night, everyone had paired off, and even Krish had left to hang out with Radhika. So, when she'd queued for a cab alone, she'd ended up exchanging phone numbers with the guitarist. She blamed Carol for making her drop her guard. Her friend was incredibly picky, and when she'd gone home with the paramedic, Meera suddenly felt lonely and agreed to meet him. She'd seen the anger on Krish's face when Duncan, the guitarist, grabbed her bottom and gave it a squeeze. She couldn't understand his reaction. He was already seeing Radhika outside the app. She'd hoped that he would admit that he liked her. That's why she had deliberately asked him about Gayani.

But, as usual, his answer was non-committal, leaving her more confused than ever.

WEEKEND AWAY

Krishan

Krishan had arranged for his children to stay with Kreena's parents in Manchester. He loved spending time with his in-laws and was now watching Natasha and her grandfather engrossed in solving a thousand-piece jigsaw puzzle at the large coffee table, something they both enjoyed doing. At the same time, he was also trying to get Neel to lie flat on the sofa and watch CBeebies. It was a long day for the children, as they'd woken up at five in the morning to catch an early train, and Neel was ready for a nap. He himself could do with a snooze after the scrumptious lunch his mother-in-law had prepared for them.

Just as he thought of Kreena's mother, a slight woman with salt-and-pepper hair, tied in a single plait, appeared at the entrance of the sitting room carrying a large tray laden with afternoon tea and snacks. Krishan immediately stood up to help with the tray, placing it on the sideboard. A smile lit up his face as he looked at the assortment of Indian sweets and savoury snacks.

Kreena's mother was a feeder through and through. Even when her daughter couldn't eat due to the effects of chemotherapy, she would bring soups and thin dals to her bedside at the hospice. Now, she prepared her husband's tea, filling a small plate of kaju katli and phulli gathia. She placed it on the small side table near them. Krishan picked up a glass of juice for Natasha, but before he could do more, his mother-in-law stopped him.

'No, Beta, you sit and rest. I can do this. You haven't stopped taking sugar in your chai, have you?'

He shook his head and went back to the sofa. She was the opposite of his wife. If Kreena was still here, she would have made everyone come and take their own tea and snacks. He pressed his aching chest at the thought. Coming to Kreena's childhood home always brought a steady ache to his heart.

He took the teacup and said, 'Thank you, Mummy.'

For a beat, she looked surprised he'd called her that. He'd always called Kreena's parents Mummy and Papa. Besides, that was how Gujarati couples addressed their in-laws. He wondered why she was surprised, and then a thought filtered to the forefront of his mind. She knew about Meera. This web of lies he'd woven was hurting more people than he'd anticipated.

Once Neel was sound asleep on the sofa, he gave Natasha a hug. 'Be good for your grandparents, okay?'

His daughter frowned at him. 'I'm always good,' she declared.

Her grandfather laughed and patted her on the head, telling her that she was right. He then told her he was seeing her father to the door.

He went ahead to collect his weekend bag and jacket

and was scrolling through his phone to check on his taxi. His father-in-law cleared his throat, and Krishan looked at him. Eyes that were the same as Kreena's held his gaze.

'Krishan, we're so glad to hear you've found someone. Kreena would have wanted you to be happy.' He patted Krishan's shoulder, his expression full of understanding.

'Yes, we are happy, Beta,' Kreena's mother said. 'I know you saw me upset when you called me Mummy, but I wasn't sad, you know. I always want you to think of us as your parents. I was just a little anxious that Meera would stop you from coming to see us.' She tentatively placed her hand on his arm.

He resisted the urge to rake his fingers through his hair. They thought he was ready to marry Meera, that he'd found his happily ever after. But the truth was, it was only a fake relationship with an end date.

He was sandwiched between the elderly couple who looked expectantly at him for any reassurance that they would not lose him or their grandchildren. He scrambled for words, but the first thing that came to his frazzled mind was that Meera wasn't like that, and before he could stop himself, his thoughts slipped out of his mouth.

'Meera isn't like that Mummy... Papa. She'd never stop me or the children from seeing you. In fact, she'd welcome you both into the family without hesitation.'

Both mouths lifted into a small, closed-lip smile.

'You've chosen well, Beta. Next time you visit, please bring our daughter with you,' his beautiful mother-in-law said.

140

His heart jolted at the mention of the word *daughter*. He felt a sudden rush of guilt. He was the worst son-in-law to feed them these lies.

Krishan arrived at the luxury spa resort in Chester earlier than the others. After unpacking his bag, he made his way to the bar to wait for his friends. The place buzzed with lively chatter from guests enjoying their little escape.

Just then, he heard a familiar laugh from the foyer. He turned his head to look at the couple nearby. Recognition made his heart thump. He blinked and rubbed his glasses before looking again.

A blond, tanned man was kissing Meera at the bottom of the staircase for an indecent length of time. Her hair was left loose, framing her round face, very different from how she usually wore it. Ever since she'd seen the photo of Kreena, every time he met her, she had started pinning her soft curls away from her face.

Meera hardly spoke about her life outside of work. It was yet another topic she'd added to the no-go area of her personal life. Was he her boyfriend? Was she dating an Englishman and hiding it from her family? He just hoped Meera wouldn't be upset to find him there, watching her with him.

He turned back to the bar, unable to shift the heaviness in his heart, knowing that Meera was with someone else. He felt a sense of unease at the mere sight of her with someone other than him.

Pushing that thought aside, he realised it had been far too long since he last saw his university friends.

They'd tried several times to meet in the past, but he hadn't been in the right headspace then. Spending time with Meera lately made him realise just how much he missed his old friends.

Taking his children to stay with Kreena's parents was the start of getting them used to being with not only his own parents but also with others who loved them just as much. He had carefully thought about it. He was planning to develop his business significantly, and with the expansion and growth, there would be considerable travel. He was looking forward to discussing his future with his friends in person instead of talking to them on the phone individually.

'Hello, mate.' Freddie, his best friend, perched next to him at the counter and signalled the bartender. 'I'll have what he's having.'

He'd met Freddie on his first day in the halls of residence at Oxford, and from that moment, they'd built a lasting friendship that had continued through thick and thin.

For Freddie, life had been mostly thick, a happy marriage, wonderful children and an outstanding career in Astrophysics that took him to different countries around the world. But for Krishan, it had been thin, as he wrestled with infertility struggles, cancer diagnosis, widowerhood, and single parenthood.

Freddie, and his other friends had met in their first week at university. All of them had one thing in common: a love for the outdoors, camping trips up mountains and regular sports.

By dinnertime, everyone had arrived at the spa resort, nestled among acres of lush gardens. The bar was buzzing with boisterous laughter and playful chiding, exactly like old times. Why had he ever been worried and hesitant about meeting up? He made a mental note to ensure that before leaving, they'd pencil in their next weekend together.

Later, once they'd eaten, they decided to walk down the lane to a nearby pub, recommended by the resort, to carry on drinking and catching up. He and his friends settled into their familiar dynamics, talking and jesting, and they cautiously brought up the topic of life without Kreena. Normally, he would have changed the subject, inquiring after their family and their lives, but this time, he told them he was trying to lead as normal a life as he could. He even told them about the dating app.

The door to the lounge opened, and his head instinctively turned toward it just in time to see Meera enter. She was wearing a leather jacket over a grass green wrap dress, paired with black high-heeled ankle boots. For the rest of the evening, no matter how hard he tried to ignore her, he couldn't keep his eyes off them. His concentration shot to pieces as his friends filled him in on the happenings in their lives. Eventually, he'd had enough. Unable to control himself, he made his way to their table.

'Hi, Meera, I thought it was you. Didn't want to interrupt you with your–'

'Matt,' the man with her cut in. 'And you are?'

'Krishan. We know each other's family.'

Matt leaned in slightly and said, 'Listen, Krishan. Forget that you saw us. Do you understand?' He had a hint of a northern European accent.

'Matt!' Meera gasped, shooting him a glare before turning to Krishan. 'Sorry, don't mind him. He has no manners.'

Then, meeting Matt's eyes, she said, 'Krish is one of the good ones.'

She inquired about who Krishan was with, and he pointed towards his friends. She smiled warmly, waving at them. He stood by their table and continued to talk to Meera, casually mentioning that he'd seen them earlier at the hotel. Matt glared at him, making a point of pulling Meera closer to his side.

Immediately, Krishan's stomach twisted into knots.

When he went back to his friends, he told them that Meera was the app developer, not wanting to share that he was also fake dating her. Their reactions were as he'd expected, some slapped his back and some raised their glasses at him. His friends had always supported him, regardless of his choices.

Except, he hadn't told them it was temporary and that he'd only agreed to sign up for the app because of Meera.

He pushed away the dull ache that rested in his chest on seeing Meera with another man. He wondered why she had never mentioned having a boyfriend and why Matt was so protective of her. He'd seen the fire in his eyes when he'd approached their table.

His instinct told him to check on them, and that's when he saw Matt with a redhead at the bar, his hands cradling her waist. Irritation and anger bubbled in his stomach. He huffed out a deep breath, his jaw tightening. Could he take him on? Matt was at least six feet three inches tall and built like a boxer. Yes, he would try. The man wasn't worthy of Meera.

'Who are you glaring at?' Freddie asked.

He pointed his thumb at the bar.

'Wasn't he with your friend?' Freddie inquired.

Krish felt rage blister beneath his skin.

'I have to find out if she's alright.' He stood up abruptly, and his friends' heads turned and fixed on Matt.

Krishan strode over and sat opposite Meera before placing his pint on her table.

'What's he doing?' he grumbled.

'He's found a redhead. Just can't resist them,' she replied, laughing.

How could her voice be so light and airy? It was as if she didn't care. Why wasn't she upset?

She fixed her gaze on Matt. Krishan's vision tunnelled as he followed her gaze. Matt's lips brushed against the redhead's neck, and Krishan's eyes whipped back to Meera. She lifted her phone and began to scroll through something, completely unaffected. Not even a flicker of emotion marred her face.

Suddenly, he felt that he couldn't leave her alone like this and said, 'Come join us, we're ordering snacks.'

A small smile danced on her lips, and she nodded. 'I could eat. Thank you. Let me text Matt.'

She quickly typed a message. Meera's boyfriend lifted his head from the woman's neck, checked his message, typed something into it and locked eyes with Meera. She raised a single eyebrow at him before grabbing her coat and bag, allowing Krishan to guide her to the table where his friends sat. Krishan's hand instinctively rested on her lower back, and it filled with warmth, as she leant into it.

As they reached their table, she held her hand out to everyone. They soon shuffled their chairs, leaving a chair next to Krishan for her to sit. His curious friends asked her how she knew him, and she told them of their complicated connections without mentioning the fake dating.

She was incredible. His friends were charmed as she asked about their families and their work. She also explained about how DMD worked and how important it was for the diverse community to find a way to meet. Even when they fell into an argument about putting people in ethnic boxes, she held her ground by making it clear that it wasn't about ethnicity but about opening up other ways to meet and connect with like-minded people.

Later, as they made their way back to the hotel, Meera sat between him and Freddie in the car.

'He's a good one,' Freddie said with a grin. 'A lovely bloke, who isn't frightened to show his emotions. You can't go wrong with him, Meera.'

'Freddie!' Krishan reprimanded him with a look. He turned to Meera apologetically. 'Sorry, he's drunk. Can't take his liquor like he used to.'

'Coz he's knackered, with four kids, two under six,' Freddie retorted.

Just then, the driver hit a bump and stepped out of the car, leaving the engine idling. Startled by the sudden halt, Krishan and Freddie followed him out. Krishan flicked on the torchlight from his phone, illuminating the space as the driver walked around the car. The cab with his friends stopped behind them and the driver turned off the engine.

Slowly each of his friends came out to check what was wrong. Freddie told them they'd hit something. They immediately split into pairs and searched the narrow country lane for any injured animal.

Meera waited inside the car; her hands clasped tightly. He leant in to check on her, and her expression reminded him of his children after a nightmare. He instinctively slid back inside and pulled her to his chest, her heart thudding against his. He stroked her hair, soothing her with words, telling her they'd found nothing.

'I saw the eyes. It was a fox. They're everywhere,' she mumbled. He looked out into the fields and saw the occasional glittering eyes watching them from the shadows.

'He's a country fox, and he's more frightened than you. Meera, look at me. Do you remember the beach and the crabs?' he asked her softly.

Her haunted eyes focused on his face, and time stood still. All he had to do was lean in a little and their lips would meet. He would be able to taste her.

Taste her? What was wrong with him? She had a boyfriend!

Even in the dark, he could see her eyes drop to his lips. Her lips parted slightly, and he felt her pulse quicken again. His heart slam against his chest. But then, she took a deep breath and pulled away.

Freddie cleared his throat as he came and sat in the

passenger seat. For the rest of the journey, he and Meera sat close, their thighs touching, her soft hand in his. He concentrated on understanding why heat surged in his blood at the sight of her. Why was his heart pounding against his chest? Why was he finding it difficult to control his need to kiss her?

When they got back to the hotel, he walked Meera to her room, keeping his distance, telling himself that she was with someone. Then why was he so desperate to kiss her? Why did he want to feel her soft lips longer than the pecks they had shared? He longed to hold her in his arms and make slow love to her.

He wanted Meera!

He was developing feelings for his fake girlfriend, and it should have felt wrong, but it didn't. It felt so very right.

The next morning, they skipped the English breakfast and opted for a morning at the hotel spa to sweat out the night's alcohol, readying themselves for more drinking later in the day. Krishan left his friends in the sauna and went to the steam room, his preferred choice. Through the mist, he saw that someone was lying on the tiled bench, and he heard a greeting.

'Hello, Krish.'

His heart knocked against his chest. Meera!

He could no longer deny it. His body was telling him loud and clear. He was deeply attracted to Meera. He couldn't even recall the last time he'd felt this way.

Should he admit it and embrace it?

But Meera was with another man. She was in a relationship, a strange one, but a relationship all the same.

'Where are your friends?' she asked, her voice coming through the haze.

He told her that they were in the sauna, explaining that he wasn't too keen on it and preferred steam instead.

'Me neither. I prefer the steam,' Meera said, coming to sit close to him, their bodies almost touching. He resisted the urge to shift, to widen his stance to touch her. She had told him explicitly that she wasn't interested in long-term relationships or boyfriends. And yet... she was with Matt.

He wanted to ask her why she tolerated him. What was so special about Matt that she allowed him to go off with another woman whilst they were together? Also, he desperately wanted to know about Kaushik. Except she'd told him she was not willing to discuss her ex with anyone. The anger that coursed through him last night as he watched Matt with the redhead, raced through his body all over again. Surprisingly, he'd felt more betrayed by him than Meera.

She was speaking to him now and he hadn't heard a word over the roar in his ears. He needed to have a word with Matt.

He apologised for not hearing a word, blaming it on his hangover. She stopped talking and they sat in silence, the steam building up between them. After a few more minutes, Krishan became too uncomfortable to stay inside the damp, hot room any longer. They both stood up together at the same time. He stepped back, allowing her to go out first before following closely behind.

As he grabbed a towel to wipe his glasses, his vision filled with the sight of her.

Meera was wearing a red bikini, the halter neck top tied at the bust, highlighting her round breast. Her curved waist, glistening with wetness and her bikini bottoms with delicate tie strings resting on perfectly rounded hips. Turning to reveal a honed arse and his gaze locked on her legs, not a wobble of the thigh in sight as she walked toward the cold shower.

He held his towel lower, trying to calm himself. The sight of her released a thirst that needed quenching, and for the first time since Kreena, he wanted a woman desperately. But the only trouble was that she was unavailable.

She was his fake girlfriend, and she was with Matt.

'Morning, Krishan,' Matt called out as he ran and knelt in front of Meera, his palms pressed together in forgiveness. Krishan resisted the urge to go and yank him off the tiled floor and throw him into the pool.

Meera pulled Matt up to his feet. In the next second, Matt grabbed Meera to him and kissed her for far too long. When they broke apart, she teasingly smacked him on his shoulder and stepped into the jacuzzi.

Needing an escape, Krishan took a cold shower and swam fast laps across the pool to release the pent-up longing that had built to a crescendo. He couldn't watch them anymore. A part of him wanted to kiss her in the same way, but another part of him knew he wasn't sticking to the rules.

What a mess! It was the first weekend with his friends in a long time, and all he was doing was lusting after Meera.

He finished his swim and left the pool area, hoping not to meet with them again; only the fates were deliberately making it difficult for him. When he came down for lunch, Matt was regaling Krishan's friends with stories about his life. Krishan tried his best to ignore him, but his ears kept homing in on his words. The more he heard about his life, the more he disliked him.

Matt was a partner in a German software company. He gloated that he travelled a lot and was on his way to New York, hence his meet up with Meera.

Freddie's eyebrow rose at the implication of what he was saying, whispering, 'A girl to call on in every port. What's Meera doing with him?'

Krishan shrugged nonchalantly, nursing his drink, his grip tightening around his glass. Meera noticed them and shot a glare in his direction. He ignored her and filled his glass with wine again, sipping in silence. Even when his meal arrived, he couldn't muster the appetite to eat it.

Later that evening, as he entered the hotel bar area, he saw Meera alone at the bar with a vodka and lemonade, no lemon slice.

'Where's Matt? Has he abandoned you again?' he said, lowering himself onto the stool beside her.

Meera shot him a look. 'You're too invested in our fake relationship, Krish. I enjoy spending time with you and your kids, but it's not real. I'm happy with my life. You just caught me at a bad time at Jaimini's wedding.'

She swirled the ice in her glass. 'I don't do relationships, especially not with Indian men. I've built my life on my own. I've paid for my home, own a little sports car, and go on a singles holiday to far-off countries. My friends support me. I don't need a man to help me. She then shrugged her shoulders. 'Matt is someone I've known for a while. We have a good time. I know he's a jerk sometimes. But show me a man who isn't? I've accepted that the universe has other plans for me. Don't try to fix things, Krish. Nothing's broken.'

'The cab's here, Meera,' Matt said, approaching them at the bar. 'Are you ready?'

She took a long sip of her drink and turned to Krishan. 'See you later, Krishan.'

Matt grabbed Meera by the hand, and they both walked towards the hotel lobby.

The next morning, the last day of their stay, Krishan headed down to ask for the bill for their late checkout, and that's when he saw them again. Kissing without a care in the world. His hands automatically fisted at his sides.

He wanted to be the man who kissed Meera. He wanted Meera to see him, not anyone else. He wanted to make her happy and cherish her. The words from when they first met resounded in his head.

'Never. Ever. Marry.'

It took all his willpower to turn his back on them and walk away. Desperation seeped into his soul. He wanted Meera to change her mind, to see and choose him.

What a mess!

The lies he had told his family were slowly and steadily turning into unattainable truths.

PIZZA DATE REGRET

Meera

A message pinged on her phone.

> **Krish: Dough, tomatoes, cheese and basil. Are you interested? Pizza?**

The phone rang, and Meera's stomach fluttered. She and Krishan hadn't gone on any fake dates recently. The last time they'd met was a few weeks ago when they were both at the same luxury spa in Chester. She'd been surprised by her response to his body, even after spending an afternoon in the throes of lust with Matt. She and Matt had a friends-with-benefits relationship, which she'd resumed after breaking up with Simon. Matthias Schneider would never commit to one single person. He was a card carrying bachelor to the core, and she was perfectly fine with that.

She'd already given Krishan the *'keep out of my business,'* speech, making it clear to him to stay out of her personal life.

'So, are you up for it? There's this restaurant in Sutton. They have a pizza oven in the garden.'

'Is this a fake date? I don't have it on my calendar?' she asked. After the incident in the country lane and the feelings she was trying hard to ignore, she had made up her mind to stick to their official arrangement. Krishan had been texting her often for an impromptu coffee or drinks, and most of the time she was too busy to accept, but not always. She'd seen how he'd reacted to Matt that weekend, and how he'd sulked at the lunch with his friends.

And yet, despite everything, what was with the butterflies in her tummy? She had to remember, Krishan was still in love with his late wife.

'No, the kids wanted me to ask,' he said. 'They've been spending a lot of time with babysitters lately, and I promised them a Friday night treat. Unless you have other plans?'

She'd missed the kids too, and she had nothing planned except packing for a weekend break in York with Lesley and Carol.

'If you're busy, we understand. I just thought we could have a friends' catch-up,' he added.

'I'd love to. What time?'

He told her the time and asked, 'Want me to pick you up? I'm in town.'

Her heart jittered, but she declined, asking him to send her the address of the restaurant instead. At least that would stop her from getting too close.

Her emotions were already all over the place, her thoughts filled with the way Krishan's arms felt around her as he held her in the car. The scent of him. The warmth of his body. She'd even had a dream of him entangled with her in her bed.

It was wrong. So, so wrong to have a sex dream about

her fake boyfriend.

The sultry breeze of the summer evening drifted through the balcony doors as she packed for the weekend. After showering, she'd dressed in her striped Breton top, pairing it with her light linen sailor pants. As she began to tie her hair back, she heard Carol's voice in her head and stopped. She quickly adjusted the layers to frame her face and tied a red bandana as a headband, knotting it with a jaunty bow.

So what if she looked like Krishan's wife? If he wanted to be her friend, he should accept her as herself. Only... why was her heart feeling strange? She gulped down her neat vodka with ice and checked the location of her cab on the app.

The restaurant was tucked away down a quiet country lane, in an old Tudor building. The air was rich with the smell of warm bread, the clatter of cutlery and hushed conversations, easing her mind. Perhaps seeing him again with the children would reset things and get them back to how they used to be.

The server escorted Meera to the garden, where Krishan and the children were already seated. As he stood up, she leant down to kiss the children and gave each of them a gift bag. They both squealed a thank you as they pulled out the notebooks. One with ducks and the other with boats that she had found whilst in Chester at a quaint little gift shop. The heat from Krishan's arm as he casually placed his hand on her lower back sent a tingle down her spine. She felt him take a step back as he pulled out the chair for her.

Krishan's gaze lowered to his hand and his eyebrows

scrunched in confusion. Had he felt that too?

Her eyes flicked to the kids as they inspected their little books. Maybe she was making assumptions. He'd probably bought them the same notebooks and was just embarrassed to tell her. Yes, she told herself, that was the reason for the look. Nothing more.

She took a replenishing breath to calm herself and asked, 'You didn't get them the same books?'

'No, we didn't go into town.'

His expression changed back to neutral and he tugged at his shirt sleeve. 'I'm not drinking. Are you?' he asked, his tone hesitant.

What was making him nervous?

The words rushed out as she told him she'd taken a cab and planned on drinking. Immediately, he called the server over, asking her if she wanted wine. She felt his sultry gaze on her as she asked the server what he'd recommend. The children were eager to fill her in on all the things they'd done since they last met and told her about Oliver, their new babysitter. She listened to them intently, unable to meet Krishan's eyes.

Suddenly, he stopped talking and cleared his throat. When she looked up, a small smile appeared on his face, and he began to tell her of his busy schedule. She saw him relax in his chair as he told her about meeting new friends through the dating app.

She knew that many of the couples who connected through the app often met outside of the experience. That morning, Craig had casually mentioned that Radhika and Krishan had met again. She bit back the question that bounced in her mind. She knew she should be happy for him that he'd found someone.

Then why was her chest filled with dread?

Since Chester, she'd felt a shift in their relationship. She'd let hope seep in and had begun to dream of a different life. She shook the thought out of her mind and concentrated on the children's excited chatter. When Krishan talked about Chester, she was grateful he hadn't mentioned Matt. She had a feeling that Natasha was listening intently to their exchange.

The pizza was excellent, made the Napoli way, with a light, fresh tomato sauce, basil leaves and creamy mozzarella. For pudding, they opted for tiramisu, and the children chose a trio of ice cream; strawberry, chocolate and vanilla. When the bill arrived, Natasha and Neel begged Meera to come home with them, and she happily agreed.

She always felt safe with Krish, and they'd slipped back into easy conversations that came so naturally to them. She just wished Krish hadn't met Matt. She preferred to keep that part of her life private. Really private. Sometimes, she craved the touch of a man, someone she could trust. She and Matt had known each other since their first year at university, long before Kaushik and her divorce. They had met again by chance a few years ago when she was working in Holland. Most of the time, Matt was attentive, except for the odd night when he'd get enamoured by a redhead. But she knew where she stood with Matthias Schneider. She knew there would never be the spectre of commitment, and it had been enough.

Later that evening, after half an hour of playing Fish, Krishan told the children to get ready for their bath and bed. She volunteered to read to Natasha, but Krishan told her to help herself to a drink and sit in the garden while he dealt with his children. The sun was setting, painting the sky in shades of oranges, reds and purples. Meera relaxed as she settled into the garden chair. She missed sitting outside the most, the fragrance from the garden, the birdsong and the quietness. During the summer, her flat was stiflingly hot, and no matter how many windows she opened, there was never enough of a real breeze.

Soon, Krishan joined her with a glass of brandy and sat at the patio table.

'I saw Radhika two nights ago,' he admitted.

'I know. I hoped you would tell me. You found a match, Krish. Our app works,' Meera said, forcing a smile.

Her chest felt heavy. She should feel happy for him. He deserved someone to spend his life with. In that moment it dawned on her that his protectiveness, his simple touches, the way he looked at her were all because she reminded him of his wife. Nothing more. The wave of hopelessness seeped into her chest. Even if she had feelings for Krish, it would never work. She had the misfortune to look like his wife.

'We are just seeing how it goes. Are you okay with it? I mean, are you really happy that I'm seeing Radhika?' he asked, watching her closely.

His hand rested on hers, and she ignored the desperate urge to turn her palm up and entwine his fingers with hers.

'I won't meet with her in public until our fake dating arrangement is over,' he added.

A sadness grew in her heart. She knew deep down that he was looking, searching for someone, even when he'd said he was only helping her out. She knew he was lonely, and as his friend, she should be happy for him and Radhika.

'Yes, I'm happy.' The words felt like sharp stones in her mouth, but she swallowed the hurt. She wasn't interested in marriage or the notion of happily ever after. This shouldn't affect her.

'Has she met Natasha and Neel yet? They'll love her.'

Honestly, she secretly hoped they didn't love Radhika as much as they loved her. But Radhika was lovely, she told herself. Of course, they'd love her. Besides, she had no right to want to stay in his family, even as his friend.

She shook the misery that was building within her. She and Krishan weren't real; they had an expiry date. They were just a convenient arrangement, a fake couple with an end. She convinced herself Radhika was right for him.

Krishan squeezed her knuckles and took a slow sip from his glass. They sat in silence, the warmth of his touch her only comfort. That was the best thing about being with Krishan. She loved the amiable silence, the simple nature of their friendship and the feel of his touch.

A loud clattering noise from the bottom of the garden made her jump, and her heart thundered in her chest. The chair under Krishan screeched against the slate tiles as he shot up and ran into the dark. She tried unsuccessfully to swallow the panic. The hair on the back of her neck lifted. What was wrong with her?

'Krishan! Krishan!' she shouted into the darkness. She heard him yelp, but it felt as if her feet had grown roots, freezing her in place, and she couldn't move. Her phone was inside her handbag in the hallway.

Someone had hurt him. *Krishan was hurt.*

Her heart raced. The feeling of dread filled her chest. She took deep breaths to get the oxygen flowing in her bloodstream.

Think. Think.

A glimmer of thought cleared her mind. The garden was too dark for whoever had hurt Krishan to see if she had a phone or not.

She croaked a shout. 'The police are on their way. Do you hear me? They are on their way.'

Adrenaline coursed through her blood. She had to do something. Krishan could be hurt, unconscious and defenceless.

Clenching her fists tight, she ran into the dark. A hard body slammed into hers and his familiar scent filled her nostrils. Krishan. She clung to him, sobbing with relief.

'Meera.' Soothing hands caressed her back, and she ran her hand over his arms, caressed his chest and finally cupped his jaw, searching for any sign of injury.

'It was just a fox. I'm alright. You're safe,' he whispered, reassuring her.

Her eyes ran over his face, and without a thought, she brushed her lips against his. At first, his lips were soft and tentative, but she craved more. Fuelled by a hunger for him, she pushed her tongue against his teeth, desperate to taste him, to consume him. His restraint shattered and his mouth devoured hers, his tongue dancing with hers. Feverish hands slipped downwards and kneaded her bottom, pulling her closer. He pushed her against the shed, his hard body slamming against her breast. She pulled his hips to hers and felt his hardness against her. Her heart raced from the heat that thrummed through, directly to the space between her thighs.

His lips left hers, and his hands pulled her top upwards. His mouth met the lacy cup of her bra, teasingly grabbing one breast in his moist mouth and then the other. She held his head closer, his hair soft under her sensitive fingers.

The need for him was too great to deny. She pulled him back up to her mouth, and the kiss deepened. He tasted divine. The feel of his tongue in her mouth and the way he held her face up to him drove her crazy with desire. Her hands explored his broad chest and slipped to the open neck of his shirt. She began to twist the buttons free and revealed his impressive chest. When she had seen him at the pool, she'd wondered how it would feel to run her hand through the tufts of hair that ran across his chest. The feel of the hair heightened her desire, and she curled the fingers on her other hand through his hair, kneading into his scalp.

He groaned as she arched herself against him. The friction of his hardness against the light linen of her trousers aroused her, and she moaned from the shiver that ran down her back. His fingers rubbed the insides of her thighs, widened her legs, and thrust her hips toward him, craving the pressure.

'Oh God, Meera.' His voice was a low plea as he knelt in front of her and deftly unzipped her trousers. He then ran his tongue along the thin material of her knickers, pushing, teasing, pressing his tongue against the damp fabric. The friction sent her into a frenzy of desire, and she gasped at how quickly she felt the shudder of release. He held her to his mouth, holding her hips firmly as her legs buckled, threatening to give way.

He slipped her knickers aside, groaning. 'I can stop,' he muttered, his voice unsteady. 'Tell me to stop, Meera.' He grumbled, 'Please... don't make me stop.'

'Don't... stop,' she stuttered, her breath hitching as he circled his thumb over her knotted spot, inserting one finger, then another inside her. Desperate to feel him, she pulled him up, unzipping his trousers and wrapping her fingers around his arousal, rhythmically caressing him. The all-encompassing need to have him sent a raw need pulsing through her, and she knew she was soaking his hand.

She moved instinctively to feel more of his fingers inside her, savouring the feeling of him in her hand, tasting the lust in his kisses. She shuddered again and whimpered, her body tensing with the sensations coursing through her. How had his touch and his mouth unravelled her so easily, releasing waves of orgasm one after the other in quick succession? It had never happened to her like this before.

He groaned wildly as her hands were filled with a moist warmth. He pulled her closer and kissed her, exploring her mouth, holding her tighter as if he never wanted to let go. Her legs were unable to function, his lips soft and luscious, his taste intoxicating. She was spent, just from the masterful touch of his fingers.

In all her life, she'd never felt this way... like she'd found her match. Her perfect man. Everything about him was perfect. They fit perfectly.

She felt his heart thumping against her, and he whispered, planting small kisses all over her face. 'I've wanted you for so long. All of you. Like this. For far too long.'

He laughed softly. 'Let's go inside.'

He zipped her trousers and pulled her top down before adjusting himself. He grabbed her hand, and as their fingers intertwined, the realisation that she'd broken her own rules hit her hard.

Krishan was seeing someone else. She was the other woman who'd knowingly betrayed Radhika, the woman he was seeing. She'd let her fright and desire for him cloud her judgement, leading to this moment. Guilt soured her mouth.

Krish kissed the side of her head and led her back to the kitchen. She told him she needed to use the bathroom. His eyes explored her features, lingering for a moment longer. Then, he kissed her gently on the lips and let go of her hand.

She washed her hands, avoiding seeing her reflection in the mirror. Leaning on the basin for strength, she finally looked up and saw the glimmer of hope, the need to belong, the desire to be wanted. And she didn't like what she saw.

Krishan had told her he was seeing Radhika, and she'd said she was happy for them. Was that a lie? How had she turned into the woman she'd tried hard not to become?

The other woman.

She'd pulled him to her, wanting the comfort of being

in his arms. He'd told her about Cynthia, although his guilt and blame were unfounded as far as she was concerned. They'd both sought out the only person they knew who would understand and help with the loss. For Krishan, it had been someone who loved his late wife, and for Cynthia, someone who knew and loved her childhood friend. But Krishan was still nurturing the blame. He blamed Cynthia and himself for not having the strength to deny comfort from each other.

Would he think the same of her now?

She was his friend, and she'd tarnished their relationship by throwing herself in his arms and slamming her mouth against his. How disgusting of her to want him to touch her in the most intimate of ways. Especially on the night when he'd declared he liked another woman. What was wrong with her? How had she let it happen?

She opened the taxi app, and luckily for her, she found one that was minutes away.

Good. She needed to leave now.

When she opened the cloakroom door, Krishan was coming down the stairs, having changed into a t-shirt and tracksuit bottoms. His eyes twinkled and his lips curled upwards into a soft smile. He pulled her into his arms, but she kept her arms close to her side.

Sensing her hesitation, he stepped back, lifting her chin with his thumb until their eyes met.

'I'm sorry, Krish. I shouldn't have kissed you,' she said, holding his gaze. It would be cowardly to shirk her responsibility.

Confusion clouded his joyous expression.

'I kissed you back. It wasn't a one-way thing,' he replied calmly, his voice firm and steady.

'You're seeing Radhika. I–'

Krishan's arms loosened around her. She missed them, but she had to pull away to get her handbag and leave.

'I have to go. I shouldn't have done that. I'm so sorry. Radhika's a perfect match for you,' she said softly.

She checked her mobile, unable to look at him, afraid of what she might see there.

'Meera?' He moved towards her, but she took a step back.

'It was nothing,' she said. 'Just adrenaline and lust. We can't let what we did ruin what you have with Radhika. Do you want me to tell my mum we broke up?'

She couldn't look him in the eye. The shame of what she had done prevented her from meeting his gaze. She shouldn't have reminded him of his wife. She was reckless... and he'd let his guard down.

'No, I'll keep to our agreement, Meera. I'm sorry if I made you feel uncomfortable.'

She lifted her gaze to meet his and saw regret. Relief eased her breathing. He'd felt the same. They'd simply gotten carried away in the moment. It was the shock and panic. Meera accepted that she'd felt frightened for his safety. That was all.

'My cab is here. I'll text you when I get home,' she said quietly.

'Sure.' He opened the front door for her, his expression unreadable.

'Goodnight, Krish. And… I'm really sorry.'

Saying that, she walked through the front garden toward the road to the waiting cab. As she slid into the backseat, she saw him stepping out onto the street, waiting for her cab to pull away, his arms hanging loosely by his side.

When she got home, she stripped off her clothes and stepped into the hot shower, washing away the shame and guilt. The shame that she had become the *other woman*, that she'd made a vulnerable man lose control.

She needed to stay professional and friendly with Krishan and Radhika. That was the only way forward.

She would miss the children, but her life was exactly as she wanted it to be, she told herself repeatedly. For a brief time, she'd fallen off the path and let herself dream of family and happiness. She was thankful that at least she was spending the weekend with her best friends. She would need all their encouragement and support to get back on track again.

Never. Ever. Marry.

She repeated the words over and over until she drifted off into a restless sleep.

SECRET CINEMA

Meera

When Meera first arrived at the Back to the Future screening, she caught a glimpse of someone who looked like Krishan, dressed in a white dinner jacket. Her stomach tumbled at the thought of meeting him, but when she looked again, she realised she'd imagined it.

She and Krishan hadn't spoken since that night a week ago. She missed his text messages and his quick phone calls. She missed how he looked at her and always complimented her. She recalled the feeling of his hand on her lower back as he guided her to a seat during their post-date debriefs. But most of all, she missed talking to the kids. Somehow, that ache was the worst of all.

She was ashamed of her actions that night. The next day, she'd confessed everything that had happened to her friends on the journey up to York, and they'd reassured her that Krishan would probably be just as embarrassed. All through the weekend, Lesley had teased her mercilessly, suggesting other romance tropes she could explore with men that interested her. She kept prattling on about the romance books she loved to read. Enemies to Lovers, Soul Mates, Secret Billionaire, Close Proximity, and in the end, Lesley had even started searching for more categories on Amazon. It would have been hilarious if she didn't feel so raw, burdened by the heaviness of knowing she would never have her happily ever after.

Eventually, Carol had put her foot down and told Lesley off for not being sympathetic to her plight, reassuring her once again that everything would be fine. She reassured her that Krishan would call her on Monday. Only Monday had come and gone. She'd waited and hoped for something on Tuesday. For the next few days, she became busy and hadn't thought about him until earlier that afternoon, when she'd gone to the Chez Shaz. Most Fridays, Krishan sent her a photo of the kids, however this week, there was still nothing.

Carol and Lesley's jaws had dropped when she'd turned up looking cute in her new hairstyle. The sleek look suited the character she was dressed as for the secret cinema experience. It was nothing like her old soft layered style, this was a short haircut that reached her jawline. She'd also asked Sharon, her hairdresser, to apply blonde highlights.

Lesley and Carol, once they found their voices, reminded her of her past disdain for the same haircut she was now wearing. They recalled how many times she'd called out women bosses who felt they needed the "prerequisite bob" to prove they were worthy of holding down a high-profile, high-worth job.

She simply laughed and told them about the dating app's upcoming launch in America in the new year, and she was that high-flying, high-profile woman who was off to bigger and better places. The cut had done her a world of good; she'd seen the complimentary looks as she strolled away from the VIP area towards the food trucks. A light breeze brushed against her neck, and she added that as another advantage of getting a bob.

As she joined the queue, she watched a group of actors sitting at a table and drinking Coca-Cola from bottles. She instinctively tugged her dress bodice up. She was wearing a strapless peach dress with a double-layered net underskirt. Carol's mother was one of the best dressmakers in Birmingham. Meera often got her to make her a dress, a reworking of an original style from the ones available in the shops. But this time, she'd surpassed herself, making identical dresses for her, Lesley and Carol in pastel shades.

The queue for the food moved forward, and a gap appeared as the people in front shifted to the side. Krish was walking towards her in a cream tuxedo jacket, crisp white shirt and black pants. Their eyes met, and her heart raced.

Would he ignore her, feigning he didn't recognise her? Or would he smile?

Please smile, please don't make it awkward.

'Lorraine Baine,' he mouthed, and a grin spread across his face as he stopped inches away from her.

'George McFly! How? Where? Who?' she said.

Krishan's head cocked to the side, and he told her it was his father's tuxedo. Shifting both paper bags he was holding to one hand, he crossed his legs at the ankle and spun in a full circle. 'It's a little snug on the waist,' he said, showing off his black socks, 'and a bit short, but it goes with the '50s vibe. What do you think?'

Meera told him she loved it and pointed to the group, pretending to drink at the makeshift café table by the side. He turned to watch them and grinned at her, '"*Back to the Future.*" Love it.' His eyes glittered with mirth, and her heart skittered. It wasn't awkward at all. Maybe she'd made too much of their kiss and more.

Just then, Radhika's voice filtered to her ear. 'There you are? I was worried you'd deserted me after my revelations.'

Krish laughed, a low rumbling sound that penetrated Meera's stomach. 'No, no, I loved that story. I wished I had the nerve to do what you did.'

He gave Radhika one of the branded paper bags.

'Hi, Meera. Want to join us? We're over there,' Radhika said, pointing towards a cluster of deck chairs. Meera declined and explained she was with her girlfriends in the VIP area. Radhika turned to Krish and said, 'Doesn't Meera look absolutely stunning tonight, Krish? That dress is beautiful. Where did you get it, Meera?'

'It's handmade. My friend Carol's mum made us matching outfits,' Meera replied, holding the side of her dress and curtseying.

Radhika elbowed Krish, and his lips thinned as his eyes roamed over her outfit. Then, he groaned and inhaled so sharply that she heard him.

'Absolutely. So stunning. Beautiful.' His lips battled between grin and grimace. Meera knew in that moment that he'd only been interested in her because of her similarity to his wife. He continued to stare at her, and Meera saw the exact moment it hit him that she was nothing like his wife. His lips twitched into a thin line.

'You look great too, Radhika. Can I take a photo? I'll send it to you,' Meera said, trying to shift the conversation, unable to ignore Krish's closed-off expression.

Radhika was wearing baggy, faded jeans, a big white shirt, and a pink jacket. Her hair was styled in big soft curls, just like Jennifer Parker, Marty McFly's girlfriend, Meera took a couple of photos on her phone.

Krish pulled Radhika closer and smiled down at her. Sharpness prickled the wall of Meera's chest. She took a deep breath, reminding herself that Krishan and Radhika were an ideal couple. She repeated her mantra. *Never. Ever. Marry.* Her confused heart didn't know whether to beat rapidly or stop beating completely.

'Now, it's your turn. Let me take a picture of you and Krish. You're one of those perfect couples,' Radhika said cheerfully, holding out her hand. Meera hesitated, then reluctantly gave her the phone.

'Put your arm around Meera,' Radhika told Krishan, and he placed his arm loosely over her shoulder.

'No, lower, silly,' Radhika teased. 'Around her waist. You're George and Lorraine.'

Meera heard him take a sharp intake of breath and hold it as his hand grasped her waist. The contact sent a tingle up her spine, but she tried to ignore it. She was relieved when Radhika finished taking a photo and gave her phone back to her. Krishan finally let go of his breath.

'Bye, Meera, don't forget to send me the picture of us,' Radhika said, taking Krishan's hand and leading them back to their seats.

Picture of us.

They are an us. *Us.* The enormity of the words hit her.

Their app was a success. Krishan and Radhika were an actual happily-ever-after couple, which was a positive outcome for their app. Only she couldn't seem to find joy. She pulled out her phone and sent a text to Craig with the picture of Krishan and Radhika, adding a pulsing heart emoji.

This was huge. She should be proud of their match.

Finally, there was a dating app created for the diverse community. She let the news sit, pushed away the sadness and mustered the feeling of accomplishment deep within her. She scrolled through the photos, selecting a few to send to Krish and Radhika. That's when she saw the photo, the one where Krish's eyes sparkled, and his smile gleamed as he looked down at Radhika. A picture-perfect couple.

She felt a wetness pooling on her eyelashes. No, she mustn't cry. They were an ideal match.

And she? She was just a *fake girlfriend*. That was all she meant to him.

INVESTIGATION

Krishan

Krishan had tried to forget the warmth and happiness that had washed over him when Meera was in his arms, and he regretted making her feel accountable for what had happened between them. He had desired her just as much.

The evening when he'd kissed her and done a lot more, she'd let her hair fall in loose, shiny curls, her face devoid of makeup except for her bold red lips. The striped navy top she wore revealed the exquisite curve of her shoulders. She was back to the woman he'd met at Jaimini's wedding, laughing, teasing and telling lame jokes to make the children laugh. She'd even brought them gifts from her trip to Chester. How bonkers was that? He hadn't even thought about it. She was supposed to be his *fake* girlfriend, of all people, yet somehow, she'd become an integral part of his children's lives.

He enjoyed meeting her, bouncing off his ideas and being with her. But yes, he was seeing Radhika, exploring his feelings for her, figuring out how he should proceed with the new relationship. But no matter how much he tried to focus on Radhika, one thing bothered him a lot. That Meera had rejected him.

When he saw her at the Secret Cinema enactment, Krishan's reaction to Meera's new haircut took him by surprise. It confused him. The sleek hairstyle skimmed her jawline, and the light highlights framed her face perfectly, making her even more beautiful than he'd imagined. Yes, she had a resemblance to Kreena, but there was also a uniqueness to Meera. The memory of her soft lips on his brought a flutter to his heart.

'Never. Ever. Marry.' The words bounced in his head as he jostled through the crowded platform to catch the train to Canary Wharf. He wanted to understand what made Meera say those words.

They hadn't been in the country when she'd split up with her husband, so the news hadn't reached him the way it usually would have. His conversation with Joshna was well overdue. He was going to find out why Meera felt inadequate. Why she felt she couldn't be part of someone's life? More than anything, he wanted to know what made her think she wasn't worthy of happiness and love.

'This is a surprise.' Joshna greeted him and kissed his cheek before sitting on the vacant chair opposite him.

The square in Canary Wharf buzzed with people enjoying the summer sun and their lunch. When the weather was good in England, everyone was a lot more friendly and cheerful. He'd momentarily forgotten he wasn't in Silicon Valley when he'd asked the coffee barista how she was. Caught off-guard, an almost smile appeared on her painted lips as she handed him a flat white with an extra shot of espresso along with Joshna's chai latte.

'Do you want to ask me something?' Her eyes danced

with curiosity.

Krishan took a sip of his scalding coffee and asked her straight away.

'What happened in Meera's marriage?'

Frown lines appeared on Joshna's forehead.

'Why? Are you serious about her?'

He didn't answer. Meera wasn't looking for a permanent relationship, but he was her friend, and he wanted to make her happy.

'We are taking it slowly. Meera struggles with relationships.' But he wasn't. It was a fake relationship. A deception for their family. She'd told him plenty of times that she wasn't interested.

Joshna sighed. 'Can you blame her? The one and only man she loved betrayed her in so many ways. She's too kind and trusting. That's her downfall.'

The one and only man she loved. Those words stung. Meera had loved her ex. Was she still in love with him?

'Where is her ex-husband now?' he asked.

Josh shrugged. 'No clue and good riddance.' She lifted her cup and sipped from it. A gnawing worry filled his chest.

'Why haven't you tried to help her? You're her family.'

Joshna told him that Meera was too independent and hurt to trust again. She reached for his hand, and patted it gently.

'We're here for her when she's ready to tell us more.' She took a sip of her chai and conflict danced in her eyes as she looked downwards.

'Did you know we had to pay Kaushik to sign the divorce papers?' she said softly, her voice barely audible.

The information left a bitter taste in his mouth. He felt anger so visceral that he felt his hand grip his coffee cup tighter and his jaw clench. Joshna continued to explain how they'd found him in Europe living the high life while Meera bore the brunt of his recklessness.

'She paid back every penny of the debt he'd accumulated,' Joshna said. 'She sold her wedding jewellery and anything that was worth any value. The only thing she's kept is the necklace she wears, the one with the diamond pendant. She bought that with her first bonus.'

After a long pause, she finally spoke again, 'You like her, don't you?'

What could he say to Joshna? He more than liked her, but she wasn't interested in marriage. And his children needed stability. Now that he'd accepted meeting someone, marriage was his only option. He couldn't subject his young children to women who came and went out of their lives.

'She's perfect for you if you're in two minds. I told you that before. Do you remember?' Joshna said, watching him closely.

He remembered it all too clearly. It was his first thought when he'd met Meera, the young woman who eerily resembled the love of his life, Kreena.

The drive home on the motorway was all stops and

starts, so he had time to think of a solution. Meera wasn't ready for a relationship, but he could at least help her get the Masi Mafia off her back.

The first person he needed to speak to was his mother. Their fake relationship would end soon, and he had to make sure the Masi Mafia wouldn't pounce on her with another suitable match. He was already heading home to pick his kids up and would raise the subject then.

'Are you and Meera getting along?' Krishan's mother asked him as he helped her tidy up the kitchen. The children and their grandfather were playing cricket in the garden.

'Yes... it's okay,' he said, trying to sound as non-committal as possible, throwing down subtle hints that they'd soon be breaking up.

'Just okay? Jasu was mentioning a widower with young children looking for a wife. He's a little younger, but he's open-minded about that. She's so kind and good-natured. She'd make an excellent mother and wife. You know I like her, don't you?'

The anger that he'd tried to keep in check at the thought of how her husband had hurt her resurfaced and the bitterness resounded in his tone.

'Why can't you all leave her alone?' Krishan blurted in frustration. 'She's already been through a lot. Are you sure you are introducing her to someone good? Did you know about Kaushik? Did you know about the debt? Look at her, she's the head of a department in a growing company worth millions of pounds. She owns her own flat, and she has great relationships with people. You've seen her, especially with the children. She doesn't need a man. She's successful on her own.

Sometimes people just want to be left alone.'

His heart was thudding. He took a calming breath and said, 'Why don't you leave her alone?'

His mother's eyes glistened at his outburst. 'Is this about Meera, or are you really telling us that you want to be alone?'

Krishan took a deep breath. 'I didn't say that, Mummy. I like her, and I want you to stop your friends from bothering her and making remarks about her luck.'

His heart pounded against his ribs as he filled a glass with water and gulped it down, willing his heart to quieten. He'd heard the whispered comments at the weddings and gatherings. He'd seen Meera disappear to avoid being told to move away.

Memories that he had almost forgotten slammed into his mind. The comments about his wife's age, career, love marriage, infertility and *bad luck* fell like fresh shards of wounds piercing through his thoughts. No one had blamed him for his wife's cancer. No one had told him he was the bearer of bad luck. Only Kreena wasn't lucky. They weren't even living in this country, but they still heard the allegation. Superstitious rubbish that made his blood boil. He'd heard from Radhika about the name-calling and blame culture that was still prevalent in South Asian communities, even in England. It angered him.

He heard his mother leave the kitchen, sensing his mood. He turned his attention to the garden and watched his children play with his father to get his anger under control.

Later, as he was leaving for the night, his mother held on to him more fiercely than usual.

'Give Meera some time, Krishan,' she whispered. 'Tara looked at your birth charts. You're soulmates. She'll come around.'

Soulmates? His mother and her friends often believed in that stuff. He'd laughed at the ludicrousness of that. Besides, he'd made his decision to marry again, and she... she had sworn she never would.

Never. Ever. Marry.

Suddenly, Kreena's voice sounded like a loud boom in his head, jogging his memory. *'Krish, promise me you'll find someone. Promise me you won't deny love. I know there's someone special waiting for you. A woman who will fill up your heart again.'* She'd coughed furiously after that conversation. He'd placed a finger against her dry lips to stop her from talking. Tears had prickled his eyes, and he'd seen tears stream down his wife's cheeks too.

The memory of Meera's lips filled his heart with a heaviness he couldn't shake. How was he ever going to get over this weight that now sat in his tender heart? *Meera.*

'Car Karaoke!' the kids shouted, interrupting his thoughts.

Taylor Swift's *"You Belong to Me"* was the first song that blasted through his car speakers as he pulled out of his parents' road. He sighed, gripping the wheel tightly.

How had he gotten himself into this situation?

At Jaimini's wedding, he'd thought his plan was brilliant. A temporary *fake* arrangement. Except now, he wished he'd never met Meera.

No. That wasn't true. He was privileged to have Meera in his life.

179

Tara Masi

Meera

Her mother's number appeared on her phone screen.

'Hello, Mummy. To what do I owe this pleasure?'

'Stop teasing. I text you every other day. Are you doing anything tonight?'

'No, why?'

'Can't a mother ask her daughter over for an impromptu dinner? I'll make your favourite food.'

Smiling, Meera agreed and told her mother that she'd come for dinner.

The dating project had been a tremendous success. Although the success rate of finding a life partner was 30%, the figures for dates leading to long-term relationships were remarkable. She felt very proud of what she and Craig had created.

At her parents' place, they'd eaten her favourite meal ever, kachori, ringda bateta nu shaak, mug ni dall, and kadhi with everything else. After dinner, her father took her in his arms, holding onto her longer than usual before planting a kiss on her forehead. She expected him to go to the front room to watch TV, but instead, he'd put on his jacket and declared he was off to the Golf Club to meet with friends.

'Aren't the wives going too, Daddy?' she asked her dad. 'If you want to go, I can clear up, Mummy,' she added, but before anyone could respond, she heard the front door close. Surprised, she turned to her mother for an explanation.

'Nah, it's a men-only thing. Go relax in front of the TV or do your usual phone texting thing,' her mummy said casually.

Meera sat in her favourite spot on the sofa and flicked through the channels to find something she could watch. Her mother hated the hook up shows she watched. She wasn't in the mood for Grey's Anatomy or House. As she flicked through the channels, she found The Great British Bake Off and followed the hashtag on social media to join the conversation.

That was what her life had become now. Conversations with fake friends, a fake boyfriend, a fake life. What had happened to all the ambitions and dreams she'd once had? The social life she dreamt of, wine bars, theatres, concerts, had faded into a distant dream. Everyone she knew had found someone special and moved away, building their own lives. That's what had happened, she told herself. The only people she met with regularly were her best friends, Lesley and Carol. As for the rest of the time, she had a very boring social life. She wallowed in self-pity and felt the boulder she carried on her shoulders dig deeper. Sighing, she switched off her phone and put it on the coffee table.

What was wrong with her? She should be happy. Happier than she had been in a long time. She was a successful app developer and an expert in creating experiences for Reach for the Sky. Yet, she felt an emptiness inside her.

Her mother brought in two bowls of chopped fruits and handed one to her. On the TV, Mary Berry unveiled an intricate cake with multiple layers for the baking challenge. For a while, they watched in silence and then her mother muted the sound.

'I have to tell you something, Meera. I'm so sorry, Diku,' she said softly.

Diku? Her mom hardly ever called her that, and suddenly, the kiwi in her mouth lost all its flavour. Too many upsetting thoughts flooded through her mind. Her mother always apologised first, even when she was the one suffering.

She remembered the day her mother had told her about her hysterectomy. She had suffered for years in silence, enduring the constant bleeding from fibroids and the fatigue from the blood loss, until eventually, her doctor finally became concerned about her alarmingly low iron count. *'I'm sorry, Diku,' her mother had said back then, 'I know you like your new flat but can you come home to stay with me after the operation?' she'd asked hesitantly.*

Snapping out of the past, Meera asked, worried, 'Are you ill? Why didn't you tell me?'

Her mother took her hand, giving it a reassuring squeeze. She told Meera that she wasn't talking about her health.

Meera took a deep breath and slowly exhaled.

'Tara had a hospital appointment today,' her mother continued.

Tara Masi was ill? She could cope with the fact that her mother's friend was ill. As it is, she wasn't one of her favourite people.

'She saw Krishan.' Her mother paused.

What?! Krishan was unwell!

'What appointment did Tara Masi have?' she asked.

Her mother skittered at the increased decibel of her voice. 'Just her regular blood tests.'

'And where did she see Krishan?' Meera tried to sound calmer, unable to slow her racing heart. Krishan was sick.

'In the coffee shop.'

Her mother's words made little sense. Krishan was in a coffee shop at the hospital. She rubbed her forehead. She couldn't believe that her mother and her friends gossiped about such trivial things.

If he was in the coffee shop, that meant Krishan wasn't sick. Her heart calmed when that realisation hit her.

'He was kissing another woman,' her mother said, her voice low.

She froze for a beat and then it clicked. She instantly realised what that meant. Krishan had met Radhika at her workplace, and the Masi Mafia had spotted them. Now their scheme was blown.

Meera took her mother's hands and confessed everything. She admitted that she'd agreed to a fake relationship with Krishan, and she also told her that she knew about Radhika. She even confessed to her mother that she was the one who'd set them up, and that it wasn't news to her. She explained that the idea

183

had occurred to them at Jaimini's wedding to stop everyone from badgering Krishan and her at family gatherings.

'I would have broken up with him after Jaisukh Masa's surprise 65th,' she said. It was ironic that they'd agreed their last fake date would be for Tara Masi's husband's birthday party.

'Why won't you allow us to find someone for you, Meera? You can't live alone. I'm worried that you'll be lonely when we're gone. I'm sorry… we didn't protect you. We should have vetted Kaushik more thoroughly.'

'Oh, Mummy, don't be sad,' Meera said softly. 'I have lots of family. Meera Fai is what I am. I won't be lonely. As for what happened in my marriage, no one knew, Mummy, not even Kaushik's family. It just happened. Maybe your Bhagwan had another plan for me.'

'It's your Bhagwan too, Meera.'

She still believed there was a plan for her. Only now, the loneliness was beginning to feel like a weight she couldn't bear any more. Her Bhagwan had found Daddy for her mother, Joshna for Harish, and even Keval for Jaimini. Yet… here she was. Alone.

She'd developed feelings for Krishan and had revealed too much of herself to him. She'd built a quiet hope around their relationship only to be misguided by his kindness and companionship. She'd made plans with him, and he'd found someone he wanted more than her. Someone he wanted in his life, in his family. Maybe she wasn't deserving of that type of love.

The thought that even her fake boyfriend had humiliated her added another boulder to the pile she was already carrying on her shoulders. Krishan was no different from all the other men she knew. Their need came first… always. Just like Kaushik and her ex, Simon. He hadn't liked her enough to protect her from the hurt and humiliation of being seen with Radhika and kissing her in public.

Then, as if things couldn't get any worse, the phone rang. It was Krishan's mother, sharing the news with her own mother that he would be introducing Radhika to the family over the weekend. Her mother looked at her and put her phone on speaker. Meera heard Kavita Masi ask Mummy if there was any hope for their children to get back together. Her mother's dark eyes settled on hers and Meera shook her head.

It was hopeless. There was no hope. Krishan didn't like her enough to care.

Her mother sighed and spoke into the phone, 'Meera is too hurt–' She switched the speaker off and added, '–and too stubborn.' Saying this, she quietly ended the call.

Driving back home from Coventry, she played out the kissing scene in her head over and over again, even though she hadn't been there to witness it. She'd told him to hold off, and he'd humiliated her by wanting Radhika to meet his parents. The Masi Mafia's phones would be hot with the gossip. She was back in their sights again. She could almost hear the hushed whispers and see the pitying looks. This was even worse than before. Unlike her other relationships, this one had played out in public.

This wasn't *just* humiliation. *This was humiliation with a capital H*. How dare he break his promise to her? She had to tell him what she thought of him.

Meera's Favourite Dinner

Mattar kachori ane ambli khajjur ni chutnee
Fried plain flour pastry encased balls of masala peas and tamarind date chutney

Ringda Bateta nu shaak
Sautéed spicy masala stuffed aubergine and potatoes

Chuti Mag ni dall
Lightly steamed split mung bean lentil cooked with mild spices

Kadhi
Thick spicy broth made from gram flour and natural yoghurt

Jeera bhaat
Fried and steamed rice with cumin seeds

Rotli
Griddled flatbread made from whole wheat flour

Roasted papad
Thin crispy bread made with lentil flour dry roasted on a flame

Gajjar no sambharo
Gujarati style stir fried carrots and green chillies

Kachumber
Salad made with cabbage, cucumber, carrots, onions and tomatoes

Dahi
natural yoghurt

Athanu
Assortment of Indian pickles

YOU DON'T LOVE ME

Krishan

He waited at their usual table. He was now part of a couple who met regularly at an eatery, a favourite of Radhika's, serving British cuisine on Birmingham's Stephenson Street. It was a small table, tucked away in a discreet corner, shielded from prying eyes. They'd begun meeting there as friends since their first date outside the dating app. He let that thought sink in.

If someone had told him six months ago that he'd start dating again, finding babysitters and going away for a weekend without his kids, he would have laughed at the absurdity of it all. But here he was.

The most astonishing part of his new life was that he had a girlfriend. Someone he was itching to introduce to his family as his *real* girlfriend. However, he also had a *fake* girlfriend. Nobody would believe that he, of all people, would do that. That he'd put himself in such a complicated situation. Only he had, and somehow, the woman who wasn't even his actual girlfriend was the only one he couldn't stop thinking about.

He pushed the sadness clouding his mind deep inside him. He missed Meera so much. She'd kept her distance from him ever since they had kissed. She had become his dearest friend and confidant, his go-to person to meet or talk to if he had a problem. Only something had changed, and she was no longer the open, friendly woman he'd grown used to. He badly wanted, needed to get back to what they had before.

Her new haircut had sent him into a tailspin. He just couldn't get over it. She was stunningly beautiful, more beautiful than he could have ever imagined. He never realised until now how much it affected him.

Earlier in the week, he'd met Meera and told her he missed their impromptu meet ups and the shared experience of watching *Grey's Anatomy* over drinks. Briefly, the teasing, smiling woman had reappeared, and all he wanted was for the fake to become real. Except, she kept mentioning how happy she was that he'd found Radhika. That comment created a gaping hole in his heart.

He told himself to be happy that he was with Radhika, the wonderfully kind woman he was waiting for right now. He had tried to talk to Meera, asking her if there was any hope of them being real. She'd hesitated, twiddling that necklace nervously and reminding him of their initial agreement to only ever fake date.

'We'd still be friends, right?' he'd asked, dreading the thought that they might not be together for long. She'd said yes, and he held onto the fact that he was lucky to still have Meera in his life.

So he had spent more time with Radhika, making sure he'd chosen well, wanting the same feeling he had with Meera when his lips had brushed hers. He reminded himself that he'd already had a full-blown love story once. Now, it was time for him to think about his children and their well-being.

Just then, Radhika walked in through the door, her hair tied in a high ponytail. She was petite, barely five feet tall, and exuded a quiet grace. He watched as she handed her thick coat to the attendant and turned to face him, her lips twitching slightly as their eyes met. She was what he was looking for, someone who would fit into his family. He stood and kissed her, it was a nice, comforting kiss. He had some news to share with her.

He and Radhika had kissed in public at the hospital during their lunch together. He'd been careless, forgetting all about his conversation with Meera. Kissing Meera had taken his breath away, filled his body with heat, igniting something deep within, and he'd had that with Kreena too. He'd never kissed Radhika on the lips before, their usual departing kiss were chaste and on the cheek. Kissing Radhika was different, and it was time for him to take his responsibility seriously. His children needed a mother, and she wanted to be a part of their lives. Not all marriages were full of passion. Companionship had its benefits too.

'I've ordered a lovely champagne.' He pointed to a bottle chilling in the ice bucket stand as she sat in the chair opposite him.

She tilted her head. 'What are we celebrating?' A small quirk appeared on her lips. 'New contract, expansion, funding approval?'

'No, it's personal.' He waved to the server, who promptly opened the bottle and poured their drinks.

They raised their glasses, and Krishan took a huge sip of his champagne. He'd planned to tell Radhika his news after the starters, but it seemed she'd sensed his need to share something. Which reaffirmed that he'd chosen well. He and she had a lot in common. She was calm, patient and dependable, a good woman to introduce to his children. Of course, there were a few differences; her taste in music, and the fact that she loathed sports. He knew he'd never find a perfect fit. He'd found that once with his late wife and had lost her. It was time to compromise. Arranged marriages worked just as well as love marriages. He'd seen that in his own family.

He was ready to accept the aunties were right. He was still young, and Radhika would make a great wife and mother. His children were young enough to accept a new mother. Immediately, the thought of his feisty, no-nonsense daughter Natasha burst into his head. She might be a hurdle he'd have to deal with, but Neel would adore Radhika. His parents would like her too. He told himself that this was the beginning of the next chapter in his life.

'Radhika's a perfect match for you.' He heard Meera's voice echo in his mind. Yes, Radhika would do just nicely.

'Did you have a good weekend?' he asked Radhika.

'Yes,' she said, smiling. 'I feel totally relaxed after spending time in the sauna. Do you like the sauna, Krish?'

He shook his head and told her he preferred the steam room. *Meera liked the steam room too,* a small voice said in his head.

The starter plates arrived at their table, and Krishan knew he couldn't delay any longer. Radhika lowered her gaze and stared at the scallops as he finally told her the news about how one of the Masi Mafia had seen them kiss. And he confessed that he'd told his parents about his fake relationship with Meera.

Radhika fiddled with the cutlery, moving the knife eschew and straightening it again, unable to meet his gaze. His brow furrowed. Something was wrong. But still, he continued, telling her that his parents were keen on meeting her. He took a deep breath and asked if she was free to join them for a family lunch on Sunday.

Once he'd stopped talking, she lifted her head. Her eyes glistened, a single tear pooling on her lower lid. She was crying.

Had Tara Masi followed her and created a scene? He rested a comforting hand on Radhika's, as she gripped her fork.

'I can't meet your family, Krish.'

'Why not?' he asked, bewildered.

'I don't want to be just *good enough*,' Radhika said, teary eyed. 'I want to be all you want. I don't want to fit just nicely with your life plan.' She paused and wiped her nose with the napkin.

Krishan was shocked. How did she know that was exactly what he'd been thinking? Could she hear his thoughts? He immediately shook the absurd thought away. Tara Masi must have confronted her after he'd left.

'Did Tara Masi say something?' he asked softly. 'Whatever it was, it's rubbish. Ignore it. She has this ridiculous idea that Meera and I are soulmates who have finally met each other. It's just how she is.'

'What if *you* are soulmates?' Radhika pressed on.

'What? Meera, my soulmate? No, I have already met my soulmate and have lost her. You know about Kreena. We've been honest with each other. I really like you, Radhika. We could work well together. And you know Meera. She's not the settling type. That bastard of an ex has destroyed her trust in people.'

His heart was racing, not only from the thought of Kaushik, but also because he'd made a huge mistake by telling his mother. His mother would tell Kalu, who'd call Josh, and then she'd tell Meera.

Meera. He hadn't told Meera. She would be upset if she came to know about it.

Just then, his phone beeped, and he looked at the message.

'What the fuck, Krish!!!?'

'Meera?' Radhika raised a thin smile, giving him a knowing look.

He showed her the message and released a slow breath. 'She's mad. I forgot to tell her that I'd told my parents, and that they want to meet you.'

Before he could say anything more, the phone in his hand rang and Meera's face popped up on the screen. He pressed the call button and hit mute.

'I have to take this call. Please don't leave,' he said to Radhika.

He pushed his chair back and stood up. 'Let me explain, Meera. I'm just stepping out of the restaurant.'

He'd never heard Meera so distraught, so upset, so breathless. He could hear her strained voice as she vented how it felt to be told by her mother that her *fake* boyfriend was serious about someone else. So serious that he'd wanted them to meet his real girlfriend straight away. She called him all sorts of names and told him he was just like the other low-life men who'd put their needs above hers. After a few minutes, she finally let go of a slow breath.

'Don't come anywhere near me, Krish. Do you understand? Just the whiff of your cologne will make me murderous.'

Silence.

He continued to hold the phone to his ear, even as the line went dead.

How could he have done this to Meera? To his children?

In the need to comfort his mother, he'd forgotten the rest of their conversation. They'd had only one more planned gathering to attend in their fake relationship. Just one.

He knew that Meera had wanted to speak to his parents, to tell them that he'd behaved appropriately with her and treated her with nothing but respect. She'd wanted to tell Natasha and Neel herself that she and their dad were just friends. She was more of a parent to his children than he was.

But he'd hated hearing or seeing his mother cry, and to comfort her, he'd blurted out that he was planning to marry the woman he'd been caught kissing. If only he had waited. He knew his mother had set her heart on Meera. She'd told him that more than once. That Meera was the ideal mother for his children and a perfect wife for him.

Yes, she was. The perfect mother. The perfect wife. She was everything.

His heart pounded, and the truth he had ignored slammed into him. He wanted to go to Meera. To comfort her. To run his hands through her soft, wavy hair and to kiss her soft, sweet lips. He had been so blind.

Meera *was* his soulmate.

'I love you Meera,' he breathed out softly, even though he knew she couldn't hear him. The realisation hit him like a hammer. He loved Meera and only Meera.

But first, there was another woman waiting for him. The kind and generous Radhika, who'd been genuinely searching for someone to love again. She didn't deserve to be in the dark. He owed it to her to tell her the truth and help her deal with what had happened.

In one evening, he'd managed to hurt both his actual girlfriend and his fake girlfriend. The only woman he wanted, had *ever* wanted was Meera. His true love.

But you lost her, you fool, the small voice in his head scolded.

Not Good Enough

Meera

Meera's misery grew after her phone call with Krishan. She knew their relationship was fake; she knew she'd developed feelings for him; she knew she'd told him their kiss was only lust. But for the first time in her life, she'd felt safe with a man. Like she'd finally found home. And somewhere along the way, she'd let herself believe that there was something special in their relationship.

Losing Krishan shattered her, and the weight of the emotions she had been carrying came crashing down, entombing her. She'd sat for hours in her car when she'd returned to her flat, unable to even call her best friends. Everything came flashing back, the things that Kaushik had done to her, the pain of her recent breakup with Simon, the man she'd thought was worth baring her fears to… and even Matt. Meeting with him again just wasn't the same.

Had she let a bit of herself fall for Krishan, even when he'd warned her repeatedly of his only true love, his late wife?

The next morning, she'd called in sick and tried to sleep away the pain. Except for the first time in her life, sleep had deserted her. The nagging voice that she would *never ever* find someone who truly cared for her gnawed at her heart. The incessant calls from Krishan, her family and his family only made it worse, hurting her ears. She turned her phone off after sending a couple of messages to her team. She wasn't ready with a response. This was even worse than the day Tara Masi had seen Kaushik with another woman. Her mind kept replaying the conversation from that day long ago.

❀ ❀ ❀

'Meera, it's Tara. Are you at home? She could hear the anxiety in Tara Masi's voice.

'I don't know how to say this…' she trailed off and Meera heard a sharp intake of breath. 'Listen, I'm in Cheltenham, and I just saw Kaushik with a white woman.'

Meera's heart crashed against her chest, pounding so loudly that she couldn't hear what was being said on the phone. She had suspected it. How could she not? The lipstick stains, the cloying perfumes that weren't hers, the way he sometime crept into bed late at night smelling of cigarette smoke.

Kaushik did not smoke. It was the only vice he didn't have.

'Meera? Did you hear what I said? He was with another woman, a blonde. And they were very close. You know what I mean.'

Fire ants crawled inside her stomach at Tara Masi's words. The shame of knowing that one of her mother's most gossipy friends had seen her husband cheating on her. Throughout her short marriage, she'd tried her best to hide her unhappiness. To make excuses for Kaushik's absences, even from his own family. But now, she finally had proof to confront him. She remembered how her response had been measured, even though her eyes were brimming with tears.

She'd convinced Tara Masi not to tell anyone, asking her to wait for a few days while she spoke to her family and his. That night, so long ago, she'd made two promises to herself, that she would never ever want to hear sympathy in anyone's voice again, and she would also never marry again. She knew that she was capable of looking after herself. After all, she'd been looking after the man-child she'd married for years; paying off his credit card bills, funding his start-ups, and bailing him out of clauses he forgot to read and negotiate.

Back then, she'd dealt with everyone. Except, this was nothing in comparison. This was different. Her whole body ached like she'd been pummelled. This time she was too fragile to deal with anyone.

All she wanted was to cocoon herself in bed and never ever step out of the house again. She was too upset with Krishan, her *fake* boyfriend.

Was she that unlovable?

She went to the kitchen, pulled out the bottle of Bombay Sapphire, unscrewed the lid and took a huge gulp. The neat alcohol seared her throat, but she welcomed the sting. She took another gulp, and tears streamed down her face. She made her way to her bedroom to drown her sorrows.

'You love me, don't you?' she said to the bottle in her hand. The night turned to day and she continued to go through her drinks cabinet, switching to intermittent water to get rid of the throbbing headache and the heaviness in her heart.

197

The incessant chirping of the dawn chorus woke her, and she lifted herself out of the bed. The alcohol had numbed her senses; there was no ache in her head or her body. Only her heart remained bruised.

As she walked along the narrow corridor, the memory of Neel's excited face crashed into her mind. She staggered from the intensity of never ever being with him and Natasha again. Maybe she could speak with her sister-in-law and arrange a play date. Would Joshna Bhabhi allow that, knowing too well that her relationship with Krishan was a lie?

How had she brought shame on herself and her family again? This was even worse than last time. At least the divorce with Kaushik was necessary. But this fake dating was despicable. A deception created by her and her alone. *No. Krishan too.*

She opened the kitchen cabinets in search of food and came across a pack of custard creams that Simon loved. Wonderful, playful Simon, who'd slowly chipped away at her guard, making her believe that perhaps she could be with someone, after all.

She had let herself hope despite the obstacles and repercussions. He wasn't Gujarati, and he was eleven years younger than her. However, he had a beautiful house in Bournville village, a holiday home in Gibraltar and was extremely wealthy due to his family's links to chocolate. They'd talked about getting the parents together on several occasions, and she'd hoped for more until that night, when she'd heard the sex noises after letting herself in the tastefully decorated turn-of-the-century home in Bournville. Fresh pain hit her chest, and she slumped on the kitchen floor, the almost empty bottle and the pack of custard creams slipping out of her hand.

Her body buckled over her legs, and she rested her head on the cold floor, waiting for the numbness to take hold again.

A relentless ringing in the distance brought her back to consciousness. The sound became louder, and with it came the thumping noise that vibrated through her body. She pulled herself up by grabbing the handle of the kitchen cabinet and staggered through the hallway to the front door. She peered through the spy hole.

Carol! A faint recollection of a lunch date wisped through her mind, hazy, like an image obscured by glass and incomplete. It can't be today, can it?

As she opened the door, Carol engulfed her in a warm, steady hug.

'I heard,' her soft voice washed over Meera's neck. 'Come on, let's get some soup in you. My Ma's Jamaican Chicken soup.' She grabbed Meera by the hand and pushed her onto the sofa.

After filling her aching tummy with food and taking a warm shower, Meera finally asked Carol what day it was. When Carol turned on her phone, a sudden burst of alerts made Meera wince. She shielded her sore ears from the sound.

'Messages from your mum, Josh, Kalpana, me, Lesley, Craig, Radhika... and over 30 voicemails from Krishan. Do you want to listen to his messages?'

Three nights ago, Krishan had called her ten times. She knew because she'd been inundated with voice message alerts, and she'd deleted them all without even listening.

What would he have said? I found my perfect match. I was too excited, and I'm sorry. Everything will be alright.

Except it never would be. He would stop seeing her, and she'd never get to spend time with the children again. Her heart felt tender. She loved the children, and a fresh wave of ache and more tears burnt her cheeks.

After spending another sleepless night with Carol staying in her spare room, her whole body ached. But this time, she knew she needed help to process her feelings. She'd done it alone once before, and she'd hated it. She wasn't scared anymore to share her pain.

She took her phone off the bedside table, and the first thing she did was delete every one of Krishan's messages, even the audio ones. Then, taking a steadying breath, she sent him three words.

Meera: Leave me alone

Afterwards, she went to her bathroom for a shower, and by the time she was out, she could smell the aroma of tea, milk, sugar and a spice blend for chai.

Carol smiled at her from the kitchen as she popped some bread into the toaster and took out eggs from the fridge.

They ate breakfast of scrambled eggs on toast and masala chai while Carol explained that Lesley would be coming to stay the night and that they would take each day as it came. Carol gave Meera a note of all the things she needed to deal with, each one colour-coded from urgent to the least important. Before leaving, her best friend hugged her so tight that it squeezed the breath from her lungs.

'I love you, Meera. I have a couple of meetings this morning but I'll be back later.'

Meera's best friends had sandwiched her between them under the duvet on her living room sofa, their presence comforting her. They'd come to spend the nights with her ever since Carol had found her drained from crying.

The doorbell chimed.

Carol's eyes widened. 'Are you expecting anyone?' she asked.

Meera shook her head, and Carol stood up and walked down the narrow hallway towards the front door.

Meera screamed in panic. 'STOP!' She scrambled out of the comfortable cocoon that had become her waking and sleeping space.

'It could be Krishan.' *Please, God, not Krishan.* She didn't want to see him and hear him. She couldn't cope with his sad face, eyes and voice. In short, she couldn't face his sadness.

There was a clanking sound from her letterbox. Carol turned to her and waited.

'It… it might be him,' Meera whispered.

Carol nodded, and Lesley wrapped her arms under her chest and pulled her from behind. 'Come back to the living room, Meera.'

Lesley guided her to the safety of the sofa.

The doorbell chimed again.

Carol came back into the room.

'It's Radhika.'

'His girlfriend Radhika?' Lesley stiffened.

Carol nodded, her lips thinning.

'Hello, Meera! I need to speak with you.' Radhika's voice called through the letterbox.

Fists thudded on the door.

'Please open the door. I know you're home. I'm not going anywhere until I speak with you.'

'What do you want to do?' Carol asked Meera.

'She doesn't want to talk to her, that's what,' Lesley answered for her.

'What if Krishan is hiding in the hallway?' Meera's heart escalated.

'I'm on my own,' Radhika yelled through the letterbox.

'For God's sake, tell her to leave Meera alone,' Lesley shouted.

Carol sighed and made her way to the front door. Meera heard the security chain clanking against the door frame as it fell away. *Why was everything so loud?*

'What are you doing?' Carol shouted. Meera winced as her ears hurt and her head started throbbing.

'Meera. Oh my god, Meera. I didn't know.' Radhika raced across the room in quick strides and squeezed into the space between the sofa and the coffee table. The front door shut loudly.

Lesley swore and Carol rushed into the room, 'She's

bloomin' fast.'

Radhika grabbed her clenched fists.

'I didn't know about the plan,' she repeated, shaking her head. 'Why didn't you tell me.'

Radhika stroked her knuckles and Lesley caressed her back gently. Meanwhile, Carol went into the kitchen to put the chai on. A cup of tea would make everything alright. Except this time, it never would.

Two women sat beside her, trying to comfort her.

Radhika was gently kneading her palms in rhythmic circles. Lesley was massaging her shoulders.

Tears streaked down Meera's face in rivulets.

'I don't know why my chest hurts,' she murmured.

'You love him?' Radhika asked softly.

'I can't.'

'Why not?'

'She has her reasons, Radhika,' Lesley interjected.

'I know about your ex,' Radhika blurted out.

'Fuck, who told you?' Lesley stood up and began to pace.

'Krishan told me when I went to see him. He's not doing too well either.'

Lesley stopped, placed her hands on her hips and stared at Radhika. 'Are you here to argue on his behalf?'

'No. I'm–' Her voice wavered. 'You don't think I'm your friend?'

Her eyes glistened, and she stood up. 'I'm sorry. I shouldn't have come.'

Lesley remained firm. 'No, you shouldn't have. You kissed him in front of everyone. He knew there was an end date. Nobody would have known about you if only you'd kept it hidden.'

'What's going on?' Carol returned to the living room with four mugs of chai, the spiced aroma filling the air.

'I was going out with him. Like really dating him,' Radhika admitted. 'We made a mistake. And that kiss–it wasn't even a proper kiss. It was nothing like what I'd expect from a first kiss.'

'First kiss? But you've been seeing him for months?' Carol frowned, adding two teaspoons of sugar into Meera's Darth Vadar mug, and stirring.

Radhika's gaze remained rooted to the floor.

'Yes, but he's been a bit. Distant. I was giving him space and the time to get comfortable. It's difficult when you've lost the love of your life.' When she finally looked up, her eyes were full of tears.

Meera stood up and pulled Radhika into her arms, hugging her to her chest.

'Don't go. You are my friend. I was stupid to let my fake boyfriend get under my skin,' Meera said.

'He might have started out as fake, but I think he's developed real feelings for you,' Radhika mumbled into her chest.

Meera froze. 'He can't love anyone else. He only has one true love. Kreena.'

Radhika's face lifted off her chest and her eyebrows

scrunched together. Then, as realisation struck, her eyes widened, and she nodded, her expression understanding.

Later, they ordered a Chinese takeaway and listened to all their favourite heartbreak songs.

As Radhika prepared to leave, she said, 'You should at least hear him out. It might help you deal with all this fake relationship stuff. I'll call you tomorrow. And again... I'm sorry. I had no idea your snoopy Masi network was so big and so vicious.'

With that, she left, and the three of them spent the rest of the night curled up on the sofa watching *Friends*.

IDEAL MATCH

Meera

Meera pulled out the narrow red belt that she'd borrowed from Carol from her dresser drawer. As she buckled it on her waist, she thought about the couple who had inspired them to build the dating with an experience app in the first place. She wondered if they were still together.

The profile of each couple on the app was assigned a unique colour and object, so it made sense that it became a secret signal for the blind date. Adding that minor detail had been a game-changer. Everyone loved the excitement of knowing that the sign meant *this* was the person they were meeting, and it got the best feedback. The other thing that made their app stand out was no photographs. In a society that spent far too much time on appearances and swiping right, this kind of approach was a novelty and hugely appealed to their growing mature demographic.

Craig had badgered her into meeting a man who was 89% compatible according to their *Design My Date* app. She was furious that he'd made her data live without informing her, but he merely shrugged, adding. 'How many nights have you stayed in since you came back?

It's been four weeks, Meera.'

He was leaning against her desk, his chin resting on the top of her screen.

'I've been out,' she replied, thinking she'd better tell him where otherwise he'd sit himself down. 'I went to the gym and supermarket two nights ago. Oh yes, and I popped into the shop to get ice cream and popcorn for movie night.'

'All on your own at home, though. Am I right?'

How could she go out? Knowing her luck, one of the Masi Mafia would be at the same place where she was and either sympathise with her or reprimand her. Her chest tightened. If just thinking about the Masi Mafia made her feel that way, then how would she cope when she'd meet him at social gatherings?

'Come on Meera. I don't like seeing you like this. It will be fun,' Craig cajoled her.

Every day, she woke up feeling raw. The slightest sounds frightened her, and the lyrics of a song on the radio brought tears to her eyes. She couldn't function. It had taken her weeks to write a report that usually took only hours.

Her exclusive diet of salt and vinegar crisps and chocolate ice cream didn't bring her any joy. They had always worked before, so why not this time?

What was wrong with her? Krishan was just a fake boyfriend. Nothing more, nothing less.

Yet, as the familiar heat of tears pooled behind her eyes, she looked away, swallowing her pain. With much resentment, she finally told Craig that she was ready to go on a date.

The wine tasting was in Birmingham's Jewellery Quarter, one of the newer wine merchants and tasting experiences on the ever expanding portfolio for Reach for the Sky. When Meera walked down the dimly lit steps and entered an exposed brick cellar with a rectangular wooden table at the centre, her gaze instantly locked on two familiar figures, Craig and Radhika.

Earlier, Meera had told Craig that Krishan could never wholly commit to anyone except his wife. His dead wife. Craig had held her gaze and shook his head as he turned to leave her office.

Now, as she stepped forward, Craig turned to look at her.

'I wasn't expecting an audience,' she murmured, glancing at them. Had they come to make sure she'd show up? Were they expecting her to behave badly with the man she was supposedly 89% compatible with?

'We're just here for the experience, that's all, Meera,' Craig said as he released her from a hug.

She arched a brow. 'Yeh, and I'm Snow White.'

Craig chuckled and reassuringly squeezed the hand he was still holding. She swallowed the lump that had taken root in her throat.

Meera went to the opposite end of the long table and told the organiser that she was meeting someone. The officious wine connoisseur then introduced himself before launching into a jazzy presentation.

Ten minutes later, the seat next to her was still empty. The wine expert's chatter bored her. She was not at all interested in soil or grape variety or the perfect climate. She just wanted a drink desperately, and her date was taking far too long.

She stared at the still empty seat. He was late. Even her blind date didn't have the courtesy to inform her of his tardiness. This was what had become of her life now waiting for a man who couldn't be bothered to show up. She should leave. Yes, that's exactly what she needed to do, but she couldn't muster the energy.

She felt her phone vibrate and rummaged through her bag. It was only a silly notification. The wine expert sent a filthy look her way. She ignored it and checked her app again, letting go of a deep sigh. She wasn't even worthy of sending a note even.

A glass was placed in front of her, and instead of sipping her wine, she gulped down the fruity Pinot Grigio, which had a hint of peach. She immediately asked the young woman to fill it up again. There was a subtle exchange between the wine connoisseur and the young woman, who then hesitantly refilled her glass. She glanced around and looked at Craig, who gave her a reassuring smile from across the table. They were awaiting fresh glasses for the next wine, and still, her so called 89% compatible man hadn't turned up.

She raised a querying eyebrow at Craig, who merely shrugged his shoulders.

The door to the darkened, dank room opened and Krishan walked in, his expression apologetic. Meera tensed. How had this evening become so intolerable? Craig, Radhika… and now Krishan. She felt a slow heat creep up her cheeks and her pulse quickened. He strode over to her and sat down.

'That seat's taken,' she said, pointing to the stool beneath him.

They hadn't spoken to each other or even met since he'd told his family he was interested in Radhika. And she had no interest in speaking to him ever again. It was a shame he'd broken up with Radhika. She was kind and was genuinely looking for someone to love. She'd even told Radhika to tell Krishan to seek help about his loss. A professional to help him move on from Kreena. To find someone to love, someone for his children to love.

But then she remembered his selfishness and his–*I have an actual girlfriend. I can't keep my lips off.* Just two weeks before their official end date.

He just needed to keep his lips to himself for two more weeks. But no, he'd gone to the hospital coffee shop and canoodled with Radhika in public, no less. Like a horny teenager.

'Urgh, can you move?' Meera grumbled as they filled her wineglass with another white.

'There's nowhere for me to sit,' Krishan whispered, his warm breath brushing against her neck.

She signalled a staff member. 'Excuse me, could you get this gentleman another stool, please? I'm expecting someone to join me.'

The man, the wine expert, who had been expounding on the virtues of the soil and climate in South Africa, sent her a disparaging look. Just then, a dark-haired woman in a black skirt and white blouse approached her.

'We're not expecting anyone else. Mr. Krishan Meghani is on the list,' she said.

'Of course, he would be on the list,' Meera muttered. 'But I want him to sit somewhere else. My date hasn't arrived yet.'

She scrutinised the other people sitting at the table. Had she missed the secret signal? Seeing Craig and Radhika had distracted her. She must have missed an eye contact she was supposed to exchange with her match.

Her red belt was clearly visible over her slate grey dress. She huffed out a breath. Now that everyone was seated, she wouldn't be able to check if anyone was wearing a red belt as a signal.

Then, it dawned on her, the thought that her match wasn't interested in seeing her filled her chest. She would *not* cry. She was worthy of someone. She just hadn't found him yet.

Why had she agreed to this? Even her 89% compatible man didn't like what he saw. She took a big gulp from her glass. At least, now she could get drunk.

'I'm sorry, Meera. Forgive me.' Krishan's face was far too close. He pulled off his glasses to wipe the lenses as he spoke quietly next to her.

Her heart missed a beat, and she took a replenishing breath.

'Have you come to watch me make a fool of myself when my 89% compatible man rejects me? Are you enjoying humiliating me?' she spoke loudly, hoping her secret date would reveal himself, even if he didn't like the look of her, even if it was to apologise.

She pushed the thought away. *She was good enough.* Sure, she was a bit on the curvy side, but she'd put that on her profile. She scanned the room, searched every man's face and even took a surreptitious look at the women. Suddenly, the thought that she was searching for the wrong gender took root in her mind. Maybe she was compatible with a woman, and she'd been looking at the wrong gender all along. She lifted the card to check the alcohol level in the wine she was tasting.

No. What an absurd thought. She was not a lesbian or bisexual. *What's wrong with her?*

The sommelier cleared his throat, breaking through her thoughts. A couple of men held her gaze, but one in particular, a dirty blonde with a tan, dressed in a maroon fitted shirt held her gaze longer than the others and smiled at her.

He wasn't her type. A bit too muscular, with long hair that was either greasy or oiled, and she couldn't help but wonder. How long did it take to wash your hair regularly? It didn't matter if their personalities was 89% compatible. He did nothing on the attraction front.

'Can you taste the earthy tones? Krishan asked, and she turned her face to him.

She read the description on the tasting card. He took another sip and made a swishing sound as he slurped the wine in his closed mouth, his cheeks inflating and deflating in a slow rhythm.

He swallowed, 'Pears.'

She also took a sip, rolling the wine over her tongue. 'No, it's more apples, and there's a hint of pine.'

He took a small sip, focusing on the flavour. 'You're

right. Pine, definitely pine.'

He nodded, smiling. 'You have a very discerning palate.'

A little joy flickered in her chest as she remembered the comment from the chocolate making class with the kids. Her combination was particularly different, as she'd added cheesy puffs with peanut butter to her chocolate mixture. She missed that the most, their evenings together and their days out with Natasha and Neel.

Her grip tightened around her glass. There was no point now in meeting with this 89% compatible man. She already knew who she wanted to be with. The only thing was that he didn't think she was deserving of his love. He'd made that clear by telling his family of how wonderful Radhika was and how excited he was for them to meet her.

She accepted she was ruining other people's experiences. And ignoring Krishan was impossible. Still, she tried her best to lift herself out of the misery trench and concentrated on the remaining wine tasting, umming and aahing when he said something to her.

As soon as the session was over, she grabbed her bag and walked around the table, discreetly checking everyone's belts. She was relieved to know that the greasy blond wasn't the 89% man. The man caught her looking at him and winked at her, making a joke about being more than 89% good in bed. Meera rolled her eyes and moved past him. She had one more person to deal with before she left the damp, cold cellar full of people. She made her way over to Craig.

'There was never an 89% man, was there?' Craig

nervously stepped back from her.

'Did you bring me here to speak with Krish?' Her voice tinged with irritation. 'Well, it worked, and I talked to him. Okay?'

She scanned the room, searching for Krish, who was talking to a young couple, and shouted, 'Tell him I talked to you.'

The couple stared over their shoulders towards her. Krish smiled apologetically at them before excusing himself and making his way toward her.

Craig sighed, 'Here's the data, Meera.' He thrust a sheet of paper into her hand. 'It's no joke. Have you checked everyone's belt?'

Something caught the edge of her vision, and she watched as Krishan's hand rested on his belt buckle.

Red.

At first, she was numb, and her legs felt hollow. Her skin crawled with humiliation. Without a thought, she turned towards the door, grabbing her coat from the stand. They'd conspired against her. Craig and Radhika knew how she felt. How she'd let hope edge into her life and had feelings for Krish.

And Krish… he had humiliated her. Not only by using her, but also by telling everyone she was unable to commit to a relationship. And she had thought of him as her friend. Someone who understood how difficult it was for a single woman in their community, but instead, he too hadn't understood at all.

She'd spent many a night analysing why she'd needed to be liked by her mother's friends. Had she unknowingly let her guard down and succumbed to the sadness in her mother's eyes at her life choices?

When Kalu mentioned the joyous retelling of days out with Meera when she'd called the children, it had taken all her willpower not to break down, not to beg Krishan's sister to promise to bring the children to meet her. Her chest hurt. She missed Natasha and Neel so much, and now she had nobody to love.

Or was it so hard to love her? Is that why Kaushik had sought comfort in the arms of other women?

She grabbed the handrail for support and pulled herself up the stairs and out into the busy street.

'Meera, Meera! Wait, I need you to listen to me.'

Tears blurred her vision as she ran into the night. She had to get away. Didn't anyone like her? She needed to get home and be safe. Krishan wasn't even a real boyfriend. She deserved better. She'd made a promise to herself she would go to America, launch the app and get that job. What good had a man ever done for her, anyway? The Masi Mafia better keep their distance from her from now on. She vowed that the next time they tried to interfere in her life, she'd tell them exactly what she thought of them and their hurtful words.

Then came a roar of an engine, a screech of tyres, and before she knew it, she was flung into the air. And then... darkness engulfed her.

My Only Match

Krishan

Krishan, froze on hearing a loud, sickening thud as Meera's body flew into the air and hit the ground.

'No, no. NO.' He ran towards her, his heart hammering in his chest.

The driver, a woman, rushed up to him as he reached Meera and held her in his arms.

'I'm so sorry. I didn't see her. She just came out of nowhere.' The woman's distraught voice broke into a sob.

Krishan raised his head. 'No... I've lost her. My soulmate. I was too much of a coward to convince her to change her mind.'

Why was he telling this to a stranger?

Radhika stepped forward and told everyone to move aside and knelt by his side.

How had Radhika got here? Krishan held onto Meera afraid to let her go. Craig covered Meera with his coat, and he saw tears in his eyes as he crouched next to him.

Hot tears poured down Krishan's cheeks, and his body

wracked with silent sobs.

'Krish, look at me,' Radhika said, squeezing his arm. 'Craig's called the ambulance.'

But his gaze was focused on Meera. 'I can't lose Meera, Radhika. I just can't. Please don't leave me, Meera. I love you.'

It felt like an eternity, but eventually, the wail of sirens filled the air, blue lights flashing in the distance. Two paramedics in green overalls rushed forward and pushed him aside. He watched in horror realising that the dampness he'd felt on his lap was blood. He looked at the road and the cold air hit him. His heart galloped from the shock when he realised that she'd fractured her skull. He hadn't even checked her. Why hadn't he thought of the consequences of holding her in his arms?

Once they lifted Meera onto a stretcher, he tried to go with her. But they ignored him, focusing on attaching her to the machines. Craig gently pulled at his arm and asked the paramedics where they were taking her. One of them gave him the hospital's name, and wasting no time, Craig immediately motioned to a passing cab. All three of them, Krishan, Craig and Radhika, climbed in and sped to the hospital.

Krishan's mind flickered back to the day Meera had called him. Instead of going to see her in person, he'd simply called her and left voice messages. Messages that she'd ignored. He should have camped outside her front door. He should have told her that he loved her, that he wanted only her. He should have asked her to forgive him and take him back, this time as her real boyfriend. Instead, what had he done? He'd sent her text messages and flowers. Flowers? As if they would mend a broken heart. He reprimanded himself for his actions.

When they reached the hospital, Meera was in a curtained cubicle in the Urgent Care Unit. Her face was covered by an oxygen mask, and she was strapped to a machine monitoring her pulse. Tubes ran from the IV bag, filled with clear liquid to her forearm. The young female doctor informed them that she was seriously injured and they needed to operate urgently. She asked them if they knew her next of kin.

Krishan nodded. He left Craig and Radhika with Meera and went to call her parents.

Meera's parents arrived at A&E, and her mother's eyes burnt into his.

'Where is she?' she demanded.

Krishan swallowed hard and told Meera's family that she was in the operating theatre and pointed to Radhika and Craig, who were also waiting nearby. Meera's father went up to them to talk.

'Radhika? Why did Meera come to meet you and your girlfriend?' Meera's mother asked sharply.

'She didn't know I was going to be there,' he admitted.

Her expression hardened. 'You not only hurt her; you shattered her. You ruined her reputation. Go, leave us alone. We don't need you here.'

The vicious tone from Shradha Masi, Meera's mother, jolted him. She was the gentlest woman he'd ever known, and he had hurt her too. How had he let himself become this person? Someone who was so selfish, so blind?

'You should go, son. You've done enough damage.' Even Shiv Kaka's eyes burnt with anger at him. The elderly man's body slumped with disappointment.

Krishan's heart broke. He had made a terrible mistake. He'd been too frightened to recognise and acknowledge his feelings for their beautiful, feisty and brave daughter.

'Come on, Krish. Let's go to the canteen. Meera's family is here now,' Craig said.

'No, I can't leave. I need to know she's okay.'

Craig sighed and led him to sit away from Meera's parents. Krish looked on anxiously as Meera's mother slumped into a chair and broke down. Her father pulled his wife into his arms to comfort her. It was only then that her father let his guard down. A haunted expression washed over his controlled features and he too began to cry.

His lap felt uncomfortable as the blood began to dry and flake against his skin. He wanted to wash it off, but he also couldn't bring himself to leave the waiting room. What was taking them so long? Why hadn't anyone come to fetch her parents?

His chest hurt, and he felt a dread too strong to ignore. Just as he was about to ask for more news, the young doctor who'd spoken to them earlier approached them and said she was still in emergency surgery. Krishan walked her to Meera's parents and introduced them. The doctor filled them in on their daughter's injuries; a bleeding spleen, a fractured pelvis, and a minor fracture in the head. She reassured them that they would do their very best for their daughter.

The moment the doctor said those words, Krishan lost control and the tears he had been holding back spilled out. His legs gave way, and he slumped into the empty chair next to them. The young doctor gave them an apologetic look, but Meera's parents ignored him. They, too, were dealing with their own grief.

Someone sat next to him and took his hand.

Radhika.

He lost track of time, his mind still anxious. He brushed the tears from his face and whispered, 'I love her, Radhika. I can't lose her. Not her.'

He was going to lose Meera. He'd only just found someone to love again. Someone he never thought he'd find. Meera had healed his heart and slowly taken up room in it. Slowly, she'd filled it with her warmth and goodness.

'She won't leave us,' Meera's mother spoke softly, 'My daughter is a fighter.' Silence filled the room again as he paced the waiting area to quieten his heart. Craig brought teas and coffees for everyone. Meanwhile, Radhika stepped away to speak to her colleague.

The waiting room door opened and his parents walked in.

'Shiv, Shradha, how is Meera?' they asked, worried.

As soon as he'd spoken to Meera's parents, he'd called his own parents to inform them about the accident and asked them to bring overnight clothes and stay with his children.

Meera's father told them of her injuries, his voice fraught with emotion. Krishan's mother kept throwing him quizzical looks, wanting to know why he was with Meera, surprised that he wasn't hurt and she was.

'Oh, Kavita! What if something bad happens to her? She's a good girl. She deserves happiness.' Meera's mother turned to face his own mother, who held her hands gently.

'We have to be positive, Shradha. She'll come through this.'

Both women cried silently, holding onto each other. He wanted to reassure them, to tell them that he was there for them, that he wasn't going anywhere. He wasn't leaving Meera alone.

Unable to cope with the despair, his father took Shiv Kaka outside for some fresh air. Krishan took this opportunity to phone his babysitter to ask her to stay longer, telling her he was sending his parents to relieve her soon.

The minute hand on his watch seemed to have jammed and he tapped the watch face. Time was dragging by slowly. He wanted to ask questions about the operation; however, Radhika had stopped him, telling him to let the young critical care doctor do her job and that she'd find out more from the medical staff. Before she left, she told him that Meera's injuries were serious and that he needed to stay positive.

Krishan's parents asked him to escort them out, and he reluctantly followed them, telling Craig to come find him the moment there was any new information.

'What did you do, Krishan? Why are you here?' His mother asked him once they were in the car park.

He let out a deep breath and explained that he, Radhika and Craig had been with Meera at a wine tasting.

'Radhika? Was she here? Then why didn't you introduce us to her?' his mother asked, puzzled.

He didn't want to elaborate on his complicated life... not now. Instead, he said simply, 'I'll explain everything later. But the only thing you need to know is that I love Meera. Only Meera. And Mummy, I made a huge mistake.'

'You love Meera?' She held her hand up to his cheek, her expression softening. 'Oh, Krishan, how could you do that to someone you love? Kiss someone else?'

Before he could reply, his father opened the car window, his voice firm. 'There's nothing you can do here, Krishan. Let's go home.' He knew by his father's expression that he wasn't impressed with his behaviour. He'd disappointed both his parents with what he'd done to Meera.

'I'm staying here. I need to be with Meera,' he said, his tone allowing no argument.

His mother reluctantly hugged him and stepped into the car, telling him to phone as soon as Meera was out of the operating theatre.

When he went back into the A&E waiting area, Craig and Radhika approached him and told him they were leaving too. Krishan nodded, unable to speak as the thought of what he'd done washed over him. This was all his fault. He was responsible for Meera's accident. He had hurt her. He hoped the woman he'd fought hard not to fall in love with would survive. He wanted to tell her he loved her and only her.

He held onto the words her mother had said. 'My daughter is a fighter.'

Please, Meera. Fight. Fight for our love.

He hoped she'd fight, hoped she still had the strength to fight.

Someone gently shook him awake. Krishan lifted his gaze and saw the steaming cup being offered to him. He looked up and saw Shradha Masi standing there. Her eyes were red from tears and lack of sleep. Deep worry lines filled her expression. She sat beside him.

'They say she went after you because of your house and your business,' she began hesitantly. 'But my daughter is not like that. She put up with the name calling and unkind remarks for years before she met you. You're not anyone special, Krishan. So why would she change now? She is very brave, very strong. Why would she persuade you to pretend to be with her? I know it was you.'

Krishan looked away for a moment, guilt kicking in his stomach.

She locked eyes with him, and her free hand fisted. 'I knew it. You're a coward. You're a man. No one would have forced you or gone after you. But for her, it was always different. She's a woman. Did you know she paid off a debt that was close to a hundred thousand pounds? She paid off every single penny they owed. She sold her shares and all her wedding jewellery. She took on extra projects and taught at evening college. And Kaushik? He took out loans here, there and everywhere. And she was naïve to support him like a good wife, approved his flighty ideas, trusting him. And then, he ran off and disappeared. Harish found him hiding in Croatia, living a life of leisure. She didn't tell us anything, but we knew. My brave daughter hid everything from us and persevered. My daughter has more courage in her little finger than you could ever have in your whole body. And what did you do? Kiss your *girlfriend* in public. You made her a laughing stock again. What's your excuse? Meera's too nice, too kind, too gullible. I thought you were different, but you are just like Kaushik,' her voice more controlled and stronger.

The last sentence felt like a slap. Shame burned through him.

'I'm sorry I hurt you, hurt Meera. I made a terrible mistake. Meera is my love, not Radhika. I love Meera. She makes me happy. I didn't realise just how much until I lost her. I can't lose her. I just can't, Shradha Masi.'

He was a coward. He was weak. He'd let the fear of falling in love with her whole-heartedly stop him from accepting his feelings for her. His eyes watered again, and tears streamed down his cheeks. Shradha Masi took his free hand and squeezed it, and that's when he knew where Meera got her kindness and forgiving nature from.

'The worst thing about all this is that I think Meera has lost her ability to forgive and fight back. If she recovers from this, she won't want you here. It was Tara who saw Kaushik with another woman. Except it wasn't just one woman. There were many women. The first time Meera found out Kaushik was unfaithful was three weeks into their marriage,' Shradha Masi recalled. 'Three weeks and she still stood by him because I'd told her that women had to sacrifice themselves in a marriage. That it was her duty to make it work. If it had been Joshna in her place, she'd have packed her bags and left long ago. But my daughter, the girl I raised, was willing to get hurt. Again, and again.'

Saying this, Shradha Masi sobbed into her hands. Hopelessness filled every pore in his body, sending a cold shiver through him. How had he not known about her past? Why had he not seen her suffering? Why hadn't he insisted on finding out about her ex sooner? The Masi Mafia were all about judging women and shouting about their behaviour. But why hadn't they damned men's behaviour too?

Meera's father came up to them and told them the operation was over, and she was in recovery. He pulled his wife off the chair and took her away to wait for more news of their daughter. Krishan sobbed in relief, and after what seemed liked hours, but was only minutes he sent a prayer to keep Meera safe. His first real prayer since his wife died.

The smell of breakfast permeated through the narrow corridor, but he wasn't hungry. Just then, he saw someone in scrubs approach her parents to inform them of where they'd take Meera next. He stood nearby to listen in on the conversation.

'You should go to your family, Krishan. Thank you for waiting. I'll take care of our daughter's needs now.' Shiv Kaka approached him and escorted him out of the hospital.

'You've done enough, son. I didn't want to say anything in front of Shradha. She's got enough to cope with. Leave us alone. You've had your fun. My daughter will never see you again. I should have protected her better than I have. I should have shielded her and stopped those women from making snide remarks about her. But I won't make that mistake again. We won't expose her to any of that anymore. She deserves better than you and your type. She deserves someone who truly loves her and is loyal to her,' Meera's father said.

His eyes shone with a fierce finality sending a punch to his gut. What could he possibly say to her father? He hadn't protected his daughter either. When Craig told him she was sad and that she wasn't the same Meera he knew, he should have dropped everything and gone to her. He should have camped in the reception area of her building and begged her to listen to him. Instead, he'd gone back to drinking and wallowing, living each day for his children, convincing himself that it was enough.

Then Radhika arrived with the biodata, explaining that if he didn't believe in soulmates, maybe the data would finally convince him to believe it and fight for Meera. He should have known Meera was meant for him. He should have told her she was similar to his wife, and nothing like his wife. That she was brave and strong like her, but different from her too. And she was who he wanted in his life. And now, he might lose her and never get the chance to tell her just how much he loved her.

LOST TRUE LOVE

Krishan

He'd arrived home hours ago and sat in his car, the cooling engine humming, trying to process what had happened. Meera's bloodstained face kept playing in his mind. The tiniest thought of losing her sent a sharp pain to his heart, the ache excruciating. He felt lost, his mind unable to focus, struggling to stay in the present. He had to see her. He needed to make sure that she was fine, but her father had told him he would not be permitted to see her. He felt untethered and suffocated, unable to take a sustaining breath.

When he eventually stepped into the house, he felt like he'd been pummelled with emotions, and even his muscles screamed for respite. Silently, he slipped upstairs to clean himself and change out of his bloodstained clothes.

The children and his parents were eating breakfast by the time he came downstairs. Natasha and Neel were in their school uniforms. He kissed them good morning and Natasha asked, catching up on his mood, 'Are you just coming home, Daddy?'

The tone of her voice brought back the guilt of what he'd done to Meera. His chest hurt, his head throbbed, and the unbearable distance away from her made him sick with worry. He slumped into a chair at the table and began to sob. Streams of tears that he'd held onto so hard finally spilled out. Tears that had threatened to burst when he'd heard about the emergency surgery; the damaged spleen, the broken pelvis and the fracture in her head. Tears for the woman who had become the love of his life.

Suddenly, his chest constricted, and his breathing became laboured. *Meera.*

He clutched his chest. 'Something's wrong with my Meera,' he choked out. Just trying to speak exhausted him. His mother looked confused for a moment, but then she quickly gathered herself and reached for her phone to type a message.

When had he started thinking of her as his? Perhaps she had always been his, and he'd made the worst mistake of his life by not convincing her of his love and letting her slip away. His true love. He wept silently, knowing that if he became hysterical, his children would be upset. But inside, there was a panicked scream calling her name in his head.

Neel and Natasha slipped off their chairs, their young faces filled with concern. His son climbed on his lap and wrapped his arms around his neck. Natasha unable to find a space held onto his arm, and he pulled her to his side, holding both of them tightly. His mother sat transfixed in her seat as messages came through her phone. She looked up at him, aghast.

'Has something happened to Meera?' his father asked, seeing his wife's expression.

'Is she–' He paused, '–was the accident too much?'

His father's face ashened.

His throat choked, and memories of losing Kreena came flooding back. With her, they had time to talk about everything important. Everything that mattered. He'd spent a wonderful life with his wife. But if anything happened to Meera, he had nothing to hold onto. No memories except the fake ones they'd created. He let his chin rest on his son's head.

'Krishan, Beta. Look,' she held up the messages to him, the words shimmered in focus. 'There was a moment, but she's back.'

'Kavita, will you excuse us?' his father said, putting both of his hands on Krishan's shoulders.

His mother nodded, taking Neel off his lap and telling Natasha to give her father a proper hug. He held his daughter tightly before she went to her grandmother's side. He stood up, but he couldn't make his legs move. His father gently guided him out of the room. As they left, he heard the children ask his mother about Meera.

His father eased him on the sofa in the living room and sat on the coffee table placed in front to face him.

'Something's wrong, Dad.' He thumped his chest. 'I can feel it here.'

The days and nights merged into an eternity of dread. It was as if his soul had slipped from his body. Nothing made any sense to him anymore. His heart and mind felt disconnected, and he wasn't able to talk, move or breath. His father helped him in and out of bed. His mother placed his favourite foods in front of him, but he only stared, unable to bring himself to eat. His children were kept occupied with play dates and hobbies. His nanny switched to staying longer to make up for his absence.

His emotions overwhelmed him, and even the slightest noise sent his stomach into knots. He stayed in his darkened room, even ignoring his children as they looked on in bewilderment. He heard their frightened voices questioning his parents. But he could not comfort them like a good parent should. His only thought was of Meera.

His Meera.

One morning, after the children had gone to school, his mother came in and opened the curtain to let the light in. Grey clouds covered the sky, and his first thought was at least it was not sunny. He couldn't bear for the sun to come out and brighten the day while his Meera was still unconscious.

'Krishan, you have to be normal for the children. Neel is okay and coping, but Natasha… she is struggling. She is holding back her tears and has started having nightmares. You have to spend some time with her, show her you're okay.'

Guilt wracked his body. 'I'll try, Mummy.' After a moment, he asked what he wanted to know, 'How's Meera today?'

His mother lifted her phone and checked her messages. 'She's stable. It's still early days, Krishan. Everyone's rallying around. It's my turn to cook tomorrow,' she said, her lips twitching upwards.

It was in times like these that the Masi Mafia came into their element. Food was cooked and delivered, and experts were contacted and brought in to consult. Everything that was good about these nosy women was revealed when a family was in crisis. They all joined in and became a pillar of strength and support. He wished they'd stick to the support network instead of spending too much time gossiping.

His mother fluffed his pillow and placed a tea tray on his lap. 'I know you all think this living inside each other's pocket isn't good. But there are people who need the help. And when it comes to marriage, some people need encouragement. Not everyone can sustain themselves on memories of love. Some people are desperate for companionship. Sometimes, all people need is a little nudge to meet with a suitable candidate for marriage. Our customs are grounded in truth, and most of the time, they'll find someone ideal for you, same background, same interests, same family connections. Marriage isn't just about two people. It is about communities.'

She sighed. 'You were lucky you found Kreena, and her family and ours got along so well. It worked.' She paused, then continued, 'I'm sorry if you ever thought we were forcing you to marry again. It's just that I saw the sadness and burden you carried with you. I just wanted you to be happy.' She picked up two cups and moved towards the armchair they'd pulled up by his bed.

'Here you go,' his mother handed him a cup of chai. 'It's sweet. Your father's been going to the office, and everything's under control. There's nothing important for you to deal with. Nothing important to worry about.'

His parents had always helped with his business. They might be semi-retired, but he needed them when Kreena was sick, and they'd stepped in and continued coming to the office for a few days a week to help run things smoothly. He was glad of their help, and now he knew he needed their help again.

He took a sip from his cup and grimaced. There was enough sugar to rot his teeth.

His mind went back to the days after Kreena's death. All that sweet chai his and Kreena's mother had pumped into him, as if sugar would ease his pain.

'You know what happened the weekend you met Meera? That burden and sadness you carried around with you wasn't as intense as before. When you told us you were dating, I was hopeful that you'd found someone special again. I saw a change in you, Krishan, and I saw a change in Meera too. She laughed a lot more, came out and spent time with everyone, and the girl who was always bubbly and lively showed herself again. It was wonderful to see that version of her return. It made us realise just how much we'd let her move away from us.'

Then she took the tea tray and told him to shower and get himself ready for a walk.

'Joshna and Harish want to speak with you. I know Shiv is angry with you, but I think he's also angry with us for not seeing the full picture. I think there was no deception on your part, but your guilt of finding someone to replace the love you felt with Kreena stopped you from recognising the love that was growing inside you for Meera.'

The days became easier with time, and he worked from home until he was well enough to return to the office. He still hadn't called Joshna or Harish. He knew of Meera's critical state. His erratic chest pain woke him up at night and disturbed him during the day. Eventually, he was forced to meet with his doctor, who examined him and arranged an E.C.G. Only to be told by the report, that everything was normal, and the chest pain was due to stress. How could he de-stress knowing that his love was in critical care, and he had no way of seeing her?

A week later, he went back to the office. The people were exceedingly hush-hush, with none of the noise and laughter he'd grown accustomed to in his place of work. All his memories from three years ago came flooding back, and he slumped in his desk chair, holding his head from the pain of reliving it all again.

Three years isn't too long. It's short. Too short, really. What made him think he was ready to find someone, even if it was only for companionship? But as soon as he'd met Meera, something had shifted in his heart. It danced when she was near him, and although his heart was sore, it had begun to beat for Meera. His aching chest felt heavy again, like someone had trussed him up in bandages, and his lungs were too squashed to take in air.

Kreena's parents had rushed to see him as soon as they heard about his chest pains, and their words bounced in his head.

'We know you loved Kreena, but you can't spend the rest of your life with only the children for company. Besides, they adore Meera. They couldn't stop talking about her when they came to stay with us. One day, all too soon, they'll grow up and leave you. We know Kreena wouldn't have wanted you to mourn her for this long,' Kreena's mother had said as they watched the children play in the park.

'It's only three years, Mummy,' he said. His guilt of wanting Meera, even after spending so little time with her, kept him clinging to that timeline. 'It's not enough. I was stupid to create these lies to get the Masis off my back. Three years isn't long enough. It's too short.'

'Wanting to be with Meera isn't a lie. Look at you, Beta. You look thin and drawn, and that pain in your chest, it's because you're holding onto fear. Talk to Joshna and ask them to help you see her.'

He ignored his mother-in-law's suggestion. How could his chest pain be anything related to Meera? He'd believed that it was his heart telling him he'd rushed into falling in love again. All he had to do was see Meera one last time and let her go, accept that his heart only belonged to his wife and not Meera. One last check that she was well and then he would walk away because that what's Meera's parents wanted.

It felt like someone had pulled his lungs out of his chest and crushed them to a pulp. Nothing flowed through his blood except toxic air, and his vision narrowed with darkness. He couldn't breathe.

Meera was going to leave him.

A sudden panic slashed through him. Where was his phone? His numb fingers desperately scrolled through his phone. He couldn't speak.

Krish: Tell Meera to stay.

'Krishan, what's going on,' his father's voice boomed. He took his phone from him and placed it on the desk as he gasped for breath. This was not a stress attack. His heart was finally giving way.

Josh: Krish? How? Shocked face emoji.

He saw his father's eyes widen with shock, worry slammed in his gaze and he tapped the green button.

Josh's distraught voice came through the speaker.

'How did you know, Krish?' Her voice was low and urgent. 'Meera's monitors have gone haywire. Her blood pressure has dropped, and her oxygen is low. But she's back. It was just a blip. Meera's fine. Tell me what happened to you?'

His father switched the phone speaker and pressed it to his ear, telling Joshna of Krishan's inability to breathe.

'Are you okay son?' He asked him as he held the phone away from his ear. Krishan nodded desperate to hear more about Meera. 'Let me speak with Joshna,' and his father walked out of the office to speak with her in private.

Krishan began to breathe out to a count of four and breathe steadily back in as his therapist had taught him. Before Kreena's parents left, they'd made him promise to see someone to help him with his grief, and slowly, he was learning to process all his feelings and to live again.

When his father returned, his chest was still sore, but the panic had subsided. He felt hopeful that at least someone in Meera's family was talking to him. He just needed to get enough courage to talk with Harish and convince him to allow him to see Meera. He needed to see her. He had to see her. He knew that his chest pain would only ease once he saw she was well.

Three days had passed, and he'd been getting regular text updates from Josh. Knowing that there was a small hope of seeing Meera eased his heavy heart. The Masis were in full community mode and everyone except his parents were on a rota to keep Meera company. His parents were on food rota, though, and that gave him hope that soon they would go and see her and tell him how his Meera was doing.

His Meera.

He buried that thought. There was no chance in hell that Shiv Kaka would allow him near her. There was still an animosity directed towards him and him alone.

As he slipped out of Natasha's room after an unusually longer bedtime read, his phone rang in his pocket. Meera's face lit up the screen, and his heart.

She was out of her coma. Meera was back, but why was she calling him?

He answered quickly, his heart pounding at the thought of hearing his Meera.

'Krishan? Are you there?'

Carol's voice cut through the phone.

'Oh, I thought…' His heart dropped to his feet. 'I'm sorry, she's still asleep, isn't she?' he asked, and then added, 'I desperately want to see her, but I have to respect her father's wishes. I have to tell her I'm sorry, that it was my fault.'

He heard Carol release a long breath.

'You did hurt her, Krish. More than anyone. Even that arsehole of an ex didn't leave her in the state you did. I really thought you'd eventually declare your love. But what the flip, Krish? Kissing Radhika? That was a low move.'

Krishan closed his eyes, shame burning through him.

'I just saw Josh & Hari. They showed me all your calls, and what's with the text messages?' There was a short pause, and she continued.

'I don't know what's going on, but every time she's stressed, you send a message. It's… inexplicable. It's strange… like you somehow know when she's experiencing pain.'

Krishan took in a sharp breath.

'I think we have to let you come and see her. We are trying to convince Uncle Shiv. But first, tell me what happens before you send those messages. My mum has a theory.'

He told Carol of the tightness in his chest that struck him at all hours of the day. How his doctor told him it was stress, but he was convinced that it was somehow linked to Meera, especially after Josh's confirmation.

That night, at 10.30 p.m., after arranging for his babysitter to come to mind the children, Krishan met Carol, Harish and Joshna.

Hari's expression was tired and reticent.

'Stop messaging, Krishan,' he said firmly. 'It's upsetting my family. You made your choice, and it wasn't my sister.'

'Hari?' Carol interrupted, 'We agreed we'd allow Krish to see Meera.'

'I'm not sure about this. It sounds too much like the stuff the aunties would say. But if you're convinced, Carol, I won't stop you. I just… I don't want to lose her. And he better not make it worse.'

Lose her… he couldn't. He still hadn't had the opportunity to tell her how much he loved her, how it had only ever been her. He clenched his fist, his nails cutting into his palm. His chest felt like the vice was beginning to tighten again.

They were nearly outside Meera's room when a siren sounded from her room. His heart jumped.

Without thinking, he ran into the room, and the sight of her fragile body, hooked to the machines, sent a pain through his chest, and his legs felt numb and heavy. He fixed his eyes on the monitor. Instead of a steady beat, her heartbeat displayed an erratic, squiggly red line.

His lungs hurt, his breathing became laboured, and tears obscured his vision. He tried desperately to gasp much needed air into his body. But nothing would allow oxygen into his bloodstream. His heart galloped erratically. A panicked voice in his head shouted, *'It's a heart attack. You're going to die before you can tell Meera you love her.'*

He dragged himself to Meera's bedside and took her hand in his. His legs gave out and he flopped into the chair beside her bed.

The alarm stopped beeping.

'Meera. Stay. With. Me,' he gasped in staccato bursts, barely audible to anyone.

'Krish, let the nurse check on you,' Joshna's voice cut through his mind. He lifted his head and met her concerned gaze.

A gentle voice said, 'Hello, Krishan. Let me check on you. It looks like you're struggling to breathe.'

He nodded weakly.

'Do you have asthma?' the nurse asked.

He shook his head as heat prickled his eyes.

'Has this happened before?'

He nodded and his eyes watered.

'Every time Meera's heart rate drops, he's sent me a message,' Joshna answered for him. She turned towards Meera.

'Meera, Krishan's here. He's holding your hand. Come back to us, Meera,' she added.

The nurse looked at Joshna with sympathy.

Just then, a young doctor with his hair in a man bun walked in. He looked at Krishan and asked, 'Who's this?'

'This is Krishan. He was with Meera when the accident happened,' Joshna replied.

'Ah. You're the *fake* boyfriend.' The doctor lifted his brow.

Did *everyone* know of his unwillingness to accept that he'd found love again?

'Why is he being examined? Was he involved in the accident? the doctor asked the nurse.

Joshna explained that Krishan had been experiencing panic attacks ever since the accident and they thought his visit to Meera might help him.

'He had a panic attack on our ward. I can't just take your word for it. He'll need to be checked thoroughly. Helga, can you take him to Admissions? I'll call A&E,' the doctor instructed the nurse.

'NO!'

Krishan didn't mean to shout, but if they put him in A&E and in another ward, he would be away from Meera. 'I'm fine, I already have a diagnosis. You can call my GP. It's just stress. I'm not leaving Meera.'

The doctor looked at him and his gaze flicked briefly toward Joshna, Harish and Carol, who were standing around Meera's bed. After a few tense moments, he nodded. 'But if it happens again, if anything feels different, you will tell one of the nurses here. Understood?'

Krishan nodded. His fingers wrapped around Meera's hand, willing her to open her eyes.

'Meera,' His voice broke down. 'I'm here. Please, open your eyes.'

SLEEP

Meera

Sometimes, she heard the sound of sirens, machines hissing, and loud voices that spoke in a language she couldn't understand. Other times, the silence surrounded her, and she felt at peace. It was the type of peace she craved, a long moment of quiet that she savoured. But the next moment, it felt like doors were flung open, and a cacophony throbbed through her body, every cell filled with the clattering that didn't give her any respite, only pain.

She wanted relief from the pain, not the pain coursing through her body, but the pain and soreness in her heart. Sometimes, she'd be swallowed up in a foggy haze, a peaceful place with a painful body. The nerves jangling in her body were the only evidence that she was still alive.

Was she dead?

Where was she?

Was *he* with her?

No. She couldn't feel the tranquillity of his touch, his voice, his smell. Time had slipped by, days, weeks, maybe even months. Eventually, she began to slowly return. She could sense her fingers again. She began to feel the weight of her body, the roughness of the cloth against her skin. There was an orange light filtering through her closed eyelids.

She recognised the voices, her mother's gentle lilt, and her father's loud baritone. She heard her brother gently cajoling and her sister-in-law's singing. She also heard Carol's raucous laughter and Lesley's gentle threats. Names she knew instinctively, but she couldn't recall their faces. Sometimes, during the night when she was in between slumber and wakefulness, she could smell his cologne, the scent she'd dreamt of so many times that it had been ingrained in her, so much so that she could conjure it up at the slightest memory of him.

She opened her eyes and saw him, but her eyelids closed too soon. What was his name? She tried to call him, but the sound wouldn't form in her throat. She gave up. The white fog claimed her again.

She felt a hand holding hers. A firm hand, a hand that belonged in hers.

Whose hand was it?

If only she could open her eyes. All she needed was for her thoughts to reach her eyelids, and then she would see him. She knew he was real. The scent of him brought back memories, faint ripples, distant memories, not yet fully formed. The feel of his chest, the warmth of his hands on her back, the comfort of his arms. They seemed real, not a dream, not something she'd imagined. She told herself… *he must be real.*

Then she heard it. Someone calling her name. A pitiful plea, urging her to come back, telling her he loved her. A voice that rumbled in her tummy and brought comfort.

For a long time, there was nothing. And then, one day she croaked a sound on seeing a woman sitting in the chair by her bed.

'Mummy.' Her mother stood up instantly, leaning over her, tear trails staining her cheeks. The moment she recognised that it was her mother, she felt a relief wash through her body. She was safe.

Faces she knew looked down at her, out of focus, yet familiar. She knew them all. A deep tiredness engulfed her, and she slept. A niggling thought crept into her mind. When she woke up again, her family and friends were there in the bright room with her, always near her. But where was he?

Some days, the exhaustion of thinking about him made her drift back into unconsciousness. Had she made him up?

Then came the time when people she knew came to visit her daily. She was glad to recognise them, but the names were hard to remember. And still, she waited for him. Watched for him. *What was his name?* The name hovered just out of reach, never forming into a solid word, and she couldn't see the elusive face on any of her visitors either. She had to remember his name; how else could she ask for him?

She knew she was in hospital, sometimes the whiteness of the walls hurt her eyes, the incessant dancing of the images on the TV felt raw. They'd told her she had an accident and every day she became stronger, staying awake a little longer, but the words were still hard to form. She smiled, nodded and hoped that the jumbled words would come out of her head and form into a sound.

But it was during the night that she heard him the most, felt him holding her hand, sensed him. At first, she thought she dreamt of him, until one morning, she smelt his familiar scent on the sheets. He was real.

She'd been practising quietly to form the words. And when the therapist came, she'd worked out what she wanted to say.

'Where is *he*?'

She heard the sound of her own voice and was surprised to know how much like herself she sounded.

The therapist replied, 'He's waiting outside. Do you want me to call him?'

Her heart fluttered in anticipation of seeing him.

But then the door opened and her father walked into the room.

'No. No. Not him,' she screamed, hysteria scrambling to unleash from within. The therapist took her hand and pressed a button. Her eyes watered, and she slumped back into the bed, turning her face away from them.

Why wasn't he waiting outside?

She needed him to be waiting nearby.

She lost track of days and nights, sleeping whenever her body needed rest. She was awake whenever people came to visit, but he was never on the rota of visitors.

Then one evening, a hushed voice woke her. 'Time for your observation, Meera.'

The nurse attached the cuff to her left arm to check her blood pressure and placed a thermometer in her mouth.

'Your man's a gem,' she said. 'He brought us a lovely Indian meal last night. I can still taste it.'

The nurse loosened the pressure cuff and added the numbers to her notes.

'How come he got the night shift?' she asked Meera.

She shook her head slightly. 'Does he come every night?' she asked, her voice rough, but still hers.

The nurse replied, 'Your man comes at 10 o'clock and stays late into the night.'

Your man. She liked the sound of that.

The nurse placed a paper cup in front of her. 'Painkillers and a sleeping pill tonight. You're making great progress, Meera. You'll be out of here in no time.'

The nurse smiled at her and left the room.

Why had no one mentioned *him*? She placed the sleeping tablet under her tongue and hid it there until the nurse was gone. Then, she spat it out into a tissue. She couldn't tolerate the pain. But she'd do it for *him*, she'd tolerate the wakefulness, just to see *him*.

The lights dimmed and the conversation turned to whispers. She waited eagerly to meet him, wondering if she would recognise him and remember his name. Exhaustion sent her into a sleep.

Soft lips kissed her palm. 'Hello, my love. How was your day? I've brought music to listen to tonight. Your favourite album, *Fearless*, just like you, Meera. Just like you.'

He sounded sad. But he was real. He was holding her hand, and she felt safe. Her mind calmed and she drifted off to sleep. She heard him singing softly. *"We were both young when I first saw you…"*

Love Story. The title sprang into her head. She knew that song. She tried to open her eyes, but it felt like they were glued shut, and she sank into a deep sleep again.

When she finally opened her eyes, he was quietly singing to *"Breathe"*, one of the songs form her playlist. His face was close enough for her to feel his breath. She could see the tiny wrinkles at the corners of his eyes, the luscious fan of his eyelashes. She knew that face.

'It's you?' she whispered, and his smile reached his eyes. 'Why do you only come when I'm asleep?'

He inhaled sharply. 'Your dad won't let me come during the day. But Josh and Hari know I visit at night.'

She tried to push herself upright on her elbow, but the effort was too much. Instantly, he stood up, flicked on the bedside lamp and used the control panel to lift the bed frame. As he leant closer to fluff up the pillow behind her, she smelt his cologne, so comforting, so familiar. In a heartbeat, his name came to her mouth, and she said, 'Krish?'

He froze.

'Yes.' He turned his face away, and grabbed his glasses and a tissue, dabbing at the dark circles under his eyes.

'Kiss me,' she whispered, and his soft lips touched hers gently. In that moment, she knew she loved him. *She had always loved him.*

They spent the night dozing, kissing, and holding on to each other. He gave her one final kiss and left at dawn, promising to come again.

She remembered everything, the dates, the time they'd spent together, the way their families had known about them.

But why was her father cross with him? Was she in his car when the accident happened? Did he blame Krish, her Krish?

When Meera's parents came in the morning, she had thought of all the reasons why they might not like him, but she couldn't think of any.

'Why won't you allow Krishan to come see me, Daddy?' she asked her father when he entered the room.

Her father stiffened. 'Do you remember the accident?'

She thought hard, but she couldn't remember anything. She shook her head. She'd been told by the neurosurgeon that it would take time for her to remember everything. He'd also warned her that she may never recover all her memories.

When her father told her that she had been running away from him as he had hurt her, she knew her father was lying to her. His retelling felt wrong. Krish would never hurt her. She knew that in her soul. She pressed her hands to her ears to drown out her father's voice. Why was he telling lies about the man she loved?

Tears welled up in her eyes and she screamed, 'Why are you doing this? I love him! You knew we were seeing each other. Why are you stopping him from seeing me? I want him here with me. Now!'

'Please, Meera, calm down and listen,' her father said, pulling her to him. 'I won't allow him into your life again. He can have as many fake or real girlfriends as he wants, but it won't be you, my daughter. I've told Tara and her friends that if they make one more comment about you, there will be consequences. They are no longer welcome in our house.'

Meera shook her head, refusing to listen to anything against him.

Her father continued, 'He was lying about his feelings. It was all a ruse to stop the matchmaking. Krishan isn't worthy of you, Meera.' Her father's eyes glistened with moisture. He told her that he wouldn't let a man hurt her again.

With a sigh, he slumped into the chair beside her bed. Just as her mother walked into the room carrying a bag.

'Mummy, please. Krish loves me. He told me before he left this morning,' Meera pleaded, trying to appeal to her mother's good nature.

Her father's back straightened. 'He was here?' he asked sharply.

'Meera,' her mother's soft voice drew her attention. 'It was what you call a fake date. He was never in love with you. Forget him.'

A fake date? She racked her brain for anything to anchor onto, to prove to them that he loved her. All she knew was that he came to stay with her every night and his kisses felt... *real*.

Later her brother came to see her, and he told her the same story they'd made up. It couldn't be a fake date. She'd felt his emotion in their kisses. She wasn't sure why they were making up the fake dating story.

Then, a memory resurfaced, a flash of his mouth on hers, her back against a rough wooden structure, the desire in his eyes as he pulled her into his house.

It was real. Very real.

LOST MEMORIES

Meera

A few months later, small fragments of her memory began to return at the most unexpected times. But the memory that she waited for, of how her relationship with Krish had started as a deception never came back to her. And yet, she felt his sadness and sensed it in the way his kisses never matched her memory. Only a soft brushing of the lips, too short, and too soft to satisfy her yearning for him.

Her father must have said something to him. What were they trying to hide? She knew about the pelvic fracture, the pins holding her together, and the ruptured spleen, but that wasn't the real problem. It was her brain that was stopping her from going home.

When the doctors came on the morning round, she asked them about her recollection of events and the people in her life. They reassured her that it was normal to be confused and told her to relax. The gaps in her mind would eventually fill. She told her to concentrate on healing from her other injuries and let her brain deal with the missing pieces in its own way.

But her unconscious mind kept filling in other gaps, even the ones she'd wanted to erase. She'd remembered there was another man. Someone who'd hurt her badly. Kaushik. With his memory, her whole body ached. She'd kept him buried, tucked away in a dark corner of her mind, but he would burst out like a dagger to her heart.

During those moments, Krish would come to visit her unexpectedly, his kind eyes reassuring her as he sat quietly by her bedside, holding her hand to ease her fear. She remembered that she had not allowed anyone to comfort her, refusing any kind of support when Kaushik had left. She had carried the pain all alone. But now, she told Krish the whole story, no editing or hiding from the truth. She told him she wanted everyone to know about her life with Kaushik. No more secrets.

Krishan listened, and when she finished, he told her she was brave and strong and that he'd never let anyone hurt her like that again. He would always be there to protect her. His reaction, his kind words gave her the confidence to tell her parents, and as she told them of her marriage to Kaushik, she saw her father's anger and her mother's guilt. But there was something else too. Pride. In that moment, she realised that her parents would have eased her burden and helped her without hesitation if only she had let them.

But there was one question that worried her. *Was there any truth to them declaring that her and Krish's love story wasn't real?*

Her first thought was to bury the uneasiness, but she savoured it, letting her subconscious float around the idea.

Then one afternoon, Krishan brought a photo album of his children, Natasha and Neel. The moment she saw the children, recognition hit her. She recognised the children and how they made her feel. With that, her memory came crashing back, along with her anger. Instantly, her mind choked with sudden heaviness.

'Don't come anywhere near me, Krish. Do you understand? Just the whiff of your cologne will make me murderous,' she had told him.

Realisation hit her like a sledgehammer. He'd told her he wanted to marry Radhika. It wasn't *real*. She'd made it all up in her head. Her parents were telling her the truth. She *had* been with him on the night of her accident. Her head burst with pain, making her wince. Then, why was he still faking it?

'Get out! You're a liar, Krish,' she declared. The photo album felt like a heavy weight on her lap.

Krishan's face fell, and a deep sadness clouded his expression. And just like that, all the light in her world disappeared in a dark tunnel and her life spiralled out of control. *He doesn't love you.* A voiced shouted in her pain filled head.

The light filtered through her eyelids, and she woke again, as she heard the scraping of a chair against the floor.

'Hello. You gave us quite a scare.' Joshna smiled down at her, gently stroking her cheek.

She used the button to lift her bed to the upright position. She knew Joshna would tell her the truth.

'It wasn't real,' she murmured.

Joshna tilted her head. 'What wasn't real?'

'Me and Krishan.' Just saying his name brought a lump to her throat. 'He doesn't love me. No one wants me.'

Joshna pulled her into a hug and stroked her hair as she sobbed, every cell in her body aching from the pain of the lie. Krishan had lied to her. But why? She needed answers.

After her tears dried up, she lifted her head to look into her sister-in-law's eyes. Joshna met her gaze and shook her head.

'I don't think that's true anymore, Meera. He has a connection with you. He was in pain when you were unwell. We understand you need answers, and he's the only one who can give them to you.'

Everything was too confusing, too painful.

And then, as if summoned, Krishan stepped cautiously into the room, his forehead scrunched, his glasses shielding his eyes.

Clark Kent. It was a silly thought, but she remembered she'd called him that once. They were in a car together, and she knew she had been happy then.

Krishan

Krishan paced the corridor outside. Meera was getting her memories back. How was he going to explain to the amazing woman, who'd already been through so much, that what had started as an idea to get some respite from the constant matchmaking had turned into forever love? A gobsmacking, aching love that hummed through his body whenever she was with him. He'd had plenty of time to relive their fake dates over and over and analyse their time together. And he knew, without a doubt, the exact moment he'd fallen in love with her.

When Harish called and asked him to lie to Meera, to pretend they were in a serious relationship for the sake of her fragile health and memory recovery, an ache had settled in his heart. He knew that this deception would make it impossible for their love to ever be real. During the nights he'd spent with her, he'd allowed a false hope to build in his mind. He'd pushed aside the nagging reminders of the number of times Meera had in the past told him that she would never ever marry again. He'd ignored the fact that Meera was recovering from a brain injury, and her mind was still processing and filling in the blanks. But he'd seen the all-consuming love in her expression and thought it was real. He pushed aside the thought that sooner or later, all her memories would come back, and she'd hate him for the hurt and humiliation he'd caused her. He was worse than Kaushik, her ex-husband.

He remembered her expression as the truth hit her and she'd called him a liar, he knew that the love story Meera had created in her mind was unravelling. He'd clung to the hope that she might forgive him, that they could start afresh. Only why would she forgive a public humiliation? He'd kissed Radhika. Yes, it was a stupid thing to do. He had always known he loved Meera, yet he had nearly chosen to marry Radhika, a selfish decision that would have ruined both their lives. Thank God, at least the Masi Mafia had saved him from making that mistake and spoiling another woman's life.

He had continued to visit Meera, sat beside her while she slept and dreaded the day her lost memories would return. Because when they did, he'd have to leave. He built a wall around his heart, thinking it would be easier than falling apart when his time was up. Now, even that wall had crumbled, and all he wanted to do was rush to her room, take her in his arms and ask for her forgiveness. To declare that he loved her more than life itself. He wanted to tell her he'd spend a million lifetimes making up for the hurt he'd caused her. But first, he owed Meera the truth, no matter the consequences. Most importantly, she deserved happiness, however she chose to seek it and live it. It was the right thing to do for the woman he loved so much.

Joshna come out of the room and told him he could go in to speak with Meera, he'd braced himself for the anger that would burst out of her. Instead, he saw the tear-streaked cheeks and the helplessness in her expressive eyes. His legs felt weak, and he slumped on the chair next to her bed, wanting to hold her hand, but too afraid to do so. It took all his willpower not to take her into his arms and tell her everything would be alright.

But would it ever be alright?

'Why didn't you tell me the truth, Krish?' she asked, her voice full of pain.

'I love you, Meera,' he blurted out, the words escaping before he could stop them.

Shock flickered across her face and was quickly replaced by anger.

'I know the truth, Krish. You want to marry Radhika, don't you?'

'That wasn't real,' he said, placing his hand on her knee. Meera had become a lot more jittery as she regained her memories, but she hadn't flinched at his touch. And now that he was touching her, his heart and head stopped pounding, and he could think clearly. Her touch had always calmed him.

'What do you remember?' he asked her.

She rubbed her forehead. 'It's all jumbled up. I remember you with Radhika.'

He filled a glass of water and told Meera to drink it. She took several gulps and quietly gave it back to him.

He sat back in the chair and met her gaze. 'I'll explain everything, Meera. Radhika is *not* my girlfriend. She's just a friend, and we enjoy each other's company. That's all.

'You–' he hesitated. He wanted to say, *'You take my breath away. You live in every nook and crevice of my brain. You fill my heart with a lightness I've never felt.'*

But he stopped himself. At this moment, she needed to hear the real reason why he'd agreed to the fake dating.

'When I stopped the car to pick you up on the road to Carlington Manor, I was speechless. All I could do was bob my head like a love-struck teenager watching the most beautiful girl in the world head my way. When I think back to that day, I knew it was a sign, but I ignored it. I still loved my wife and felt guilty as hell that you'd stirred all these emotions buried deep within me. How could I let a woman whose face I'd seen in a window of a restaurant on Gas Street make me feel that way?

But that weekend, you kept surprising me with your words, your honesty and your ability to stir my emotions. I loved spending time with you and thanked the gods for destroying the flowers and for our road trip to Bristol. We got on so well that weekend. It was like I'd found my safe place. A glimpse of happiness. And that's when I hatched a plan. I knew about the dating app. You'd asked everyone on the night of Sanji to join it except me, and I was upset. Not because I wanted to be on the dating app, but because I was jealous of the time they would get to spend with you afterwards as Beta testers. That weekend, I saw how much the gossipy aunties' remarks hurt you, and honestly, I was fed up with the introductions too. But more than that, I was desperate to see you again.'

He paused for a second and asked, 'Do you have any memories of our trip to Bristol and when I walked you to your room that night?

'You're so sweet,' she'd told him, unlocking her door. 'I'm not looking for anyone. Never. Ever. You remember?' She'd smiled at him. Now, those words flashed in his mind, hoping she wouldn't remember saying *Never. Ever.*

'Yes, I remember,' she said, surprised, and he saw the memories bombard her just as they had when she was looking at the photo album earlier.

'Krish, help me,' she gasped, and suddenly she was in his arms. He felt her relax into his embrace. At that moment, he felt a tinge of hope that perhaps she would forgive him. After what seemed a long comfortable embrace, her breathing calmed, and the thought he had to let go of her made him release her from his arms.

'Hold me.' Without thinking, he slipped off his shoes and got into the bed facing her, his arm wrapped around her waist.

'After our goodbye, I spent the whole night thinking of a plan to meet with you again, and then I had a brilliant idea. A dating arrangement, a fake dating scenario,' Krishan continued, reminiscing that moment.

Meera's eyes widened.

'I do know romance tropes, Meera. I listen to Taylor Swift,' he laughed at the recollection. 'You said those words 'Never. Ever. Marry.' back to me so many times. It felt like you knew I was secretly hoping for more. However, you dug up the growing seed of hope and tossed it onto the compost heap to wither and shrivel in the heat. Every time I thought that we would finally admit that the fake was real, something would come up and set us back.'

He took a nourishing breath to calm his racing heart. 'I'm sorry I hurt you, Meera. But you blew me off, even after we'd kissed without inhibitions in my garden. You ran away from me. And then I thought… who was I to take you away from your happiness? You enjoyed your life. So what if you had Matt as your friend with benefits? I had to respect your decision. I would do anything to make you happy. You know that, don't you?'

He pulled her to him, hoping she could hear the love in his words, his embrace, 'You are my world, Meera. And if you can't love me back the way I love you, then be happy. Go to New York and live your life to the fullest. Your happiness will make me happy too.'

Her head rested against his chest, and he forced his heart to quieten, even though it felt like he was having a heart attack again. He was letting her go. The universe had sent someone special to him and he'd messed it up.

She lifted her head off his chest. 'Tell me what

happened on the night of the accident?

He exhaled slowly. 'We were on a blind date. Your *Design My Date* app Meera. It matched us, even better than with anyone else. The universe and statistics brought us together again.'

He told her gently that when Radhika and Craig had come to see him, at first, he wasn't happy with the idea. Only his need to speak with her was greater than his reluctance. He admitted that he'd made the mistake of hurting both her and Radhika on the same day. Instead of texting and voice messages, he should have camped outside her flat, her work place, her gym, until she was ready to hear him out.

As he spoke, his voice became quieter, almost breathless. He rubbed his chest, reliving the night he'd nearly lost her for good. His chest hurt, and he gasped for breath as he realised that the thought of losing her that night had been terrifying, but this–this was worse. She would still be alive, but he would have to learn to live without her.

TRUE LOVE

Meera

'I... I can't breathe, Meera.' He gripped her hand tightly, and she saw tears pool and run unhindered down his cheeks. She watched him gradually regain his breath and felt his heart steadying, only hers had begun to race, hurtling towards the pain of that night.

She tried to ignore it, but the weight of it was too much. She didn't have the strength to hold her head up, and weakly, she slumped against his chest.

'Meera!' His breathing became laboured as if he was experiencing her pain. How was that even possible? How could such a connection exist?

They lay on the bed until both their hearts quietened, and their breathlessness eased into a stable rhythm.

'I'm sorry, I can't seem to control the panic. I didn't mean to scare you,' he murmured.

She had been running away from him that night after the date. A proper blind date that Craig had said would be her ideal match. Except it had been Krishan. How had her life become so entangled with this man's?

His eyes spoke volumes to her. He loved her, that was the truth. Now that her memories had started to return, she couldn't stop the floodgates. Right after their drive to pick up the flowers, she had noticed the change in the way he stood closer to her and rested his hand on her back with ease. But more than anything, she'd noticed how his eyes softened whenever they caught each other's gaze, as if she was precious.

And then, there was the memory. He'd asked her if she was interested. And she had said no, except she'd very much wanted to say yes.

'What about you? Would you be interested?' Krishan had asked, his face full of anticipation. She'd felt a flutter in her tummy. But then, she remembered Simon and Kaushik, and she felt the pain and betrayal all over again. So, she had forced herself to sound lighter, almost indifferent, and told him she'd never ever marry again.

Krishan looked into her eyes. 'I fell in love with you the day you turned to speak to me on the road to Carlington Manor. I should have told you then. I should have persuaded you to rethink your Never. Ever. Marry. mantra. When we met on our dates, I hoped you felt the same. Our dates may have started as fake, but my feelings for you are real, Meera. I love you and only you.'

She couldn't deny him the knowledge of her feelings. She loved him too.

'I love you too, Krish.'

His eyes widened.

'You do?' His entire face lit up. 'You love me?'

She nodded. 'But I'll need time. These memories are too much,' she said, rubbing her throbbing forehead.

He immediately slid off the bed, grabbed the water jug and filled her glass again.

'Drink this, and I'll ring for the nurse to get you some pain relief.'

'Has anyone told you why I could only come to visit you in secret?' Krishan grinned. 'You'll want to hear this… unless you're too tired and want to sleep?'

She gave him a weak smile and told him she needed to rest. He held her hand as she drifted into a peaceful sleep, knowing that Krishan loved her, and she loved him back.

For the next few days, she struggled to cope with her past, the memories of her life playing out as a silent film. She saw everything, but it was the painful feelings she'd learnt to bury that bombarded her like hailstones on soft leaves.

Every time Krishan came to see her, they talked more and more. And then, one day, he asked her if she would move in with him. She said yes, without hesitation, her heart vibrating with joy. She knew she belonged with him and he belonged to her.

Her hospital stay was coming to an end. Her recovery had progressed quickly once she'd processed her memories. Earlier in the day, she'd been given the all-clear as far as her motor neurone functions were concerned. There was none of the sudden numbness and loss of grip that had plagued her since she'd started moving with the aid. And even the tilt to the left when she walked had become sporadic. In her case, it was the fractured pelvis that was more problematic than the injury to her brain. And the healing would take time. It would require an outpatient rehabilitation process.

Before the minute hand on the clock hit the hour for visiting time, she sensed him and pulled herself to her feet from the edge of the bed, the walking frame within grabbing distance.

He stopped at the door, a smile spreading across his face as his eyes explored her body. A trail of goose bumps followed his gaze and the kaleidoscope of butterflies in her tummy danced in response to his appreciation.

In seconds, he was by her side, his hands gently taking hers.

'You beautiful, brave woman. You got out of the bed on your own?' he whispered.

She couldn't speak. Those butterflies had decided the only way out was through her throat, effectively stealing her words. Meera had changed out of the hospital pyjamas into one of her soft cotton summer dresses that she remembered wearing on one of their dates. She'd sensed that today was going to be important, and she wanted it to be etched in her mind as a new memory.

Krishan stepped back, still holding on to her hand, his other hand slipping into the breast pocket of his jacket. Then, he knelt on one knee and pulled out a small red velvet box, opened to showcase a solitaire diamond ring.

'Meera, will you *never ever* agree to marry me?' he asked, gazing at her adoringly as he slipped the ring onto the third finger of her left hand.

It was unfortunate that at the same moment, her parents arrived. Meera watched in horror as her father's face darkened with rage. He yanked Krishan up by his shirt collar and pushed him out of the room.

Her mother told Meera to sit by her side and held her, apologising softly for trusting Krishan again. She tried to reassure her mother that it was a joke, but soon, their attention was drawn to the shouting outside the room.

Her father's stern baritone telling Krishan that he'd trusted him too readily and that he would not allow Meera to agree to an arrangement with him ever.

Krishan calmly said, 'Shiv Kaka, I love Meera. This wasn't a joke. It was a real proposal of marriage. Only Meera insisted she wouldn't marry me until she could walk unaided.'

He continued, 'And Shiv Kaka, you missed the real surprise. Meera was standing on her own, without the help of the walking frame.'

'She was?' Her father's tone softened.

The door to her room opened, and Meera once again stood up from the bed, unaided. It felt so good to see the joy in her father and mother's eyes, making the moment even more precious.

Krishan stood a short distance away, watching as they hugged her gently. They made her sit back down on the edge of the bed, tears streaming down both their faces.

'Daddy said you're going to be our Mummy and that

you're coming to stay with us?' Neel ran into the room and stood in front of her. She looked at Natasha, standing by the door, holding her father's hand.

'I would like to if you're both happy with that?' she said to the children.

Krish pushed Natasha towards her. Neel turned around to face his older sister.

'I knew you'd be our Mummy. You and Daddy are perfect together,' she said excitedly. 'I've already told him off for taking so long.'

Krish chuckled as he stood behind his children and kissed their heads.

'We made a picture,' Neel announced, lifting a small rucksack from his back. 'It's got us, with ducks, boats, castles, crabs, and slimy seaweed.' He scrunched his nose at the last two words.

'All my favourite things,' Meera said laughing, and Krishan bent down to kiss her.

'I love you. You are perfect, my true love,' he murmured against her lips.

GOOD NEWS

Krishan

'Where are we going?' Meera asked, listening to his travelling playlist as *Atomic Kitten* blasted through the car's speakers.

'It wouldn't be a surprise if I told you, my love,' Krishan replied with a grin.

'Can't you give me a hint? One tiny one?' she pleaded, holding her thumb and forefinger close together to show how tiny she meant.

He chuckled. In the past six months, his life had completely changed. Meera had returned to work recently, and her new position allowed her the flexibility to work from home. And Angus, her boss, was already hinting at bigger responsibilities, nudging her toward managing DMD's entire operations team as they expanded. Sometimes, she still exerted herself too much and would have to recoup, but the children were attuned to her needs and would fuss over her. He thanked the universe for making his family whole once again.

After a quick rest stop at the service station, she'd fallen asleep. As he slowed down to turn off the M5, a soft squeal escaped her lips as she realised where they were heading. Excitement jittered in her body, her leg bouncing with anticipation, until suddenly–it stilled. He saw her smile falter.

'We should have brought Natasha and Neel, Krish.'

He reached for her hand, reassuring her. He told her that he wanted to spend a weekend together, just the two of them. Yes, she was their Mummy now, and his family was complete again because of her. But she was also his lover, his partner. They'd never been away alone since she'd moved in with him. His heart swelled at how easily his children had taken to her, as she nursed them through their colds and scrapes, loving them as her own.

As soon as they'd parked, Meera leaned in and kissed him, thanking him for bringing her to fill in yet another important memory.

She clung to his arm as they climbed the stairs to their room, her body vibrating from excitement. As soon as they entered the hotel room, his lips found hers, and his hands began to work on her clothes. She laughed, a soft, guttural moan escaping her, as she tugged at the buttons of his shirt. Soon, they were naked, unable to control themselves. There was always an urgency when they first made love, a fierce need to reclaim each other's bodies. And once that hunger was sated, they would luxuriously slow down, taking their own sweet time, letting each touch linger.

He savoured every moan, every breathless whimper as his tongue moved in slow circles over her sensitive knot. He teased, drawing out her pleasure until the urge to explore her soft opening with his fingers took over. She was wet. So wet, so ready and his own need to be inside her grew.

'Krish,' Meera gasped, scraping her nails over his shoulders, and he knew she wanted to kiss him. He shifted on top of her, their bodies perfectly aligned, all the while keeping his finger inside her as he bent it just right, hitting that sensitive spot. She released a soft, low scream as her orgasm built, her hips rocking in tune with the motion of his finger, his thumb circling her swollen knot.

'I love you,' she breathed. He caught her mouth with a kiss, sealing the words between them. He loved to hear her say those words to him, and wanted to shout it back so everyone could hear and know that she was his, but first, he trailed kisses down her body, taking her nipple into his mouth.

He was desperate to be inside her, aching to feel her soft tightness around him, but more than that, he needed to see her unravel, shudder, surrender. And he could wait. He was a patient man.

She melted against him as an orgasm rippled through her, her body softening in his arms.

Meera stood with something in her hand. He'd dozed off after they'd woken up and made love again, simply because he couldn't resist her. Every day, he sent a silent prayer to the gods for bringing her to him. The girl who had always been meant for him.

Not that he regretted his life with Kreena, his beautiful wife. He was the luckiest man alive. Two beautiful, brave women had chosen him to be with them.

His eyes travelled over Meera, drinking her in. Her

silk nightdress skimmed the top of her thighs, and blood rushed to his groin. He reached for his glasses to get a better look.

'Is that…are you? Meera?' His voice faltered as he focused on the white plastic stick in her hand. He jumped out of the bed and moved to stand in front of her. Sweeping her in his arms, he lifted her up and swung her around before kissing her deeply. She held onto his shoulders, laughing.

'When? How?' he whispered in wonder.

'I don't know. I just felt I ought to check. Everything's been a little out of sync,' she said, smiling down at him. 'I'm in my forties, Krish. This sort of stuff happens to twenty-year-olds.'

He lowered her against his body, feeling her soft warmth against his. 'Only just forty, and clearly, the universe has a different plan for us,' he said as he led her back to the bed.

It was still too early for breakfast. Krishan turned on his side and watched Meera as her expression changed from confusion to joy and then fear. He pulled her to him and kissed her gently, easing her fear. She responded with a soft kiss, then her tongue danced with growing desire, returning his kiss passionately with equal fervour. He explored her mouth with his tongue, hungrily worshipping her luscious breasts and her scrumptious body. She moaned as his mouth moved lower, exploring her stomach and hips, paying extra attention to the scars she carried. His lips moved further down, easing her thighs apart, and he couldn't help but groan at the taste of her. She raked her fingers through his hair as he began to use his tongue to worship her. How had he ever survived without her taste, her touch, her lips, without her?

His Meera.

Then, and only when she'd gone limp with ecstasy, did he finally join with her. She tightened around him, her expression softened with bliss. He loved watching her, especially when she pleaded for him to be inside her, to take her to that final, complete contentment.

'Krish, please,' she moaned as he paused to adore her.

'Be patient,' he murmured. 'I want to stay inside you, especially today.'

After too short a moment she began to roll her hips, and he couldn't control himself and burst inside her. Their moans blended in perfect unison, and she pulled his lips to hers as they kissed tenderly and quietly, acknowledging the new life that was growing inside her.

'I love you, Meera,' he whispered, his voice husky with the happiness surging through his blood.

He held her close to him and waited for her breathing to steady before she fell into a deep sleep.

She was pregnant. It was perfect. Today was perfect.

He'd persuaded Meera to take Friday off. He remembered how she'd laughed with joy at his surprise when she saw him pull up to Carlington Manor. He'd booked the biggest room, and as soon as they stepped inside, he'd stripped her naked and made frenzied love to her, before driving to a nearby village for a quiet meal.

It had taken all his willpower not to blurt out that he'd planned an even bigger surprise. His Meera was blissfully unaware of the hustle and bustle in the manor's gardens and orchard.

He woke with a smile on his face. Nine months ago, he'd almost lost her. Now, she slept beside him, stirring as the alarm went off. He kissed her forehead and propped himself up on one elbow.

'I love you, and today is a very special day,' he whispered.

'Why? What have you planned?' Meera's eyes narrowed at him.

He needed to steer her away from the secret, but the only trouble was that his Meera had a sixth sense when it came to his thoughts.

'A stroll on the beach, lunch and your favourite 99 with all the sauces,' he said with a grin. Then he added, 'And we're having a baby. You and me.'

She smiled back at him and whispered, 'I love you, but we can't get too excited yet! It's too early to celebrate.'

Practical Meera, she was still wary of happiness. Any time he said anything optimistic; she'd tell him to be careful.

❋❋❋

As they walked past the reception desk after breakfast, someone was putting up an easel with a notice.

Orchard and Garden Closed for Private Wedding.

Disappointment washed over Meera's face. 'Oh, I wanted us to go to the gazebo. I can't quite picture it, and I thought seeing it would help trigger that memory. We put up bunting that day. Is that the right memory?'

'Yes, it is. And it doesn't matter. We're here for another day. We can go visit tomorrow,' he said, drawing her to his side as he led her to the car.

Once they were beside the car, she asked him if he would tell her the exact moment he'd fallen in love with her.

'Yes, I remember every moment, every minute of that weekend,' he said without hesitation, lifting the palm of her hand to his lips.

'No, you don't. What was I wearing the day we met?' She leant against the car door, waiting for his answer.

He grinned and began to describe what she'd worn the day he first met her on the road, 'A ruffled-neck yellow top with black trousers. I love that top. It shows off your exquisite shoulders and this–' He slid his finger on the dip that held the diamond pendant of her necklace and felt her goosebumps. He loved how she reacted to his touch.

'You hardly said much except that you were Jaimini's guest. I couldn't help sneaking glances at your face; your full lips with just a hint of lip gloss, and your hair... My God, your hair glowed in that light. I kept racking my mind for a memory of you, trying to place you, and then it came to me as clear as day. The moment Josh pointed you out to me.'

He watched as her expressive eyes widened and she recalled her brother's wedding, her face filled with incredulity. She threw her arms around his neck and kissed him.

'How do you remember that far back? We hardly knew each other,' she whispered, nuzzling into his neck.

He wrapped his arms around her. 'I frequently dream

of our near misses. And the day I met you again, and fell in love with you, is etched in my mind. Now, are you ready to celebrate the good news at the beach?'

They walked along the beach and talked about their new future. Meera had recovered quicker than expected. Her fitness regime had helped, as had her determination. There were hurdles with the pregnancy, her pelvis had fractured, so natural birth wasn't an option, and she was still on medication for her spleen.

They discussed how and when to share the news with the children, and she also told him she wanted to be married before the baby arrived. They talked about their wedding and agreed on a small gathering: a legal ceremony in the morning, followed by a Hindu ritual in their garden with an exchange of haar and the sacred walk around Agni Dev, in the presence of their friends and family, and ending with a small party afterwards.

She didn't know it yet, but she would love what he'd planned, Krishan mused. A wedding at the house where they'd first met. The place where two soulmates had united and found each other again.

On the way back to the country hotel, Meera asked him, 'Should we call the kids?'

He told her that his parents were taking them out for the morning, which was a lie. Their children, along with their family and friends, were already at Carlington Manor, waiting for the bride and groom. Them. The private wedding in the garden was *their* wedding.

As they drove up the winding drive, Meera turned towards him. 'Thank you for bringing me here. It means a lot to me. The place where I found you.'

He squeezed her hand and said, 'It's special to me too.'

He stopped at the entrance of the manor, and they saw Jaimini running towards them.

'Meera Fai, you're here. Krishan Kaka, I've put your change of clothes in room thirty-two,' she grinned, thrusting the key into his hand.

Krishan jogged around the car to open the door for his soon-to-be-wife.

'Happy wedding day, my love,' he said as he helped her out, his eyes shining with love.

Meera's eyes widened. 'Is that. Are we? Krish?' she asked, grabbing his hand, her gaze searching his.

Before he could reply, Madonna's *"True Blue"* blasted through the sound system, and the rest of the wedding party surged out of the entrance. Natasha and Neel ran up to them for a hug, dressed in their Indian wedding outfits.

'Daddy, Mummy, we came in a big bus,' Neel excitedly rolled out information about their early morning start, singing on the coach, breakfast at a service station and getting ready.

They hugged the children to calm their excitement.

'No hugging or saying hello. We have a lot to do,' Jaimini declared, holding out a palm to stop the others from coming up to them.

Meera's hand caressed his cheek. 'Happy wedding day, my darling,' she said lovingly. Then she looked at

Jaimini. 'Okay, Jaimini, I'm all yours. See you in the orchard, everyone.'

Krishan's heart swelled with joy. Meera deserved the best wedding day ever, and he'd made her nearest and dearest swear to secrecy, including the Masi Mafia. *Especially the Masi Mafia.* He was very thankful to them. If not for their meddling, Krishan would never have pretended to fake date Meera, and he would never have found his true love.

Every child who called her Meera Fai was there. He counted his blessings that he'd met Meera, the kind, forgiving and strong woman. His life partner. And now, the universe, or her Bhagwan, had sent them yet another sign that they would soon be a complete family with their unborn child.

She deserved all the happiness in the world, and he vowed to give it to her for the rest of their lives together.

The End

Playlist

When You're In Love With A Beautiful Woman – *Dr Hook*
I Want To Break Free – *Queen*
Banke Tera Jogi – **Alka Yagnik, Sonu Nigam**
I Knew You Were Trouble – Taylor Swift
Whole Again – *Atomic Kitten*
Suraj Hua Maddham – *Sonu Nigam Alka Yagnik*
Uptown Top Ranking – *Althea and Donna*
You Belong With Me – *Taylor Swift*
Breathe – *Taylor Swift*
True Blue – *Madonna*

Soundtrack

To enhance your reading experience, you can listen to the soundtrack, search and scan on Spotify.

Glossary

Words

Agni Dev – God of Fire

Anarkali – a long dress made with panels worn over tight fitting trousers.

Ba – mother or grandmother

Beta – a term of endearment for a child usually boy but can be used for either male or female

Bhabhi – brother's wife

Bhai – brother

Bhagwan – God

Chaniya choli – traditional long skirt and blouse worn with a long scarf

Chandlo – a jewel like ornament on the forehead of women

Chundadi – a scarf worn with chaniya choli or salwaar / churidar kameez

Churidar – tight silk / cotton trouser worn under kameez or sherwani

Dabo – a metal round tin

Dada – paternal grandfather

Dandiya – short pair of wooden sticks used in Gujarati folk dance

Dandiya Raas – traditional Gujarati folk dance using short wooden stick

Dhoti- a traditional garment for men in the Indian subcontinent.

Diku – a term of endearment for a child

Diya – a single flame or a lamp created using a cotton wick and clarified butter

Fai / Faiba – paternal aunt

Fua – paternal aunt's husband

Ganesh Puja – a worship for Ganesh to bring good luck and to remove all obstacles for the auspicious day. All Hindu religious ceremony begins with a prayer to Ganesh

Gangajal – water from the sacred river Ganga and Jumana

Gopi – women devotees of Krishna

Haar– fresh flower garland placed on bride and groom neck by each other

Jabho/Jabha pyjamas – long or short shirt and trousers worn by men

Jai Shri Krishna – praise be to Krishna, often used by Gujarati Hindu community

Janam Kundli – horoscope chart prepared at birth

Kaka – paternal uncle

Kaki – paternal uncle's wife

Kameez – long shirt/dress worn over trousers traditionally worn by women

Kem Cho – Gujarati greeting meaning how are you?

Kediyu- A traditional upper garment worn by men, particularly in the coastal areas of western Gujarat, India.

Mehfil - a social gathering where poetry and songs are recited

Masa – Husband of Maternal aunt

Masi – Maternal aunt and in this instance a phrase for aunties

Mama – Maternal uncle

Mami – Wife of a Maternal uncle

Mehndi – paste of crushed leaves of the Henna plant used to create intricate body art during wedding and festivals

Nah

Nana – Maternal grandfather

Nasto – savoury snacks

Nehru suit – A collarless jacket worn with trousers or jodhpurs

Pallu – The decorated end of a saree that is left loose or displayed at the front

Puja – Worship

Pithi – A blessing ceremony where a paste, traditionally made from turmeric, sandalwood, and rosewater, is applied to the bride and groom's bodies.

Saree – Traditional garment that is worn by women.

Sanji – A vibrant and festive pre-wedding ceremony dedicated to music, dance, and entertainment.

Sherwani – a long coat that is worn at weddings and special occasions

Tika – an ornament worn on the parting in a woman's head.

Tilak – auspicious mark on the forehead using vermilion or sandalwood

Foods

Ambli Khajjur ni chutnee – tamarind date chutney

Athanu – a variety of sweet spicy and sour pickled vegetables, fruit and chilli

Baath – steamed rice

Badam nu dudh - milk with ground almonds, sugar and ground cardamom

Barfi – sweet made with milk powder and sugar

Bateta nu shaak – Potato curry

Bateta ni chips – deep-fried potato chips

Bharela Ringda Betata nu shaak – spice stuffed aubergine and potatoes

Bombay Sandwiches – a toasted sandwich made with tomatoes, cheese, onions, boiled potatoes and coriander chutney and special spice blend

Boondi na Ladwa – beads of gram flour fried batter soaked in saffron and cardamom infused sugar syrup formed into balls with raisins and chopped pistachio

Chai – brewed tea with milk, sugar and spices

Chuti Mag ni dall – dry split yellow mung

Dahi – natural yoghurt

Dhana Marcha ni chutnee – coriander and green chilli chutney

Farfar – fried tapioca crisps

Ganthiya – fried gram flour noodles with spices

Idly – a steamed dumpling made from ground lentils and rice

Jeera Baath – fried rice with cumin seeds

Kachumber – a salad made with cabbage, cucumber, carrots, onions and tomatoes

Kadhi – a thick stew made from gram flour and yoghurt

Kaju Katli - sweet made with almond powder and sugar

Lasun Mogo – fried cassava chips with garlic and chilli powder sauce

Masala Chai – brewed tea with milk, sugar and spices

Masala Dosa – Rice and lentil pancake with dry potato curry

Mattar Kachori – fried plain flour balls filled with masala peas

Mithai – generic name for traditional Indian sweets

Pani Puri –fried wheat breaded hollow spherical puri filled with potatoes, chickpeas, and a special water made with a blend of spices.

Paneer Pakora – fried gram flour batter coated fresh Indian cheese squares

Papad – dried thin bread made with lentil flour eaten either fried or dry baked on flame

Pau Bhaji – fried bread rolls with mashed spiced vegetable and butter

Phulli Gathiya – fried gram flour shaped noodles with ridges

Puri – deep-fried small rolled flatbread made from wheat flour

Rotli – rolled bread cooked on dry griddle pan usually made with wheat flour

Shaak – any vegetable curry

Sukha betata nu shaak – dry potato cumin curry

Talela Murcha – fried green chillies

Tameta ni chutnee – Fresh tomato chutney

Theekhi Puri – deep-fried spiced small round rolled flatbread made with wheat and gram flour

Topra Paak – sweet made with ground coconut sugar and milk

Topra ni chutnee – Coconut chutney

Waatidall na Bhajia - ground black-eyed peas and mung split lentil fritters

Acknowledgement

There may only be one author listed in this book, but I couldn't have written it without the support and constant encouragement of my family and friends.

To my beta readers and my early support team, your feedback, support, and constant friendship are more than I deserve. Thank you all for allowing me to fulfil my dream of writing stories.

To Sejal, I enjoyed working with you on this book immensely. It felt like we were honing the story together. Our conversation about the book and all things Gujarati and beyond were the best moments during the editing process. I'm sure that we'll continue working together on my next romance.

To Sarah, my cheerleader, my friend and the best proofreader ever, thank you for always agreeing to the silliest of requests I throw at you.

To our son, who came into our life briefly, but gave us the opportunity to nurture him and help us grow into better people. For leading me to what I do now, raise my voice through storytelling in my community.

To my family: my constant, including Hassy, my best friend. You've been through my life's tribulations and helped me tremendously. I don't say it often enough, but you are my rock, and I love you always. My life would be empty without you.

To all the musicians and lyricists whose songs are always playing in my head. Your words are my inspirations for the characters that feature heavily in my writing. Krishan came to me singing a song by Atomic Kitten. I've created a playlist on Spotify for this book, songs that feature and songs I listen to when I'm writing my books.

To all the authors who have inspired me and keep inspiring me. I am a reader first and foremost. These last few years more than any other I have discovered many new authors both traditional and indie. Many of your stories and characters have helped me discover new worlds to escape to, whether real or imaginary.

Finally, and most importantly to you, my readers, THANK YOU so much for reading my story, I hope you liked it. I am always interested in connecting with you.

Please leave a review as an author your reviews mean a lot to me and help other readers find new stories, especially self-published or small press authors like me to reach new readers.

To find out more about my books, free chapters, deleted scenes, recipes and much more, please sign up to my newsletter.

About the Author

Saz Vora is a passionate storyteller, wife and mother, and a proud voice of British Asian in multicultural Britain. Born in East Africa and raised in Coventry in the heart of the Midlands, Saz grew up balancing the vibrant rhythms of her Gujarati Indian roots with her British upbringing. This rich cultural tapestry infuses every word she writes.

Saz's powerful debut novels, My Heart Sings Your Song and its sequel Where Have We Come, a finalist in The Wishing Shelf Book Awards 2020, weave a deeply emotional tale of love, loss, family, and resilience. Based on true events, her work fearlessly explores the often-unspoken realities of baby loss within South Asian families in Britain, shining a light on stories that need to be told.

Her talent has also been recognized in short form, her poignant piece on a childhood memory, Broad Street Library was long listed for the Spread the Word Life Writing Prize 2020.

Before embracing her calling as a writer, Saz enjoyed a successful career in television production and teaching. But storytelling has always been her true passion. Today, she crafts heartfelt narratives that reflect the layered complexities of multicultural identity, family expectations, and women's experiences, especially those often shrouded in silence.

With a love for music, food, and film (from Bollywood to Hollywood and everything in between), her books are rich with references that connect readers to her world. Each story is a soulful blend of emotion and authenticity, written for readers who appreciate the depth and drama of South Asian family life and the power of voice in confronting taboo topics.

Stay connected with Saz through her blog and

newsletter, where she shares personal reflections, recipes, playlists, and behind-the-scenes glimpses into her creative journey.

Website: www.sazvora.com

Facebook: www.facebook.com/saz.vora

Instagram: www.instagram.com/sazvora

TikTok: www.tiktok.com/@sazvoraauthor

YouTube: www.youtube.com/@sazvora

Books By Saz

If you want to immerse yourself in the world of British South Asian multicultural romances with family gatherings, mentions of mouth-watering foods, and sprinklings of music, you might like her other books.

"My Heart Sings Your Song "– A coming-of-age romance set in '80s Britain.

'I enjoyed reading this book. It was full of happiness and heartache in equal parts. The reference to parties, student life and songs was so good.' *Amazon Reviewer*

"Made in Heaven" – A story of forbidden love between an au pair and her millionaire employer.

'This Jane Eyre-inspired romance with an Indian flavour will make the perfect light beach read.' *Wishing Shelf Book Awards - Red Ribbon Winner.*